PRAISE FOR NANCY PICKARD'S

DEAD CRAZY

"A well-controlled sense of the absurd runs beneath the surface of the narrative, and Pickard is also deft at sharply rendering her characters' strong personalities. The plot eventually widens to include extortion and blackmail, all adeptly ferreted out by Jenny, as independent and imaginative as ever in her fifth mystery."
—*Publishers Weekly*

"Jenny's sardonic asides are delightful. . . . a sprightly mix of social issues and amateur detection."
—*Kirkus Reviews*

"Pickard nicely balances the action with her complex portrayal of Jenny. . . ."
—*The Kansas City Star*

A MYSTERY GUILD "EDITOR'S CHOICE"
SELECTION

———

Look for Nancy Pickard's

Marriage is Murder • Generous Death
Say No to Murder • No Body

Jenny Cain Mysteries Available from POCKET BOOKS

Books by Nancy Pickard

Dead Crazy
_Generous Death
Marriage Is Murder_
No Body
Say No to Murder

Published by POCKET BOOKS

DEAD CRAZY

Nancy Pickard

POCKET BOOKS

New York   London   Toronto   Sydney   Tokyo

POCKET BOOKS, a division of Simon & Schuster Inc.
1230 Avenue of the Americas, New York, NY 10020

Copyright © 1988 by Nancy Pickard
Cover art copyright © 1989 Richard Bober

Published by arrangement with Charles Scribner's Sons
Library of Congress Catalog Card Number: 88-15324

ISBN: 0-671-64337-1

First Pocket Books printing June 1989

10 9 8 7 6 5 4 3 2 1

POCKET and colophon are trademarks of Simon & Schuster Inc.

Printed in the U.S.A.

For
Phyllis Brown and Lewis Berger

ACKNOWLEDGMENTS

I wish to thank my friend Jane Van Sant, who is the director of the Transitional Living Consortium in Kansas City, Missouri. Thanks to the TLC and Network staffs for being so patient and helpful not only to me but also to the clients they serve so well. Thanks to those clients, who are some of the most courageous men and women I've ever met. Thanks to Barbara Bartocci and Sally Goldenbaum for "picking all nits." Love to my family. And special thanks to Lenore Hammer, from whom I stole a great line.

DEAD CRAZY

1

The woman was driving me crazy.

I should have been grateful to her because her unexpected visit to my office was allowing me to postpone the next item on my schedule—the one I'd been dreading ever since I decided it had to be done. But I wasn't grateful. She was annoying me beyond tolerance.

Her name was MaryDell Paine—appropriate, since she was one—and she was seated across from me, on the other side of my desk at the Port Frederick, Massachusetts, Civic Foundation, where I'm ostensibly the boss. Her mission, on this cold, gray October day in "Poor Fred," was to persuade the foundation—as represented by me—to purchase a site for a recreation hall for former mental patients and to do it immediately, this very week. It was a ridiculous, an impossible request—we may be small, but we're still a bureaucracy. We don't just instantly write out checks for thousands of dollars to anybody who walks through the door with a sad story.

"I am the president of the board of directors of a local organization which is devoted to helping these poor people mainstream back into society,'' Mrs. Paine had informed me, pompously, straightaway.

First of all, the ''which'' annoyed me—it should have been ''that.'' *Which* just proves how tightly strung I was that day. Second, ''mainstream'' is psychologists' jargon for living like a normal person. Ever since she'd rushed into my office half an hour earlier, without an appointment, she'd sprinkled her conversation with pseudowords like that, as if there weren't enough plain and simple ways to say the same things. Every time she did it, I wanted to mainstream her back into the interpersonal socialization from which she'd come. I knew it wasn't fair of me, but I did have an excuse for my antipathy toward this messenger, if not toward her message. My own mother was a resident of a psychiatric hospital and had been for years. Having lived with the ugly reality, I had little tolerance for people who sentimentalized it or who detached themselves from it with words like poles. But Mrs. Paine was impassioned, and it's my job to listen to impassioned people plead for money, even when they annoy me. I reminded myself that it was not the fault of the crazy people that they were represented by a patronizing fool of a patron.

It is also true that I was in a foul mood even before she barged in, and she was, innocently in a way, only making it worse. I—equable, even-tempered, famously sweet-natured I—was in the sort of mood that's blamed on premenstrual syndrome, but on this day raging hormones had nothing to do with it.

My visitor was at the upper end of middle age and the lower end of rich; short, chubby as a cookie jar, expensively packaged, and enervatingly energetic. From her red leather pumps up through her red silk suit to her stiff, dyed blond hair, she radiated kinetic energy and resolve. Just being in the same room with her made me want to go home and take a nap. Through luck and planning, I had managed to avoid serving on any committees with her, so until now we had had only a formal, nodding acquaintance. She was the sort of woman who did so many good works around town that I felt guilty for not liking her any better than I did, which was not at all. This meeting was accentuating the negative.

Ever since she had barged into my office, she had been trying to impart a sense of urgency to her request. So far she had not said anything to convince me to rush tens of thousands of dollars of foundation money to the aid of her cause.

"I beg you!" she was exclaiming now.

She seemed to have a habit, when saying melodramatic things like that, of widening her blue eyes to full moons. It produced such a soulful look of sincerity that it automatically made me doubt that sincerity. In addition, it's very difficult to reply without stuttering to somebody who looks at you like that. I was, of course, perversely tempted to point to the carpet and bark, "On your knees, then!"

I told myself I was being a creep.

She was still gazing soulfully at me, and I was beginning to stutter some reply, when my assistant director, Derek Jones, strolled into the outer office, forty-five minutes late from lunch. Instantly, my blood pressure rose another ten points.

"Derek," I called out. My voice sounded brittle. It startled Mrs. Paine, so that she jerked her head around to see who I was yelling at. "Come in here, please."

He stuffed his hands into the pockets of his baggy khaki trousers and sauntered in, nodding at my visitor before offering to me his best irrepressible, I-know-I'm-impossible grin. He wore old, scuffed Italian loafers on his feet and a sweater that also looked old and Italian. The total effect was that of a man who should have been sitting under a café umbrella in Paris, rather than walking into an office in New England. He said, in lazy tones of no particular regret, "Sorry I'm late, Jenny."

I had heard that phrase so many times in the last couple of years out of the five that he had worked for me that I had by now lost all curiosity as to *why* he was late. Flat tires, dead batteries, slow waitresses, bad traffic—Derek had run through them all innumerable times. Because of that and because of his increasing tendencies to skip Mondays altogether and to slough off his assignments onto other people, I had finally placed him on a three-month probation six months earlier and then extended that for another three-month period that was up today.

His grin, his cocky Derek-walk, his general insouciance informed me that he had forgotten—or didn't give a damn about—the significance of this date. I had not forgotten. It was on my calendar, staring up at me now.

It was the original source of my agitation.

"Mrs. Paine, this is Derek Jones . . ." I found myself pausing, before completing the introduction, "our assistant director. Derek, this is Mrs. MaryDell Paine. . . ."

He grinned charmingly as he slipped into the empty chair beside her. Ironically, or perhaps not, he had become cuter—there's no other word for it—as he got more irresponsible. By now, short, trim, and curly-haired, thirty-year-old Derek, resembled nothing less than the most popular boy in some senior class. I tended, cynically, to think of it as a high school class.

"I think we may have met at the last fund-raising dinner for multiple sclerosis, Mrs. Paine," he said in a mock-respectful tone that fooled only her.

"Oh?" she replied, with a stiff hint of nobility responding to peasantry. But a dimple appeared in her fat cheek, the side that faced me. Derek had that effect on women: they (we) wanted to pinch one of his cheeks but slap the other.

Briefly, I explained her mission to him.

In upper-class accents, Mrs. Paine now deigned to include Derek in her plea.

"Mr. Jones, Mrs. Cain . . ." She'd been in my office forty minutes, and she hadn't gotten my name right once. "Plead with your trustees. Persuade them to contribute funds to our recreation hall. Really, you simply must." Her voice dropped dramatically on the last word.

"Really, it's not so simple," I said.

"But this is so dreadfully important!"

As if the foundation's other projects weren't, I thought sourly just inconsequential little jobs like a pediatric surgery center and cancer research. (God, I thought, you are a bitch today, Cain.) But Mrs. Paine had a reputation for bulldozing through people, projects, and committees to get her way.

I exchanged glances with Derek.

He widened his eyes at me in a dangerous imitation of our guest. In spite of everything, I had to stifle a laugh. I felt some of the hot air of irritation seeping out of me. Derek could still punch a hole in my bad moods, even when he caused them. Would he make a joke when I fired him?

She said, "I'll admit this is short notice, Mrs. Cain, but we didn't know the landlord would try to sell the building out from under us! And so soon!"

She didn't speak, she exclaimed. I wondered if that's what she sounded like all the time. When she pulled up to a gas pump did she cry: "I want unleaded! Oh, fill it! Do it right away!"

She was saying, "There's no way we can come up with enough money in time!" To which she added coyly, "At least, not without your help. We simply must put a deposit on the building immediately—this week, the sooner the better, tomorrow if possible . . ."

"Whoa," I said.

But this horse was at full gallop and didn't respond to my tug on the reins.

". . . or we'll lose the best site in town! Mrs. Cain! If the foundation doesn't help us, we'll have no defense against the opposition, and if we don't open the hall, there will be no safe refuge for our clients!''

"Safe refuge," I said.

Derek, who knew redundancy was a pet peeve of mine, scratched his side and smiled down at his lap. And suddenly, I experienced a surge of helplessness, frustration, and sadness. I had given him every chance, hadn't I? I had tried everything I knew to motivate him. This was the consequence of his own actions, wasn't it? But I was going to miss his grin, his devilish wit, even his irreverent attitude toward me, an attitude that usually contained just enough respect to restrain his natural impulses toward flirtation.

Mistaking my echo for interest, Mrs. Paine nodded so violently that her pinked cheeks shook.

"Exactly right," she said, compounding the error.

Safe refuge. Baby puppies. I dislike redundancies in speech, and I am trained to avoid them when spending foundation money on charitable grants to good causes. Furthermore, I'm suspicious of people who don't recognize them in their speech or lives: once is enough for almost everything but sex and chocolate; history only repeats itself for people who aren't paying attention. And that was why I was going to fire Derek this afternoon: his procrastination, his tardiness, his failures, his laziness were all infuriatingly, boringly redundant by now. I was exhausted by that history. It wasn't going to repeat itself anymore.

I realized I wasn't paying attention to her.

"They'll be lost, Mrs. Cain!" She widened her eyes dramatically. I narrowed mine. I knew I was being nearly as obnoxious as Derek was, but I couldn't help it. "They'll wander the streets, they'll end up eating out of garbage pails, they'll become beggars and bag ladies! They'll be lost to themselves and to society! But if we obtain the recreation hall, we'll have a place for them to come in out of the weather, a place for them to be with each other, to socialize . . ."

In mental-health jargon, that meant make friends. I dislike jargon, and I'm suspicious of people who use it.

". . . have a hot meal, learn simple crafts . . ."

If she was such a patron, I thought, why didn't she spend her own damn money?

"Who's the opposition?" I asked.

"Oh, the neighbors, of course." She turned down the corners of her plump red mouth and flicked a manicured hand at me, then at Derek. "They're getting up a petition. A petition! The way they carry on, you'd think we wanted to move homicidal maniacs onto the block."

"Do you?"

"Mrs. Cain, these dear people are perfectly harmless!"

I should have recognized Famous Last Words when I heard them, but then, I should have been paying more attention to her altogether. But I wasn't, not at that moment. I wasn't even taking her seriously. I was focused not on her but on Derek and on myself.

"It's Ms. Cain," I said, with emphasis, and not for the first time. Her glance flickered to my wedding ring, still fairly shiny, then back up to my face. Derek grinned and coughed behind his fist. I sighed. "I'm married to a man named Geoffrey Bushfield—a policeman. He is Lieutenant Bushfield. I am Ms. Cain. We thought that was better than Cain-Bushfield or Bushfield-Cain, which sounds like something you'd plant in the spring." I couldn't bring myself to invite her to call me Jenny—it might result in my having to call her MaryDell. That sounded like something you'd name a sheep.

She had failed to laugh at my little witticism.

Derek, however, was now grinning openly at me. He was safe in doing that; she'd never get the joke—she probably never got any joke. I wondered if MaryDell Paine knew any of those "dear people" personally, or if she only administered her good works from the safe and sanitary confines of a boardroom. And had she bothered to speak personally to any of those antediluvian neighbors? Had she tried to understand and assuage their concerns, or did she just take it for granted that she was compassionately enlightened and they were reactionary idiots? She probably never got her fat little hands dirty by actually touching any real people with real feelings. Just by looking at her, all dry-cleaned and permed, I could tell she was one of those professional volunteers who go to meetings to learn how to hold better meetings. If she had been a football, I'd have kicked her.

She was pleading prettily again, an ugly sight in a middle-aged woman. "Do give us the financial backing we need, Miss Bushfield! Oh, do! It would simply make all the difference in the world!"

Do give. Simply make. She needed a good editor and a tough aerobics instructor to excise the flab that puffed out her red silk suit and her sentences.

"I'll have to talk to a few people," I said.

"They'll agree with me!" she declared.

"And then, if I think this is a project the foundation might fund, I'll have to present it to our trustees. As it happens, they're meeting this week, so it's possible that I might have their decision by as early as Thursday."

She actually brought her hands together and clapped them, arcing the tips of her fingers so she wouldn't knock off any of her red fingernail polish.

"But"—I affected a warning tone; I didn't have to fake the frown that accompanied it—"that's less than four days away. I won't even have an opinion until I take a look at the site for the recreation hall, or until I talk to some of the other proponents and the neighbors as well. You're asking me to work this out a good deal faster than we usually move, and I don't want you to get your hopes up about whether or not I can manage it."

"I know you will!"

"Even if I manage the groundwork, there's no guarantee that I'll recommend this project to my trustees, or, that if I do, they'll approve it. I hope that's clear, Mrs. Paine?"

Her smile was a simper. "Oh, call me MaryDell."

I was afraid of that. Out of revenge, I went for the jugular: "And how did you come to be so involved in this business, MaryDell?" I knew what she'd say, something civic and pious. But between her syrupy words about helping people, there would lie, like a greedy snake, her own neurotic need for attention and for something, anything, to occupy her empty, unfocused days.

Sure enough, her eyes filled like ice-cube trays, and I thought, Here it comes—how she just feels so sorry for all those poor, sad, crazy people, and if she can just do her teensy-weensy bit to help them, she'll feel she's done something to help clean up her little-bitty corner of the—

"My brother is paranoid-schizophrenic," she said.

2

She had finally got my attention, all of it.

I stared at her, and then I glanced away with a feeling of contrition. Unable for the moment to meet her eyes, I watched her soft hands roll into fleshy balls on the arms of her chair, then creep into her lap. The hands huddled together, like frightened or angry animals, on the hills of her thighs.

When I looked up, MaryDell had closed her eyes, so that for a moment the full blue moons were eclipsed. I felt as if I were, in fact, staring at a dark, private side of her. Derek and I exchanged glances again, but of a different sort this time. Neither of us spoke. We waited for her.

When she opened her eyes, they were dulled, like her voice.

"It isn't a secret," she said, although her strained, hushed tone gave it the feeling of one. "I suppose you might as well know. Everybody else does. I . . . I used to be ashamed of him, but . . . I'm . . . older now." She shook her head, as if somebody had disagreed with her. Not a hair of her lacquered bowling ball moved. Even then, I found it difficult not to observe her cynically. "So's he, Lord knows. Older." She took a breath, like a diver plunging into deep water. "My brother is forty-six years old. And he's insane. He's been in and out of institutions since he was sixteen. They released him again last month, and they won't take him back because they say he's not sick enough. Not sick enough!" A little of her old energy came back into her voice and eyes. "He can't support himself, he won't come home, he won't even talk to any of us in the family about it! The last time I saw Kitt, he was sleeping on a park bench!" The face she turned toward Derek was shocked, indignant. "Did you know that people from decent homes really do that? He doesn't have a place to live, he can't hold a job, heaven only knows what he finds to eat. . . ." She shuddered; a fold of red silk fell from her lap, making a soft swishing sound on its way down her leg. "Winter's coming! What's he going to do then? What are any of them going to do then?" She beat her small, fat fists on her lap. "He doesn't want the family's help. He yells and says simply terrible things if we try to help him, but he's my only sibling."

Sibling. My teeth clenched involuntarily at the pompous sound of the word.

She opened her hands then, and frowned at them as if she didn't recognize them. They snapped shut like turtles. She raised her chins, and some of the old arrogance returned, but not enough to hide the naked pleading.

"I'd buy the damn hall myself," she said, surprising me again, this time with the profanity that seemed out of character. "If I could. But it's all we can do to keep him in psychiatrists now. I just can't ask my husband to do more than that. I can't!" She leaned toward me, reaching out her right hand to me, across my desk. "If you don't help us, if you don't help Kitt and all those other crazy people just like him, I don't know what we'll do, I just don't know. You simply must help us, Mrs. Bushfield!"

"Jenny," I said quickly, reaching across my desk to meet her halfway, to pat her hand. I ignored the base feeling I had that even that impassioned speech of hers had seemed canned. I felt my voice go softer. "Please, call me Jenny." I pushed my telephone across my desk toward Derek. "What's the landlord's name?"

"George Butts," she murmured.

Derek, taking my hint, reached for the receiver with one hand and dialed Information with the other.

"Oh, I do thank you," MaryDell Paine murmured. She leaned back in her chair and dabbed at the corner of her eyes with her knuckles. I had the fleeting, unworthy thought that it was a practiced gesture, to keep her long red fingernails from poking her eyes out.

Butts couldn't see me for an hour and a half.

That allowed more than enough time for MaryDell Paine to leave my office, for Derek and me to discuss her request, and for me to reach the property in time for the appointment. Unfortunately, it also left enough time for me to move on to the next piece of business on my agenda.

"Derek," I said, as if to stop him from leaving my office. In fact, he had propped one leg on another, slouched down in the chair until his blond head rested on the back of it, entwined his fingers over his chest, and looked, generally, as if he might spend the rest of the day at ease there.

He cocked an eyebrow at me.

That small gesture, so typical of his minimalist approach to his job, annoyed me so much that regret and guilt slipped instantly away from me. If my decision needed clinching, that raised eyebrow did it.

When I had hired him five years previously, I had figured him for an ambitious young man who might use the foundation as a stepping-stone. In the meantime, I hoped we would benefit from his talents, which seemed to include initiative and ingenuity. He had those skills, all right—he used them brilliantly to concoct his excuses. I'd also hired him because he seemed to have the spunk to disagree with the boss, to say no even when everyone else around me was saying yes. Eventually, I'd come to view even that as merely a remnant of adolescent rebelliousness. Five years earlier, I had thought I was hiring a man, but he had turned out to be, in many ways, still a boy— cute, funny, mischievous, bright, thoughtless, unable to commit himself fully to anything meaningful or to anyone, self-centered, and impulsive as a monkey.

"It's October fourteenth, Derek," I said.

His attitude didn't immediately appear to change, but something in his blue eyes—a change in the pupils, some slight movement at the corner of his mouth—betrayed an awareness.

"Your final probation period ends today," I said.

He slid to a sitting position in the chair, placed both feet on the carpet, straightened his shoulders, his back, his posture. Like a schoolboy, he grinned at me with mock innocence and said sweetly, as to a schoolteacher, "You look real pretty today, Ms. Cain."

"You're fired, Derek."

The words felt like bullets coming from my mouth. They stung and burned me. But I also had to acknowledge a tingling feeling—a small, vicious electrical charge of spite, of getting even, of power, or why else would I have chosen to say it so bluntly?

He blinked—an involuntary reaction, I think, as if something unexpected had blown into his eyes. Then he started to grin at me, as if I'd made a joke. But the grin dissolved before it reached his eyes; the corners of his mouth turned down, imparting to his mobile face the appearance of those theatrical masks that display comedy and tragedy. He leaned forward slightly, as if to see me better.

"What?" he said.

I gazed back at him, biting my lip to keep my mouth shut. I had decided earlier that I would not rationalize, I would not justify, I would not defend, I would not apologize. I had said it all before, he had heard it all before. I had his employee evaluations in my desk. I had his signature on his probation agreement, where he had agreed in writing to clean up his act within a specified time, or be, as they say, terminated. He had not kept his word, and so this time had arrived.

He laughed briefly, the most popular boy turned down for a date and not believing it.

"You're not really going to do it, Jenny?"

I couldn't help it—I cocked an eyebrow at him.

"Oh, come on, Jenny, so I'm late a few times. So—"

In the face of whatever he saw in my expression, he stopped cold. And laughed. Then stopped laughing just as abruptly. Laughed again. Looked at me, stopped again. It was finally sinking in. I would know that he believed it, and accepted it, if he didn't try to charm me out of it.

He was breathing fast and lightly, like a skier after a long run. He made several odd, disjointed motions with his hands and body, movements that probably reflected the chaotic state of his mind and emotions. Suddenly, I wanted to be anywhere but there, doing anything but this.

"Five years, Jenny!" he said.

At that moment, I hated being boss. Strangely, this was the first time I'd ever had to fire anyone. There are some experiences in life that I'd rather gain vicariously, and this was turning out to be one of them.

"I can't believe this!" he said in a loud voice. "You can't—I can't—"

He shook his head, as if to clear it. When he finally spoke again, it was to ask, in a voice that was characteristically cocky but uncharacteristically gruff, "So, Boss Lady. When do you want me out of here?"

I started to reply, but he continued, his voice rising as if some fury had exploded, "Do I leave today? Pack it up and get the fuck out? Tail between my legs? Tarred and feathered—" He bit his lower lip to regain control of himself, laughed, shrugged, grinned strangely at me. "Sorry. I mean, when do I have to go?"

This scale of emotions he was playing—and trying to control—was unnerving and upsetting me. Did you think this was going to be easy? I asked myself. Did you think he'd just say, "Oh, well, of course, you're right, Jenny. So sorry about being such a jerk, but I see your point." I had known this would be rough, but I hadn't counted on the raw emotions that were playing unpredictably across his face: first surprise; then disbelief, anger, sadness; then anger, surprise, all repeated again and again, as if he'd completely lost control of his internal emotional thermostat. It occurred to me then: But of course, if Derek had any real control over himself, he wouldn't be losing this job to begin with.

I wanted to say, "Take all the time you need, Derek, to find another job," but I knew instinctively that was wrong, so I said, "Two weeks. That should give you time to clear your desk."

He put his hand over his mouth and chin, as people do if they're trying to keep from throwing up, but he nodded.

I glanced at my watch, noticing as I did so that my hand was shaking.

"I'll go with you," Derek said suddenly. His voice was still rough, edged with self-pity and resentment.

I looked up at him, surprised. "To see the landlord?"

He nodded again, though grimly. "Sure. Why not? If you hadn't fired me, I'd be going along, right?"

"Right. If you want to. Sure. Okay."

Shut up, I commanded myself, before you turn into a blithering idiot and start apologizing for his failings. It was going to be awkward riding over and back in the car with him, but I didn't see how I could turn him down. Besides, he was good at site evaluation. What the hell, I thought wearily, let him earn some of that salary before he goes. I reached for my briefcase, then stood up behind my desk.

"We'd better go," I said.

He looked at me, and for a moment we simply stared at each other. I was aware suddenly of everything that lay unfulfilled between us. Not just the job, but a friendship that never entirely took root, because we were employer and employee. Even a sexual attraction we had both suppressed for the same reason.

I felt an impulse to put my arms around him, to hug him, and to say, "Derek, I'm so sorry. I didn't want this to happen. I hoped it would turn out differently. I'm just so damned sorry." But he'd always had a tendency to misinterpret any physical gesture from me, so I held back. I wish I hadn't; I wish I had followed my instincts. But I was thinking, rather bitterly, If he doesn't already know how I feel, then he doesn't really know me, and that would render my regret pointless after all. What I didn't consider, but should have, was: We don't any of us really know how anybody else feels.

Unexpectedly, he laughed, breaking the mood of regret, which maybe only I was feeling. He pushed himself up slowly from the chair. "Well, what the hell. Easy come, easy go." The moment passed as if it had never been. In a voice that was near enough to his normal casual tone to deceive a stranger, he then merely inquired, "So what was that landlord's name again, Jenny?"

3

"George Butts." The landlord, a tall, thickly built man of about fifty-five, held out to me a hand as rough and gnarled as a tree stump. He was dressed in a tan workshirt and tan trousers, and he showed us an ingratiating smile in a face full of wrinkles and stubble. "You folks want to see the place?"

"Please," I said, having already introduced myself and Derek.

We were standing outside the building, on Tenth Street, which was a residential block of New England saltbox-type houses, a few blocks south of downtown. There were maybe twenty houses on the block, most of them as gray and dingy-looking as the October clouds above us. The only exception to the predominant architecture was the one-story cement building we were about to enter through a double door. It was an odd-looking structure, sitting half out of the ground and covered partially—on top and down the sides—by dirt and grass, like an old sod house on the prairie. Instead of walking up stairs to reach the front door, we walked down a few steps.

"It looks like a basement," I said.

"It is a basement." Once inside, Butts flipped a switch to his left. Fluorescent lights revealed a short entryway leading into a large open room with a cement floor, cement walls painted industrial green, and insulated water pipes running floor to ceiling. Just to our left was a door marked, "Men," and another marked, "Women." Brown metal chairs had been folded up and stacked haphazardly against the wall in the big room, which also contained a blackboard, wiped clean, and a stage with curtains pulled to either side. "You want to shut that door, Mr. Jones? I don't heat this place."

"Aren't you afraid the pipes will freeze?" I inquired.

"By the time the weather gets cold enough to freeze 'em, they ain't gonna be my pipes." The wrinkles around Butts's eyes closed into a wink, and he smirked at me. "Anyway, as I was sayin', this is a basement, and with that dirt on top, the temperature pretty much stays the same all year round. Don't take much to heat n'r cool 'er. There was a church built it about fifteen years ago, never raised the dough to finish the job, so they just piled on the dirt and used it like you see here. Members kept dyin' off, though, buncha crazy old holy roller coots, and they run out of dough to keep it up, so I bought it off 'em. Kind of unique, ownin' a basement, kinda hate to give the old girl up."

"I'll bet you do," I said.

He caught my wry tone and grinned again.

Derek and I glanced at each other, the first time we'd really looked at each other since we left the office, and I saw immediately that he was thinking what I was: MaryDell Paine was right, this would make a perfect recreation hall for her former mental patients. Right size, good facilities, great location.

"Is there a kitchen?" I asked. In the Sunday school memories of my childhood, church basements always had kitchens. I recalled huge pots of coffee perking and great, steaming trays of hot rolls emerging from vast ovens. Sometimes I think the only thing I miss about religion is the potluck dinners.

"Yeah, a big one, and a couple of other rooms off this hall." Butts led us farther into the building, talking all the while, and jerking his head back now and then to wink at me over his shoulder. "You folks understand, I don't give a good goddamn, excuse me ma'am, who buys this place. I ain't got nothin' against those crazy people. I suspect they ain't no nuttier than some of my tenants, and, anyway, ain't their money that's crazy. But I'm a businessman, and when somebody makes me a good offer, why I don't want to be rude and refuse them, you see what I mean?"

"Who made you an offer?" I asked.

"Nordic Realty and Development Company."

That wasn't the name of any of the Port Frederick real estate companies I knew, but it sounded vaguely familiar anyway.

"Never heard of them," Derek murmured. Now every time he spoke, which wasn't often, he sounded hesitant and sulky, as if he weren't sure he had the right to an opinion, as if he'd lost his self-confidence, knew it, and resented it. Nice work, Cain, I thought unhappily, you've just neutered Derek.

"They're outa state," the landlord was saying.

That was interesting—it was unusual for buyers from out of town—much less anyone from outside Massachusetts—to show any interest in Port Frederick properties.

"What do they want it for?" I inquired.

"Fifty-five thousand," Butts said, and grinned.

That wasn't what I meant, and he knew it, but he'd given me some information I needed anyway. So, if we wanted this strange bunker, we'd have to do better than that fifty-five-thousand-dollar offer from the Nordic Realty and Development Company. MaryDell Paine had told us he was asking sixty-five thousand dollars for it, so maybe we could get it for fifty-eight or fifty-nine.

By this time, we had arrived in the kitchen—it was all industrial stainless steel that was filthy but possibly operable. Depending on appraisal, it might indeed be a great buy for our purposes. I crooked my index finger over a greasy handle of an oven door, opened it, and peered in: no hot rolls, but it was spotless. All the dirt in this kitchen was on the outside. That shining stove interior gave me a pang—whoever had cleaned it must have loved this kitchen, and the church, and it must have hurt to see it fall into the warty hands of this old rascal. I closed the oven door, took a tissue from my raincoat pocket, and wiped the inside of my finger.

Derek was standing by, his hands stuck down in the pockets of his black ski parka, staring at the floor in an attitude of resentful dejection.

"Nordic, they want to build them some apartments on top of this basement," Butts said. His eyes flicked rapidly between Derek and me as if he hadn't figured out yet who was the final decision maker. "Funny thing is, if they buy this place, they'll take my lot next door, too. You see that empty lot when you come in? Had a house on it, burned down. These apartment fellows, they'll grade it, pave it, use it for parking. Offering me a pretty good deal—this place, plus that lot, too."

"All right," I said, and sighed. "How much?"

"For the lot? Half again as much."

"So we're really talking about ninety-seven-five."

"Thereabouts," he said cagily.

"Do they have zoning for multifamily units?"

Butts pursed his chapped lips and looked canny. "You got zoning for a recreation hall for loonies?"

"Mr. Butts, I'm sure you know even better than we do exactly how this neighborhood is zoned." Which was one way of getting around the fact that I had a lot of information to gather before recommending this purchase to my trustees at their quarterly board meeting on Thursday.

He nodded sagely. "That young fellow who's representing Nordic—one of the partners—he's got his hands on his checkbook, practically got a pen in his hands; you know what I mean. I ain't gonna be able to hold him off much longer, probably not no longer'n Thursday."

"Friday," I countered.

"Noon."

"Right," I said, and smiled at him.

"Here." He began to dig around in the many pockets of his tan trousers until he came out with a silver key on a string. "Tell you what I'll do—got nothin' to hide here, you take this here key, let your people in anytime you want, take a look around." He flipped the key to Derek, who looked startled and nearly dropped it. Derek took out his wallet and placed the key inside. "That way," Butts continued, "you don't have to be botherin' me about nothin' until you got an offer to make. You got my numbers, home and office."

"We'll call you," I said.

"Look forward to it," Butts replied, and winked at me.

Derek and I let ourselves out the front door and locked it behind us. The landlord departed via a back door that led to the alley between Ninth and Tenth streets. As we climbed the front steps to ground level again, Derek glanced at me, and, although his tone was dry, a hint of the imp showed itself in his eyes.

"Old George sure liked you, Jenny."

"I found him pretty irresistible myself."

When he smiled at that, I felt again a sadness that things hadn't turned out differently. We paused on the top step. As usual, he seemed to be waiting for me to tell him what to do.

I said, "What next?"

He blinked, glanced at me suspiciously, but then looked around, suddenly seeming to notice our surroundings. "Well," he said, making a visible effort to bestir himself. "We're here. As long as we're here, I guess we could talk to some of the neighbors, and see how they feel about it."

"Good idea," I said, with enough enthusiasm to embarrass both of us. He looked away from me and laughed. Quickly, I added, "Which one first?"

He shrugged, but then he pointed right, then left, then right again.

This time when he laughed, it seemed to be at himself.

"We'll start there," I agreed.

The clouds were thicker and whiter now, the air was colder and beginning to smell like snow. I set us a smart pace down the sidewalk, partly in response to his sulky, foot-dragging gait. But also because I was beginning to feel a sense of urgency about MaryDell's project, an urgency I attributed to a suspicious lack of objectivity on my part. It was difficult not to think about what might have happened to my own mother if she'd ever been released from a hospital prematurely. What if she were one of those who needed "safe refuge"? Suddenly, the phrase didn't sound redundant so much as it did emphatic.

4

The house just to the east of the church basement was a one-story saltbox with a red lacquered door and a bright blue doorknob that were unexpectedly cheerful notes on this drab block. I was prepared to like the owner—basing my judgment solely on those touches of individuality—even before she responded to her doorbell.

She wasn't, however, as ready to like us.

"No, thank you," she blurted, and began to close the door on us. "I already belong to a church."

"No," I said quickly, and smiled as ingratiatingly as George Butts. This neighbor was a tall, thin redhead in blue jeans, a paisley shirt, and braids, whom I guessed to be about thirty years old. "We're not selling salvation, at least not directly. My name's Jenny Cain, this is Derek Jones, and we represent the Port Frederick Civic Foundation. We're studying the building next door as a possible site for a recreation hall for former mental patients. We'd like to know how you feel about those plans."

I braced myself for a barrage of hostility.

She reopened her door and shrugged. "It's okay."

"Is it?" My surprise made me stupid.

"Everybody's gotta be somewhere." Her tone was philosophical. A small child, a girl, thrust her face between her mother's knees. The woman smiled and was suddenly pretty. "I guess the only thing is, I do have a couple of these monsters, and I wouldn't want anything to, um . . . you know. I guess I'd like some kind of assurance the patients won't do anything crazy." She laughed when she realized what she'd said. "I mean, I'm an artist, so I understand normal crazy. And I don't mind gentle crazy. But I could get a little nervous about *crazy*. You know what I mean?"

I nodded, making no promises.

"Listen," she added, "I don't really belong to a church, I just said that to get rid of you. Oh, God . . ." She clapped her ringless left hand to her mouth in embarrassment. "I mean . . ."

We were all smiling inanely at one another as Derek and I turned to go down her front steps. The sound of children's giggles followed us down the front walk. When their mother closed the front door, it was as if she'd shut the lid on a merry music box. Derek and I were once again surrounded by the still, white silence of impending snow. But it's only *October,* I thought.

"Wonder if she's married," Derek murmured.

"I didn't know you liked kids, Derek."

"Sure, if they're accompanied by a pretty mother." He stuffed his hands in his coat pockets again and glanced back at the bright red door. He seemed to have perked up a little. "Hell, she's probably taller than I am."

"That's okay," I said, "her children are shorter than you are."

He shook his head in mock disgust.

"You never paid me nearly enough, Jenny."

It was the first hint of ambition I had heard from him in months.

* * *

We walked past the church basement, past the vacant lot, toward the tiny, shabby saltbox to the west. No red door there, or blue knob, just unpainted wood and a general air of decay and neglect. After we knocked—the bell was only a wire hanging out of a hole—it took the occupant a long time to respond. In fact, we would have thought nobody was home, except that strange clumping noises alerted us to the presence of someone within. Gradually, the clumping got louder as it seemed to draw closer to the door. I had the feeling then of being observed through a peephole. We must have appeared respectable, because two bolts slid back, a lock turned, and the door opened a crack. A rheumy blue eye peered out at us through a hole in a thick metal chain, and a thin, querulous voice demanded, "What do you want?"

I repeated my spiel, turning up the volume in case our questioner was hard of hearing.

The chain dropped, and the door opened to reveal a tiny, elderly woman leaning over an aluminum walker that was two-thirds her size. Her hair, thin and gray, was contained by a hairnet, and her stockings were rolled up just below her knees. She was wearing grubby white terrycloth mules on her feet and a blue flowered nylon housedress that zipped up the front. Her hands were arthritically deformed, but they gripped the walker as if it were a shield against our invasion of her home. With her head bent to the right, her tiny, unbelievably wrinkled face peered up at us like a mole's through a hole in the earth. The old lady was suspicion personified, but she said strongly, "Come in!"

Her house, which was suffocatingly warm, suffered from the same decay that afflicted the outside, but here, you could smell it—dust, unswept carpets, dirty dishes, unmade beds, medicine, and old age. But that alone wasn't what caused us to stop dead just inside her door, and to stare. The weird part was that we were being stared back at—by dozens, maybe even hundreds of little piggy eyes. She had amassed a staggering collection of porcelain pigs of every description, and nearly every one of those porkers had been turned so that it faced the front door. There were pigs everywhere—on tables, shelves, on top of her television, on the bare wood floor, even suspended from the ceiling, hung by their little piggy necks. It was like walking into an overcrowded, weirdly silent sty. Or slaughterhouse.

"My goodness," I said, stunned.

I knew, I absolutely knew without even looking at him, that Derek was restraining an overwhelming urge to snort. Please, I thought, just let us get through this without making asses of ourselves. That was an unfortunate choice of metaphors, however, since it brought barnyards to mind, which nearly brought a chortle up my throat. I knew it would be polite to compliment her extraordinary collection, but I couldn't, I just couldn't. I knew I'd never make it past, "My, what a nice . . ."

She introduced herself as Mrs. Grace Montgomery.

"Sit there," she commanded, pointing to an overstuffed sofa with a cruelly twisted index finger. Walking carefully among the pigs, Derek and I followed her instruction. I still didn't dare to look at him.

She lowered herself into an armchair so faded with time that you almost couldn't tell that it had originally been upholstered to match the sofa. Her face puckered with the pain of movement.

"I've hardly slept since I heard they might put that insane asylum next door." Her voice was high, quavering, agitated. "We'll be killed in our beds, I know we will, I'm just so upset about this I can't eat or sleep." She pointed to a scrapbook on an end table at my side. "I want you to look at that, girlie."

Nobody had called me "girlie" in thirty years. I'd nearly

forgotten the word existed. I picked up the scrapbook and opened it. Taped to the first page, there was a yellowed newspaper clipping about an old murder. The dateline on the clipping was February 17, 1977, San Francisco, California. The tape that affixed it to the page was also yellowed and curled with age—like the clipping itself and the old woman who'd put it there.

"Do you see that, do you?" Her agitated voice rose nearly to a sob. She was extraordinarily upset. Any impulse I had to laugh, because of the pigs, had already vanished. Hers was the kind of deep, abnormal, irrational fear that demands serious attention. "That man in San Francisco there, he stabbed that old woman on the street! He was crazy, they knew he was crazy, but they let him out! And look, turn the page!"

I did, and discovered a clipping about a murder in Texas. Also 1977. Houston. I turned more pages and found clippings on every one—all stories about violence committed by people who were alleged or judged to be insane at the time of their crime. The pages of the old scrapbook were frayed, as if Mrs. Grace Montgomery spent her days thumbing through them.

I passed the book over to Derek.

"You see, do you?" Angry, frightened blue eyes glared at me from the wizened little face. "There's that girl who went crazy in that shopping mall, shot up the place, killed three innocent people, her mother knew she was crazy, tried to get the girl committed, but they let her out anyway! Just look, just look! My book's full of them! And I have more, more here. . . ." With her arthritic fingers curled under, she patted a small pile of clippings that lay on a table beside her chair. Beside them lay dainty, filigreed scissors, which I wondered at her ability to use. "This is proof. This is proof of what I say. I'm not some old kook. No, no, this is real life, this is what happens when you let the government turn those people loose on our streets. Well, I won't have it on my street! I've lived here all my life, right here in this very house. I was born here and married here, I lost my babies here, and I'll die here, too. But not too soon! Not at the hands of a murdering lunatic. I'll die at God's will, not the devil's!''

I watched in dismay as she began to cry. Tears found their crooked way down the eroded cheeks, then into the corners of her mouth.

"Oh, Mrs. Montgomery," I said, feeling helpless in the face of her frantic, miserable paranoia.

"It's bad enough to be old and live alone." She wiped angrily at her tears with the backs of her crippled hands. "Nobody to talk to, take all my meals alone with only my dear piggies to keep me company, but this, this! I tell you I can't bear to think of it, I can't bear it. You've got to stop it. Tell them they can't do this to me."

I tried to comfort her, but she was past all hearing. When it was clear there wasn't anything we could say to make her feel better, Derek and I made our careful way out of her house. This time it was the sound of bolts shooting home, instead of children's laughter, that followed us down the front walk.

Back on the sidewalk, Derek opened his mouth to speak. I could almost see the flip words forming on his tongue.

"No," I warned him.

"Hell, she's as crazy as any mental patient, Jenny."

"So we shouldn't take her any more seriously than we do them?"

He started to reply, then smiled slightly. He knew he was caught in the trap of his own paradox. "Right." He sighed, deeply, as if he were letting out a lot more than carbon dioxide. His shoulders had been tightly bunched under his black jacket, but now they relaxed a little. "Jesus, I hate being fair-minded. It kills all my best jokes. It's unmasculine, you know? Hell, I should have been a lawyer—lawyers don't have to be fair, they only have to be good.''

He was cussing more than he usually ever did on the job. I had a feeling he was beginning to let go of it now, of the job, of his relationship to me, of whatever image he'd had of his future at the foundation.

"That sounds like my old Derek," I blurted.

He flushed and said quickly, as if to avert a discussion he didn't want, "Okay, Mother Teresa, what next?" It came out sounding hard and sharp.

I was heartened to hear him display a little spirit, even if it was only prompted by his attraction to the red-haired artist in the house on the other side of the basement. Sex had always been the best stimulant for Derek. He used to do his best work when he had a steady woman friend. Maybe that was the problem, I mused briefly, because as far as I knew, it was a long time since he'd been in love. There'd been plenty of women, but not much love. Maybe if I fixed him up with a nice—or not so nice—woman, maybe that would—

Oh, stop it, I thought, this is ridiculous. Sex is not a perk. The boss does not pimp for the employees.

"Let's try one more, Derek." I pointed to the house across the street, a run-down, two-story saltbox with a "For Sale" sign in its scrubby front yard. "I want to know if the recreation hall is chasing them away."

5

Across the street, the young man who answered our knock confused us at first with agents of a somewhat larger bureaucracy.

"You from the city?"

Before we could figure that out and then deny it, he pointed a dirty finger at us, and laughed snidely.

"Don't be bringin' us any more of your effin' notices," he said. "I got enough of your effin' notices to paper the effin' bathroom. I've sold your effin' notices, lady, along with this house. You want it painted? You want it a-lume-i-num sided? You want gold-effin'-plated plumbin'? You want the weeds cut down? You tell the new owner to do it, baby, 'cause I ain't responsible no more." He raised the long-necked beer in his hand and drank from it, all the while holding my eyes with the sly, laughing look in his own. "Sold!" he exclaimed, and then he blew a toot on the mouth of the beer bottle.

It takes a rare and cavalier disregard for the opinions of others to use any form of the, as mothers say, "F-word" that many times on first meeting.

"We're not from the city," I told him. I was tempted to insert his favorite adjective, but I restrained myself.

"I ain't joinin' no church, either." He tooted on the bottle again. This was one happy fella. Viewed through the brown mesh of his screen door, he looked shabby and ill cared for, like his house. His breath—like the open trash bags on his front porch—smelled of beer and last week's lunch. He had a languid, lazy diction that slid over consonants, and his lank greasy hair curled low over his forehead. He appeared to be in his late twenties, but he hadn't outgrown his teenage acne. His fingernails were bruised, horny, and framed in black grease. When I explained our mission, he acted as if he couldn't care less about what happened to this neighborhood.

"Hell, like I said, we've already sold this place," he said blithely. "We just ain't got up the 'Sold' sign yet." At that moment, a very pregnant blonde who looked about sixteen walked up behind him and stared at us—or rather, at Derek—over the young man's shoulder. She was beautiful in a sluttish way, and silent—although the slow, small smile that she directed at Derek, was expressive enough. The young man said, "This place is too big, we can't afford to keep it up—hell, nobody could." He glanced back over his shoulder at her and laughed. Her mouth curved in an amused, sly smile. I felt the joke had somehow been at our expense, but whatever it was, I didn't get it.

"Hell, I don't care what they move in over there," he claimed with a young man's air of bravado. "I'm gettin' the hell out of here, me and Sammie here—" He lifted his right shoulder to indicate the girl behind him. "We're gettin' the hell out of this dump. They can move in fuckin' orangutans"—he pronounced it "tangs"—"for all we care."

He was laughing when he shut the door in our faces.

I stooped to retrieve an unopened piece of third-class

mail from the floor of the porch so that I could read the name on it: Mr. Rodney Gardner. I passed it to Derek, who looked at it and then slipped it into the mailbox beside the door.

"Another charmer," I said.

"Fuckin' charmer," he corrected me, and we laughed.

The girl's face appeared at the cross-paned window in the door. She stared at Derek, ran the tip of her tongue over her full upper lip, smiled lazily, and then disappeared from view.

"*She*, however, could steam-heat an entire office building, all by herself," I observed as we walked off the porch. I smiled at him. "Did your temperature rise, h'mm, Derek?"

"She's just a kid," he said, but he seemed out of breath as we walked back down the front steps. We stopped at the sidewalk. He looked everywhere but at me as he said, "So where the hell's the opposition? I guess the pig lady's it, huh? So much for that petition Mrs. Paine was going on about." And then he tensed, smiled slightly, and touched my arm. I started to turn around, but he said, "Uh-uh, don't look now. I think the loyal opposition is coming our way in a three-piece suit."

I turned, casually, to look.

A tall, portly man was approaching us—marching, really, both arms swinging. He was wearing brown shoes, a brown suit and matching vest, a tan shirt, and a tie that was striped in shades of, you guessed it, brown.

"A cigar with legs," Derek murmured.

In one of his beefy, swinging hands the man clasped a thick sheaf of white paper.

"You there," he called out to us. "Wait up."

We waited, up on the grass beside Derek's car.

When he reached us, the man planted his brown shoes wide apart as if to break the forward motion of his own stride. Up close, he was the spitting image of the Las

Vegas singer Wayne Newton, complete with pompadour. I half expected him to break out in a chorus of "Danke Schön." He didn't, however, seem to be in a mood to entertain us.

"Listen up." He had a resonant voice that would not have required a microphone to be heard at the rear tables in a cocktail lounge. I realized that some women would find him attractive, but I was not one of them. Maybe it was the tie. He said forcefully, "I ran into George Butts in the alley just now, and George says you're from some charitable outfit that's going to finance the recreation hall for those lunatics. I want to tell you people right here and now that you won't get away with it. We have us a nice family neighborhood here, decent people, safe streets, and we won't have any loonies comin' in to rape our wives and murder our children."

"In their beds," Derek murmured, behind me.

The brown man glared at Derek.

I had at first guessed him to be in his fifties, probably because of his Las Vegas–businessman appearance, but now I realized he might be considerably younger than that, maybe no more than thirty-five. Clearly, this was a man who had skipped his own generation.

He was pugnacious in his rebuttal to Derek: "You live on this block? Well, I do, smart guy, that house on the corner." He pointed to yet another saltbox, painted brown, that was in better repair than most of the others. "And I don't plan to look out my window and see maniacs pissin' in the bushes. So you can just take your bleeding-heart money, and you can stuff it down MaryDell Paine's fat throat, and you can tell her I said so, tell her Perry Yates said so. Her and her crazy brother. Crazy like a lazy fox, that's what he is. Do you people know there are psychiatrists, top psychiatrists, who say there's no such thing as schizophrenia? They're just lazy bums, that's what they are, living off my taxes, walking my streets, eating in soup kitchens that I pay for, sleeping in flophouses on my tax money.''

"Yeah," Derek said in a tight voice, "it's one hell of a life, all right. It's the envy of all my friends. Isn't it the envy of all your friends, Jen?''

"What's your business, Mr. Yates?" I inquired.

"None of yours," he shot back. "The folks around here, we want that nice apartment built on top of that basement, it'd get rid of an eyesore, be good for real estate values, bring in a good class of people. You get in the way of that sale, and you'll be in trouble like you won't believe. I got signatures here." He waved his sheaf of papers at us. "Hundred of signatures . . ."

"Hundreds?" I said.

I ignored his retort as I opened the door to Derek's car, got in, and shut it. Derek didn't follow my lead at first, but stood on the sidewalk, fists clenched, staring at the man. I had a sudden, awful feeling that he was about to take out his emotions on this stranger. But just as I started to roll down my window to distract him, Derek turned and moved off the sidewalk. He strode quickly around to the driver's side and got in. When I breathed deeply, I realized I had been holding my breath.

As we drove off, Yates was still waving around his sheaf of papers. Derek glanced in his rearview mirror and said, furiously, "Bastard! They don't have all the goddamn crazies locked up.''

This time I didn't reprove him.

The first flakes of snow fell on the windshield like a cooling touch on a hot brow.

"Is that what I think it is?" Derek demanded, as if it were a personal affront.

"What snow?" I said, lightly. "I don't see any snow."

6

"It's only October," I said. "It's too early for this."

Nevertheless, the flakes were getting bigger and wetter, and falling faster.

"Damn it!" Derek, still in an impotent, misdirected fury, slammed the palm of his left hand against his steering wheel. "I haven't checked the goddamned antifreeze in my car."

"Or changed the filter on the furnace," I said.

He glanced at me. "Changed my damn tires."

"Had my winter coats cleaned."

He was calming down a little. "Chopped wood."

"You really chop your own?"

"No." He paused, smiled a little. "But I haven't found the mates to my gloves."

"Put gas in the snowblower."

"Hauled down the electric blankets."

"Moved to Miami."

We laughed a little then, both of us nervously, but still, it was the familiar, rueful, comfortable sound of New England natives facing winter. His anger was dissipating, but it had served the purpose of shooting more life back into him along with the adrenaline. I felt almost at ease with him again.

He turned his windshield wipers on and then jacked the heater up another notch.

"It's almost five o'clock, Derek. Let me off at the office, then you go on home. Tomorrow I'd like you to go back to Tenth Street and interview more of the neighbors. See if you can locate some of those 'hundreds' of signatures that Yates claims he has. All right?"

"I'll do it tonight," he said unexpectedly. Derek had never been one to volunteer for extra work. "I'll probably find more of them at home."

"That's true," I agreed. "But I didn't want to ask. We've never paid you enough to justify overtime, and I certainly can't expect it of you now."

He was quiet for a moment, and then he said, almost lightly, "That's all right. I never worked hard enough to justify you *paying* me any overtime."

We were silent all the rest of the way to the office. When he had stopped his car, and I was about to get out of it, he said, "So what are you going to do now, Jenny?"

"I'm going to find this Nordic Realty and Development Company," I told him. "Who are they? That's what I want to know. Why do I think I've heard of them somewhere before? Why this sudden move on Poor Fred?" That was the affectionately contemptuous nickname we natives had long ago dubbed our town. "And why do they have to have that particular basement anyway? I'll find out who the partner is who's trying to make the deal. Maybe I can play on his sympathies, Derek, and get him to withdraw his offer."

"Just smile at him, Jenny. Once'll do it."

I dropped my gaze, pretending to get a better grasp on my briefcase.

"I fucked it," he said, in a dull voice. "I've fucked it

all up. I've got no job. No family. No wife and kids of my own. No reason. No . . . nothin'. I got a one-bedroom apartment and some friends. That's it. I've fucked it.''

I wanted to reach across and touch his arm, to squeeze it. But I didn't. I wish I had. All I did was ask, ''Derek, do you want me to tell Faye, or do you want to do it?'' Faye Basil was my secretary, a motherly woman who was nearly as fond of Derek, and as forgiving of his faults, as she was of her own sons.

He shook his head and didn't look at me. ''You do it.''

''All right,'' I said.

The Nordic Realty and Development Company was so new, it wasn't even listed in the telephone directory, but a call to Information earned me the telephone number and the address. It was only a few blocks out of my way home, although the detour was made slower because of the snow that was beginning to accumulate on the side streets of town.

The company was lodged in a small, freestanding building that somehow managed to look like Colorado in the middle of New England, an effect that was heightened by the snow on its shake-shingle roof and on the wooden floor of its homey little front porch. The sign out front was a discreet little thing with orange and blue lettering. ''The Nordic,'' it said, with a painting of what looked like a Swiss chalet under construction. The artist had topped each letter with a dollop of painted snow. It all looked clean, respectable, modestly successful, quaint, and it gave me an overwhelming urge to yodel.

I walked into an empty office.

''Yoo-hoo,'' I called out, unable to resist the temptation. ''Is anybody home?''

An arm, clad in plaid wool, emerged from a door that led farther into the building. It waved, then held up its fingers as though to say, ''Five minutes.'' I gathered, from the red light on a phone in the front office, that the arm's owner was on the telephone.

While I waited for him—the arm had been long and muscular-looking, and the fingers decidedly male—I looked through the brochures that were scattered about the reception area. They told me that Nordic's headquarters were in Gunnison, Colorado, and that the company specialized in the sale and construction of commercial buildings. The four-color brochures featured photos of several of their projects—a small ski lodge in the Rockies, an office building, a warehouse, a town library, a city hall. On the back of the brochures there were photographs of the two partners in the firm. I looked up from their pictures just as the partner in the plaid shirt hung up the phone and walked in on me.

"Hello, Michael," I said to him.

He stopped, put a hand on the desk nearest to him, and stared at me. If he had only walked over to me at that moment, I would have hugged him gladly, kissed his cheek, and we could have told each other how wonderful it was to see each other again. But maybe because of the surprise of the moment, he didn't move. Michael Laurence, a partner in the firm of Nordic Realty and Development, and the man I'd abandoned in order to fall completely in love with Geof, just stood as if frozen, and the moment passed. Immediately, an awkwardness set in between us. I didn't seem to know what to do with my hands or feet or mouth. Finally, he took mercy on me, and smiled—the wonderful smile that warmed those brown eyes that used to make my secretary feel like a heroine in a romantic novel. And then he did walk over to me, hold out his hands, take mine, and squeeze them.

"Hi, Swede," he said, kissing me lightly. "How'd you find me?"

"Were you hiding?" I tried for a light tone to match his. "Actually, I didn't come looking for you, Michael; I came looking for the Nordic company, only to find that you're it.'' But then I gave in to the sheer delight of seeing him again. "Oh, Michael, you look wonderful! You look as if you go skiing every day, and hiking every other day. You look so good to me! How are you? What are you doing back in town?"

He smiled again. "Well, I wasn't run out on a rail, Jenny, so I assume I'm allowed to come back to my hometown." When he saw how that flustered me, he stepped in to save me from embarrassment again. "We're opening this Port Frederick branch, Swede, at my instigation. I think we can do some good business here, and it'll give me a chance to get back home more often. See my mom and dad. See my old friends." Again he flashed that smile that could have melted every glacier west of the Continental Divide, though it had never managed to unthaw my heart, oh, stubborn organ. "By the way, congratulations." He lifted my ring hand to look at the plain band on it, then looked at me again. "From the way you look, I'd say it suits you."

"Thank you," I mumbled.

He released my hand and pointed us over toward a couple of chairs. When we were seated, he asked me why I'd come looking for his company. Michael had once been a foundation trustee—the young man among the elders—so I didn't have to explain that part to him, only that we were interested in purchasing the basement and why.

"There must be other sites in town, Jenny."

"They would be harder to find than you think," I said. "Can't you find some other site for your project?"

"That basement is not the project, Jenny, the whole neighborhood is. We're going to rehabilitate those properties, starting with that block, starting with that basement. I've already done the legwork, Jenny, I've already put in an offer, and I'm not inclined to back down at this point."

"Not even for the foundation?"

"Not even for you."

"But Michael . . ."

He smiled, fractionally. "Where have I heard that before? But Michael, she'd say, just before she demolished my arguments. But Michael, but Michael . . ."

". . . it's already snowing, it's already cold, these people need daytime shelter now. We can't wait. We need that basement . . . they need it . . . more than you do."

He stood up, walked over to a front window and stared out for a moment. I waited, hoping he was thinking it over, hoping he was changing his mind. He turned, and said, "You can't have everything your way, Jenny."

I stood up, too, and said as mildly as I could, over the surprise I was feeling, "This isn't personal, Michael."

"I agree, it's business. But I will make a personal effort to help you locate another site in town, how's that?"

I shook my head in a gesture of frustration that brought with it a sense of déjà vu. "You weren't listening to me, Michael. And when have I said that before? *You* can find another site, on another block. We want that basement, before somebody freezes to death. Are you willing to let that happen, just so you can make a quicker buck?"

"You never did fight fair."

"It is fair, damn it. It's also true."

He shrugged and glanced out the window again. "You'd better get home to your cop, Jenny. He'll be worried that you got stuck in the snow."

I drew a deep, calming breath. I forced myself to smile and to say as lightly as I could, "I'll outbid you, Michael. The foundation has deeper pockets than you do. But listen, I'll send you an invitation to the open house the day the recreation hall opens its doors."

He put a hand on my shoulder as I walked past him toward the front door. "They'll be holding it in my basement, Jenny, the basement of my apartment building."

We traded tight if-looks-could-kill smiles. "Drive carefully, Swede."

"Welcome back, Michael."

Once outside, I got the front door partway shut against the snow. From the inside, Michael pulled the door out of my hands, closing it the rest of the way.

7

I slid home on a low burn of anger that took my mind off Derek and that should have melted the ice under my tires and defrosted the car windows. For the past few years I had been remembering Michael fondly—conveniently forgetting how infuriating he could be. He had come home from Colorado tanned, muscled, fit, even better-looking than before, but no more reasonable and fair-minded than he'd ever been. Once, he'd seemed like a saint for pursuing me for many months of date-but-don't-touch. Inevitably, sainthood had become martyrdom, a less attractive condition. He still carried an air of petulance—at least, around me—that made me want to kick him in the shins. Clearly this was not a case, and never had been, of two people who brought out the best in each other.

I skidded the Accord into the garage, then I walked—stalked—into our cold, empty house in which a telephone was ringing. I let it ring while I shrugged off my coat, hung it on the coat tree, turned up the thermostat, and kicked off my heels; only then did I reach for it.

"Mrs. Cain? Jenny?"

That could only be MaryDell Paine. The wonder of it was that she'd been able to find me in the phone book at all.

"Hi, MaryDell." I took a deep breath to cleanse me of my encounter with a former lover. "I'm glad you called. You'll be pleased to know that Derek and I were both very impressed with the basement. If everything else checks out, we will probably recommend it to the board for purchase. We got the landlord to give us until noon Friday to make an offer."

I thought she'd be pleased, even excited, but she didn't react to my news. It didn't even seem to be the reason she'd called. Instead, she went off on a nearly incoherent diatribe about the weather and her brother.

"I found him today, Jenny. I found Kitt, my brother, you know. After I left your office. I'll admit it to you, I just plain drove around until I found him. After all this time I do know some of the places he hangs around! So I made him get in the car, and I drove him past the church basement, and I said, 'There, *there*, would you go there, get a hot meal, if you could?' And he surprised me, Jenny, he really surprised me, he said he would! Well, I'll be honest, he said maybe he would, maybe he would if he felt like it. But I was so encouraged by that, really I was, because all the good intentions in the world, you know . . . but this weather! It's too soon; we can't have all this snow and cold so soon! What will he do between now and when we open the recreation—"

I was confused; I couldn't figure out why she'd called me.

"I'm not sure I understand, MaryDell. Do you want us to help you find emergency shelter for them? Is that it?"

"No," she cried, "I want to know where he is! I lost him again, he got out of the car and ran off, and I don't know where he is! I've just got to find him—he'll freeze to death in this weather."

"I wouldn't know where—"

"Did you see him at the church basement?" she interrupted. "I thought maybe he went back there—"

"I don't *know* him, MaryDell, I wouldn't recognize—"

"You'd know him! He looks *different.*"

"Well, I don't think I saw—"

"I offered to bring him home with me, give him a warm bed, but he wouldn't have it, heavens no, it was *only* starting to snow, it was *only* freezing outside, but he had to be dropped off on a street corner, like some . . . some hitchhiker, some bum that I'd picked up off—"

I interrupted her this time, in a firm voice, trying to exert some control over the conversation. "He's probably used to this, MaryDell."

"He's . . . what?" She came to such a screeching halt it was almost funny.

"Used to it. Listen to me. From what you've told me, I'd guess that it's nothing new for your brother to be on the streets. If he has to find shelter, he will, because he knows where to look. Assuming he's rational enough at the moment to do it. Do you think he is?"

She reluctantly agreed that he had seemed to be.

"Okay, then. Here's what I would do. Call the police department. Tell them he's on the streets, that you're concerned about him, and ask them to keep an eye out for him and to take him to the mission if they see him. You might even call the mission tonight and ask if he's there, to put your mind at ease about him. Chances are, he'll go there. Your only other choice is to go out in the snow and drive around and look for him yourself—and take the chance of getting stuck or having an accident. So make the calls, do that, but then let it go, MaryDell. He has survived other nights like this, hasn't he? In all likelihood, he'll survive this one, too."

I knew I sounded cold-blooded, but I was not unfamiliar with reality.

"Yes," she said doubtfully but fairly calmly. "Yes, I suppose so."

"MaryDell?" I wanted to distract her, but I was also thinking of my "pig lady" and of the pretty redhead's concerns about her children. "Tell me again about how harmless these people will be."

"Oh, well." She sounded more like her authoritarian, arrogant self now. "They will be like my brother, which is to say different, definitely a little different from you and me, but not violently so. Jenny, these are extraordinarily sweet and docile people we are trying to help."

"Why? Are they drugged?"

"Oh, well, yes, I guess you'd have to say most of them are on medication of one sort or another."

"What sorts? Lithium for your basic manic-depressive is one thing, MaryDell, but Thorazine for your basic raving psychotic is quite another."

There was a slight pause before she said, "You seem to know an unusual amount about this subject, Jenny."

"As I think I told you, my mother—"

"Your mother?"

"Oh, I didn't tell you. Well, MaryDell, would you prepare a report that answers the following questions. Hold on." I put down the phone long enough to reach for my briefcase and to remove from it a small notebook in which I'd been hastily jotting notes to myself at odd moments throughout the day, ever since my meeting with her. "MaryDell? Ready? Average age of the clients who'll use the recreation hall—"

"Wait! All right, now I have a pen."

"Percentage male, female; percentage white, black, other minorities; average age at onset of mental illness; average frequency of hospitalization; average total lifetime duration of hospitalization; percentage schizophrenics, personality disorders, affective disorders, etc; present living situations—that is, do they live with family, friends, in group homes, alone, on the streets, whatever; average financial capability; average employment history; how many clients you expect the hall to serve at any one time, and try to project that into the third year; specifically what services the hall will provide for the clients; describe the staff that will be required; hours of operation; start-up cost; yearly cost of continued operation." I had read upside down and sideways from my notes, and now I put them away. "That's all I could think of immediately, but please add any other information you think we'll need. Can you possibly do this for me, MaryDell?"

"Oh, of course," she said easily, as if I had only asked her to step outside to see if it was still snowing. I was not dealing with your average volunteer here, that was obvious. "We gathered that information and wrote it up before we searched for a site, Jenny."

"I'm impressed." Truly. "Now, this is important. I know you'll be as objective as you can, MaryDell, but I'd better warn you that my trustees will want to be informed about all sides of the situation. If there are disadvantages to this project or this site, be honest about them. Don't be afraid to mention them in your report. They won't necessarily militate against approval. The important thing is that if we anticipate them, we can deal with them. But if we get surprised by them, my trustees will be exceedingly unhappy with you and with me. So give me the warts as well as the beauty marks, agreed?"

"Oh, of course, Jenny."

Her voice throbbed with a deep, rich sincerity that should have alerted me but didn't. I was too eager to get off the phone, change clothes, fix supper, open a beer.

MaryDell Paine seemed much calmer when we hung up than she had been when I first answered the phone. I, on the other hand, was haunted by the image of a ragged, crazy man scuttling through the night, the cold, the snow. I wished he had an old church basement to repair to, a warm and well-lighted place that might stay open late on evenings like these, so he'd have some place to huddle until the mission opened its doors and offered its beds for the night.

There were two messages on the telephone answering machine; one informed me that my husband would be working late at the office. He was, I knew, up to his lieutenant's bars in paperwork, one of the prices he paid for his last promotion. When he had agreed to move from being a detective into administration, I'd hoped it would give him more time to spend at home. Silly, optimistic me.

The other message was an apology.

"Hello, Mrs. Bushfield." The speaker had a hearty, jocular tone that immediately set my teeth on edge. "This is Nordic Development calling to apologize for our little misunderstanding this afternoon. We would certainly like to be able to help the foundation, and I hope you'll let us know if we can at any time in the future. In the meantime, thanks for dropping by our office. Come again."

It was Michael, of course. It was also history repeating itself—he used to call me all the time to apologize for behavior that he later regretted. But why was he taking such a formal, anonymous tone this time? Just to be amusing, or maybe to fool a husband who might be listening? Damn. I had liked Michael, nearly loved him, in fact, and I expected better of him—or my memory of him—than this.

My stomach growled. I opened a can of lentil soup and a light Beck's beer and grilled a ham-and-cheese sandwich, all of which I downed while slouched in front of the television, in a terrycloth bathrobe and sweat socks. I watched a detective show, the last influence in the world I needed.

8

It was on nights like this that I missed my mother's house, where I'd lived after dad had remarried, and she'd gone into the hospital. In their house, I could light the fireplace in the den, curl up in a chintz rocking chair with an afghan—the blanket, not the dog—on my lap and a good mystery in my hands. All it had lacked was a cat. Here, in the ultramodern house Geof had when I met him, the coziest room was the bathroom.

So, partly it was the detective show, but partly it was the house that drove me back into my clothes—coat, hat, boots, and gloves—and out into the snowy night.

I'd called ahead, so I was expected where I was going.

As I kicked my way down the street, making fresh prints in the snow and sticking out my tongue to catch flakes on it, I thought how there are a couple of nice things about marriage—or at least some marriages—that nobody ever confides beforehand. One is that you don't have to worry about dating anymore, or about whether you're ever going to marry. A decision has been made. There's less turmoil. And all that emotional and mental energy that you used to pour into dating—or into hoping to—you can now apply to other, more interesting things in life. Your job. Your garden. Your computer. Your slug collection. Whatever it is that you feel you neglected for so long. I was trying to devote more time to my women friends.

One of them, going clear back to grade school days, lived three blocks over, in a house a little like my mother's. Marsha Sandy greeted me at the door with a bear hug. There was a man standing behind her—her current beau, evidently—who looked bearish himself.

"I'm glad the doctor is in," I said to her, sighing.

"This is Joe Fabian." Marsha took one of her date's hands and one of mine, briefly, as if to join us. "Joe, this is my buddy, Jenny."

He had the sort of looks that Marsha and I, had we been alone, would have insufferably called cute—average height; losing a little of his curly brown hair on top; full beard and mustache; warm, intelligent, lively brown eyes; the kind of build that was made for cuddling up against. He exuded energy and purpose. At the moment, judging from his grin, his purpose seemed to be to ingratiate himself with me, Marsha's oldest friend. And who could blame him? Marsha, dressed in a burgundy-colored jogging suit that brought out the color in her cheeks and didn't hide her figure, was well worth whatever effort he put into wooing her.

Joe Fabian followed us into her recreation room, where there was a bowl of popcorn on her coffee table and a fire in the fireplace. He immediately endeared himself to me by excusing himself from the room.

"Marsha says she hasn't had a chance to see you for a while, Jenny," he said, "so I'll leave you two alone while I wash up in the kitchen."

I felt my eyebrows rising.

"Thanks, Joe," Marsha said, straight-faced.

When his back was turned, she grinned at me.

I whispered, "Does he do windows?"

Her smile turned lascivious. "He doesn't have to."

We settled ourselves at opposite ends of her chintz couch. Marsha was already in her stocking feet, and I had removed my boots at the door. Now we sat back against our respective ends of the couch, and stretched out our feet toward each other, with Marsha's legs on the outside, mine inside. We had sat this way as teenage girls, giggling at the slightest provocation. In those days, she'd been a big, plain, smart girl about whom adults said, "You wait, you'll come into your own when you're older, and then the boys will flock around." She had, and they did. The one she married had eventually left, however. Now he shared with her the care of their adolescent children. He had them this week, so we had the house to ourselves. And Joe.

"Here's your apple for today, Jenny." Marsha, who was a psychiatrist in private practice, raised her mug of hot apple cider in a toast. "So"—she put on a thick Viennese accent—"vat'z new vit you, kid?"

"Michael's back in town."

She leaned her head back against the armrest and laughed out loud, an irresistible sound. Once I realized why she was so amused by my simple announcement, I guffawed, too.

"Oh, God," she said, wiping her eyes. "Do you think we fool anybody? Forget the briefcases and the suits. Let's talk about what's really interesting—men!"

That set us to giggling again. It felt good and satisfying, like being best friends and teenagers again. I felt as if one of our mothers should walk into the room at that moment and say, "Now, girls."

We talked about Michael. We talked about Geof. I told her about firing Derek. We talked about her ex, and—quietly—about her present boyfriends, including the forty-year-old domesticated teddy bear in the kitchen. Then, having exhausted all the gossip, we played grown-up.

"I don't know if community placement is *right*, Jenny," Marsha said in answer to a question. "I only know it is a fact of life these days. In another decade, trends will undoubtedly change, but now, morally and politically, community placement is the fashion." She shifted herself into a more comfortable position at her end of the couch and inquired rhetorically, "Is it good for patients to be released from hospitals so soon?" She shrugged. "Beats the hell out of me. You read the journals, and you'll see a study one month that claims it is beneficial for them and another study the next month that says it screws them. Hell, Jenny, you know we used to warehouse the mentally ill for lifetimes, but now they're in and out of hospitals like revolving doors. I know of state hospitals that ten years ago housed two thousand patients, and now those same hospitals are down to five or six hundred residents—"

She shook her head and continued her lecture.

"And where, you ask, because you are a concerned citizen, are those fourteen or fifteen hundred former patients now? I mean, hell, that's a lot of crazy people to release from hospitals, to say, 'Hey, good-bye, good-luck, write us when you get there.' Well, we call it community placement, which sounds all warm and fuzzy, not to mention civically enlightened in the best Aristotelian sense, but the reality can be something quite different. The money hasn't followed them out of the institutions. So, at best, they're living with their families—although that is certainly not always in the best interests of the patient or the family—or in group homes, nursing homes, or their own apartments. At worst, the sickest ones are living in parks, cars, or doorways, and there are a good many of those people, too many."

She stared for a moment into her cup of apple cider.

Joe Fabian had quietly come back into the room and taken a chair across from us during her last speech. When she looked up, it was at him first, and then over at me, with sadness and anger showing in her wide brown eyes.

"There are no group homes in this town. At night, for the real down-and-outers, there's only the mission. During the day, there's nothing. If you don't believe me—"

"Of course I do."

". . . ask Joe."

I looked over, inquiringly, at him.

"Joe's the director of the Wayne County mental health association," Marsha explained. So he lived out of town, I thought, even out of our county. That explained why I didn't already know him. Marsha smiled ironically at him. "Our friend here wants to finance a recreation hall for the folks who get released from psych wards. She wants to know if it's a good idea. Tell her how it is, Joe. Let's say she's a thirty-four-year-old man, chronically mentally ill, unemployed, broke, recently released from the hospital, on medication, and she lives in Port Frederick, Massachusetts. What is there for her to do with her days and nights?"

He looked from her to me, unsmiling now.

"Let me say first that I'll bet I know about this project of yours." He had a gruff, growly voice, and an intensity, that suited his appearance. "I'm also on the state board of mental health. Mrs. Paine consulted with us about it when she first got the idea. We're all for it, although I'd have to say that anybody who works with that woman is going to go bonkers himself."

He grimaced and shook his head.

"But okay," he continued. "So what do you do, if you're the fellow that Marsha just described? You could jump off the Seventh Street Bridge." He leaned forward, placed his forearms on his thighs, and radiated intensity. "If that doesn't appeal to you, you could stare at the walls in your room, assuming you have a room. You could sit on a street corner until somebody moves you along, or you could find a stretch of shoreline and a pile of rocks to lie down on. If it were me, I'd probably just walk, just keep walking, probably in circles, all day long. And then, when I got tired of all that deeply pleasurable and meaningful activity, then I'd do what I probably should have done in the first place, which is to go jump off the Seventh Street Bridge, an act of great and merciful savings to the taxpayers of the Commonwealth.''

"Aren't there any programs?" I asked.

"Programs? What do you mean, programs?"

"Organized activities, sheltered workshops, clubs . . ."

"Clubs, Jenny?" He laughed harshly. "You're talking maybe country clubs for the crazy? Rotary clubs? A fraternity of the fragile, a sorority of the insane? Not in Poor Fred, not lately."

"Joe . . ." Marsha said in a quiet tone.

He looked at her, took a deep breath, and stared at the floor between his feet for a moment. "Sorry," he said to me, looking up and smiling slightly. "I get a little carried away sometimes. My wife says I'm living proof that mental illness is contagious, Jenny. She says she has the evidence, which is that I'm obviously crazy to stay in a profession that takes so damned much out of us and pays so little of any sort of reward in return. Hell, she's right." He leaned back in his chair, closed his eyes for a moment, then opened them to look at Marsha. "Isn't she, Shrink?"

Marsha only smiled benignly, like any good psychiatrist. But to me she said primly, as if he weren't in the room, "Joe was separated from his wife before we started dating. They're getting a divorce." She didn't have to tell me that; I knew her well enough to assume as much. Marsha returned to the previous subject and said in that same rather formal tone that told me she was feeling uncomfortable about something, probably him, "I think the recreation hall is a fine idea, Jenny. You can count on my support for it, mine and Joe's. Isn't that right, Joe?"

He nodded, but then he was obviously besotted with Marsha. He would have agreed to carry me home through the storm on his shoulders if she'd asked him to. Nevertheless, I raised my own cup of cider in a toast to both of them. "Thanks."

"There's no charge for the speeches." Marsha smiled.

"MaryDell Paine says the clients will be, in her words, perfectly harmless. Do you think that's true, Marsha?" I included him in the query. "Joe?"

They glanced at each other, and Marsha said in a rueful tone, "Jenny, who can tell? You might go along for years with nothing happening out of the ordinary. All sweetness and light. Or you might get a couple of suicides, or attempted suicides. You might get clients going into psychotic episodes and attacking each other, or staff members, or, hell, we might as well admit it, the neighbors. When you hear that psychiatry is not an exact science, you'd better believe it."

"Would you welcome the hall next door to you?"

"Yes," my friend said seriously, "I sure would."

"When your children are here?"

She leaned her head back and laughed again. "That sounds like the old line, 'but would you want your daughter to marry one?' Yes, even with my children here, I'd be happy to have that hall—provided the clients were well screened and the place was well run—right next door. You want some more cider? The defense rests."

"No, thanks. The prosecution's got to get some rest, too." I untangled myself from her couch, and we padded in our stocking feet to the front door. Joe said good-bye at the door of the recreation room and then retreated tactfully to the kitchen. As I redressed for the blizzard, I said to her, "He's cute. Intense, but cute."

She whispered, "He hates to be called cute."

I gave her one of our old straight lines: "Would you call me a taxi?"

"You're a taxi."

We hugged. I trudged home.

On the telephone-answering machine, there was a new message from Geof, advising me not to wait up for him. A second message, from Derek, asked me to call him back.

"Jenny," he said when I reached him, "I went over to Tenth Street tonight, but I couldn't find any really violent opposition to the recreation hall. It makes them a little nervous, I'd say, but they seem pretty impressed by MaryDell and her group; they seem to feel she'll do a good, safe job of running the place." Derek sounded nervous himself. "Besides, like they told me, it's the sort of neighborhood where there are already a couple of halfway houses—one for parolees, I think, and another for druggies—so this sort of thing is not all that new to them, so it's not so threatening. And the few who are opposed seem to have been talked into it by Perry Yates."

"Who?"

"Wayne Newton. The cigar with legs. Anyway, they seem willing to listen to reasonable people with reasonable ideas. I'd say that as far as the neighborhood is concerned, all systems are go, Jenny."

Except for the pig lady, I thought.

"That's great, Derek." All of his systems seemed to be on go as well, as if he might be making a last-ditch effort to keep his job. "That was really above the call of duty to go out in the storm tonight. Thank you."

"Glad to do it," he said, in an overly hearty tone of voice. "Well, good night, Jenny. Stay warm! I'll see you at the office in the morning!"

He really was trying very hard, so hard that his eagerness made me cringe a little. For some reason my mind made a fleeting connection between him and Joe Fabian, but what was it? Granted, they both fell into the category of cute, but Joe seemed a stronger, more intense, possibly even more intelligent man than Derek. I couldn't, in that instant, put my finger on what it was about each of them that reminded me of the other.

"Good night, Derek."

I ran an exceedingly deep and hot bath and remained soaking in it for a sinfully long time. Then I switched on both sides of the electric blanket and crawled into bed, feeling fairly relaxed. I hated the thought of the pig lady being so frightened, I thought drowsily. Tomorrow, tomorrow I'd visit her again and try to assure her that . . .

9

I woke up the next morning to find that the storm had whirled away from us. It was now out over the Atlantic Ocean, having left behind a clear blue sky, freezing temperature, and fierce sunshine that glistened on the eight inches of snow on the ground. We hadn't even seen Halloween yet; it was beginning to look like a long winter. But it was beautiful, the first snow of the season is always beautiful, the way Southerners imagine it should be. This was a fantasy snowfall, where everything sparkled so that it hurt my eyes to gaze too long at it. Do Southerners, the ones who've never seen snow, realize that you have to wear sunglasses on days like these?

I discussed such weighty questions over breakfast at the kitchen counter with Geof that morning. We were having an actual meal—unusual for us toast-and-coffee people—of scrambled eggs, bacon, orange juice, and toasted bagels. It was fuel for navigating the ice floes, I guess, for killing seals, pounding blubber.

I also told him about Derek, about encountering Michael Laurence again, and about the recreation hall project. He told me how many times he'd signed his name to paperwork the previous day, and then he said, "I don't suppose he's gotten ugly while he's been gone?"

"What? Oh, well, no."

"Probably looks all tanned and healthy, one of those disgusting Colorado types. Wears cowboy boots and blue jeans. Turtleneck sweaters and tweed jackets. Grew a mustache and a beard that he trims every morning. Drinks Coors. Eats Grape-Nuts cereal. Plays the guitar. Walks around with a pickax over one shoulder."

"Right. Rappels down the side of tall buildings, catches mountain trout in his bare hands, hunts elk with a bow and arrow, sits around campfires with John Denver." I grinned at him. "You've got him pegged, all right."

He grunted, took a drink of his coffee.

"You've also got me."

He smiled. My husband was looking particularly sexy this morning, in brown corduroy trousers and a green-and-yellow plaid flannel shirt that made him look, ironically, like one of the western outdoor types he had just mocked.

"Geof," I said, "what would be the police attitude toward this recreation hall of MaryDell's?"

"Changed the subject, didn't you? You can't fool me; I used to be a crack detective." He considered my question while he chewed and then swallowed a chunk of bagel that he had slathered with blueberry preserves from the state of Maine. "This policeman's attitude is that it would probably be a good thing because it would get some people off the streets."

"Would you worry about an increase of crime in the neighborhood?"

He shook his head and cocked an eyebrow at me. "You're not talking about the criminally insane, are you?"

"I don't think so, no."

"Well, then no, why would we? They won't be any more likely to steal hubcaps than your average citizen.

They're only crazy, not criminals, right? If anything, the crime rate might decline, because we'd patrol there more often just to keep things copacetic. In fact, you can promise the neighbors that, if you like. It might calm down some of the irate ones. It could also discourage them from doing anything unfriendly, like that fellow you said Derek calls the cigar with legs.''

"Perry Yates."

"Yeah. And your pig lady."

"I don't think she'd hurt anybody."

"You said she strangles pigs from her ceiling."

I laughed. "Porcelain pigs, Geof."

We exchanged buttery kisses. We helped each other on with our overcoats and then supported each other on the icy walk to the garage. He guided me out of the garage; I made tracks in the snow for him to follow. We waved good-bye to each other. It was nice. It was married. I liked it.

I liked driving in the snow a lot less. The storm had moved on too late for our road crews to clear the streets in time for rush-hour traffic.

My car slipped and slid for three blocks, with me alternately holding my breath and gasping at each near-miss. It finally fishtailed one too many times for my nerves, and—while staring at the bumper of the Chrysler with which I had nearly collided—I decided the better part of valor was to abandon my car.

I'll take the bus, I thought, and call it research.

So I let the Accord slide into a semicleared area of an elementary school parking lot, got out, and locked the doors. Derek could bring me back to get it later, assuming he managed to drive his own car all the way in to work. I set off for the nearest bus stop, which turned out to be four arctic blocks away.

Already, the bitter cold was forming a thick crust on

top of the snow, so that with every step there was a moment of suspension before my boot crunched down into the softness beneath. I lurched forward—pause, crunch, oof, pause, crunch, oof—wondering if Southerners have any idea how exhausting it can be to walk through a winter wonderland. Thank God I'd put on boots, I thought, instead of just wearing heels and counting on the protection of my car. Without boots, the crust would have bit and sawed at my ankles like alligator's teeth, an image that probably shows only how little this Northerner knows about swamps.

At the bus stop, I stamped my feet and clapped my gloved hands to fend off frostbite. I felt like a backup dancer in a Russian folk ballet. Finally, a big gray belcher hove to, crunching snow under its tires and farting air from its brakes.

The doors folded open, inviting me inside.

"Good morning," I said, looking up to the driver.

"Not so's you'd notice," she replied, gazing stoically down at me. She was a bruiser of a woman, middle-aged, bulky and tough-looking, wearing a yellow ski parka, unzipped, over her black uniform, and brown leather driving gloves. I climbed the rubber-coated steps. The folding doors whooshed shut behind me. The floor around my feet was puddly with melted snow from the other passengers' shoes.

I hadn't taken the bus in years, so I had to ask her what the fare was. She gave me a look she might have given a Martian, before saying, "Six bits."

"I've only got a dollar bill."

"The company don't let me make change."

So I bought a token and lost a quarter in the deal. What that told me was that we'd have to be able to provide change—or tokens—for the clients at the recreation hall.

"Hold on tight," the driver advised me, assuming a

more friendly manner once I was a paid customer. "It's bumper-car city this morning."

I heeded her advice as I sat down on the bench directly behind her. Although there were quite a few empty seats on the bus, it seemed full, what with the passengers swaddled in thick coats, wool hats, boots, gloves, and mufflers. Some of them stared curiously at me, the newcomer, not one of the regulars. I felt like the heathen who only goes to church at Christmas and Easter. Well, hell, they'd have to tolerate me—I had, after all, put an extra quarter in the collection plate.

I looked over the driver's broad and padded right shoulder, and out the front windshield. Everything out there looked white and confused.

If I had, as I hoped, picked the right bus, our route would take us near Tenth Street, by the old church basement. I didn't think that many of the hall's clients would have cars, so they would need easy access to public transportation.

As we crossed Ninth Street—and I had nothing else in particular to think about—I tried to imagine what it might be like to be just out of a psychiatric ward and nervous about being back in society. I imagined myself as a middle-aged woman who was taking this bus to a place where she might feel more comfortable than any place else, where she could be with maybe the only people in town who'd really understand her. It made me—imagining myself as that woman—feel comforted, safer, to know the recreation hall awaited me at the end of my bus ride.

The bus approached Tenth Street, which I had only intended to view from inside the bus. But suddenly I had an urge to live out this fantasy of mine a little more.

When the bus screeched to a halt at the intersection of Tenth and Jefferson, I got off. Dodging cars, a couple of which honked at me, I jaywalked across Jefferson and started down Tenth.

The first house I passed was brown and, even under the snow, almost obsessively neat—Perry Yates's home. When I glanced at it, trying to see it through the eyes of the mental patient I was pretending to be, I felt waves of hostility flowing from it toward me.

It was startling and a little scary.

If I were the woman I was imagining, I would have walked past that house as quickly as I could, with my hands in my pockets and my head down, trying to look inconspicuous so that I wouldn't cause offense or attract Perry Yates's venomous attention in any way.

I did just that, playing the role.

The woman I was pretending to be felt nervous, and she felt as if she were being watched. Was he glaring at me through one of his windows? Would he come out on his porch and shout at me, frighten me, and embarrass me? Why did he hate me so?

Once past the brown house, "I" felt as if I had narrowly escaped something.

I scuttled along the sidewalk, but it was difficult to make any speed through the crusty snow. And suddenly I realized that I, Jenny, was better fed and in better shape physically than she'd be, that I could step more lightly and breathe more easily in the cutting air than she would be able to do.

I slowed to her pace, breathing through my mouth, becoming "her" again.

Trudging now, I passed two more houses, keeping my head down, and knowing I was going to have to walk past the pig lady's house. I felt like a child who had to walk past the neighborhood "witch's" house every day. She was frightened of "me"—my friends at the recreation hall had told me so—but I was a lot more frightened of her. Please, I thought, just let me get past her house one more time without any trouble. I didn't want to cause trouble, I didn't want anybody—not any of my friends—to cause any trouble. I needed the recreation hall. I needed some place to go every day, some reason for getting up in the morning. I didn't have any place else. Sometimes it seemed like it was the only thing that stood between me and being crazy again. Please, don't let there be any trouble.

Was the witch watching me?

I wished that mean boy across the street would hurry up and move out of his house. I remembered boys like him—younger boys, but just like him anyway—who always looked like they were going to throw rocks at me, or trip me or push me down, and call me ugly names. The names hurt more than sticks and stones, that was for sure. Sometimes, when I was alone, I thought of names to call them back, but it was always too late to do any good.

To erase the thoughts about the mean boy, I looked up at the house where the artist lived, the pretty lady who even brought her children over to play with us now and then. It was so wonderful to be around children. A lot of people wouldn't let their children even talk to us, but she would. I liked her. Her children were so cute and funny. I hoped she liked me.

My muscles bunched up with cold as I crossed in front of the vacant lot where the wind blew unobstructed. Maybe "we'd" have softball games there with the staff, next spring. "I" hoped nobody would ask me to play, I'd be too scared and clumsy, but it would be fun to watch. Only a few more yards to go now to reach warmth and safety. I'd got past the brown man again, and the pig-lady witch, and the mean boy across the street, and if I just hurried a little more, I'd be inside where nobody from the outside could get me and hurt me.

The front doors of the recreation hall beckoned to "me," but they also repelled me. The staff would smile at me and try to get me to smile back at them; somebody might tell a joke that I didn't get; and what if they wanted me to help in the kitchen today? I might drop something, or break something, or they might ask me to cook something, and I wouldn't know how! And somebody was always wanting to carry on a conversation, when I could barely remember the beginning of my sentences by the time I got to the end of them. Oh, everything was so hard. Even the mostly good times, they were just so hard. So hard. But I had to try. If I didn't want to get crazy again, I had to try. I would. I'd try. They'd be proud of me. I'd show them. But I was still scared. Everything was scary. Life was scary.

So immersed was I, Jenny, in my imaginings that at first it didn't seem odd to me that the double front doors of the basement were slightly ajar. Somebody, some client, had just forgotten to close the doors, that was all, and the staff would be proud of "me" when I remembered to do it. By the time the fact of the doors being ajar finally registered with me, I had nearly stepped right into the bloody footprints in the snow.

"What?" I was myself again but shocked and disoriented. With my eyes, I tracked the footprints to the front doors. There were smears of blood, looking vaguely like handprints, on the doors.

I didn't scream, but I did turn and run like hell to the home of the artist next door.

10

I joined the artist at the bay window in her living room to watch for the police cars that would soon pull up in front of the bloody basement. The artist's name it turned out, was Marianne Miller. When she had discovered the nature of my errand, she had sent her two little girls into another room with the instruction, "You *will* watch 'Sesame Street'!"

"What do you think happened in there?" she asked now, in a scared, excited, whispery voice.

I could only shake my head and stare.

She, very kindly, had handed me a cup of strong coffee as soon as I had hung up the phone from calling the police station. While I was at it, I had also called my office, so that my secretary, a born worrier, wouldn't be concerned about me. I didn't tell her why I was so late—that would really have given her hives—only that I was delayed and that I would be in the office fairly soon.

"Did you hear anything going on?" I asked Marianne.

This time, it was she who only shook her head.

I gazed out at the church, and realized the cops would

have a hell of a job getting in there without destroying evidence. There were no windows in the dirt-covered building; they'd have to go in through the front or back doors. From where I stood, I could see my own footprints in the snow. They were only one of several sets, but they were the smallest prints, and I don't have a particularly dainty shoe size.

"Oh, here they come!" Marianne breathed.

The police, she meant.

"I'd better get out there," I said, regretting the need to leave this warm, cozy home. "Thank you for helping me."

"Anytime," she said politely. Then she clapped her hand over her mouth, having embarrassed herself again. "I mean, I don't mean . . ."

"I know," I assured her.

Once outside again, I waited at the edge of her sidewalk until the police needed me. Their sirens had brought several neighbors outside, too, including the sluttishly beautiful pregnant girl from across the street. She stepped out and watched from her porch. The "For Sale" sign in her front yard was nearly unreadable because of the ice and snow on it. She wore a hooded red cape that bulged over her belly and black tights that disappeared into black high-heeled boots. The red hood was pushed back, framing her mass of blond hair, which looked disheveled, as if she'd just gotten out of bed. She looked like a ruined Red Riding Hood. The girl stood with her hand on the railing, staring across the street. There was, in more ways than one, an expectant air about her.

"Bitch."

I wheeled around, startled, to find Marianne Miller standing at my back. She'd put on an extra sweater and slipped up silently in the snow behind me. In an intensely bitter voice, she said, "Somebody like that shouldn't have kids. That baby would be lucky if she'd abort it."

When she realized I was staring at her, she grimaced, a little shamefaced, at me.

Old Grace Montgomery, the pig lady, was also watching from her front stoop, leaning on her walker. She wore the same thin housedress I'd seen her in the previous day, without even a shawl to protect her thin, humped shoulders from the cold.

We were all watching, then, like a circle of women around a blood rite, when the police carried out a body, covered in plastic, on a litter. Behind me, Marianne Miller gasped, and said, "Oh God! Who is it?"

"I said so!" old Grace Montgomery shrieked from her porch. She lifted her aluminum walker and began to pound it onto the floor of the porch. My own shoulders ached, just imagining the pain that movement must cause in her arthritic joints. *"I said so!"* she shrieked. *"Nobody listens to an old woman! I told you so!"*

One or two of the cops stopped to stare at her, and then a female cop began to trudge across the snow toward the old lady's house. The other officers returned to their duties, seemingly impervious to the racket, though I suspected it was shredding their nerves as well as mine. I watched an officer I knew, a detective, flip open a billfold he was holding in his hand, pull a card out of it, and study it for a moment.

He looked back at the church, as if scanning it for the address, and then he looked across the street. His gaze came to rest on the porch where the pregnant girl stood, and he started to walk toward her.

The girl saw and stood bolt upright.

"No!" she screamed. She waved her hands frantically in front of her big belly, as if to ward off an evil spirit approaching her. "No! No!"

Now the old lady's shrieks turned wordless and hysterical.

"It's Rodney," Marianne breathed at my back.

The girl turned and fled to her front door, opened it, and ran inside. She slammed the door shut; I imagined her bracing herself against it, trying to hold off what was coming toward her, like a woman holding a cross against a vampire.

The detective ignored it all and just kept walking inexorably through the snow to her house. He knocked steadily, insistently, until she opened the door.

When I turned to say something to Marianne Miller, I discovered she had slipped silently back into her house.

"Jenny?"

It was a detective I knew, standing in front of me.

"I called it in, Frank," I told him.

"Tell me about it," he said, taking out a notebook.

I shrugged. "I just walked up and almost stepped in the footprints and blood, that's all. The doors were ajar. I saw blood, like a handprint, on one of the doors. And then I ran over here and called you guys."

"Why were you here this morning, Jenny?"

Since the real answer—"I was impersonating a crazy lady, Frank"—was embarrassing, I just said, "Oh, the foundation was going to put some money into this place to turn it into a recreation hall for former mental patients. I was just taking another look at it."

He nodded, bless him.

"What did you find in there?" I asked him.

"You sure you want to know?"

"I'm a cop's wife, Frank," I said with a mock bravado that made him smile a little. "I can take it. I'm tough."

"Well, let me tell you, it was enough to make a tough man puke. The deceased was a young guy. Somebody really sliced him up good. It looks like somebody just went crazy in there, Jenny."

"Oh, Frank." I sighed. "You could have talked all day without using the word *crazy*."

He looked at me quizzically, but I only shrugged, and he slipped off to more important tasks.

I looked back at the strange, snow-humped basement, seeing it again with the eyes of the former mental patient in whose shoes I had tried to walk for a little while. ''She'' gazed sadly at it, feeling as if her dreams were melting before her eyes like icicles in the sun. I agreed with her— the heat this murder produced would surely evaporate the plans for the recreation hall.

Two plainclothes detectives and one uniformed officer emerged from around the back of the building, half rolling and half lifting through the snow the blackboard that I had seen the previous day in the central meeting room in the basement.

When they got it to the curb, they stopped, seeming stymied. It was clearly too large a piece of evidence to fit into any of their cars, and the evidence van hadn't arrived yet. They didn't seem to know what to do with it. They stood it in the snow at the curb.

Why did they want to take it to the station at all? I wondered. Couldn't they just check it for prints and photograph it as part of the crime scene?

Curious, I edged around the perimeter barrier to get a better look at it. The side nearest to me was completely covered in a scrawl of white chalk, writing so cramped and tiny it was unreadable until I got up close and squinted at it.

I stood in the snow that was over my ankles and read what seemed to be a long, rambling letter.

''*Dear God,*'' the strange, cramped scrawl began . . .

I am called Mob because I was inhabited by a legion of demons. You know the biblical allusion? No matter. The demons have fled at the insistence of a plethora of psychiatrists. I no longer hear the voices of the demons—how they argued!—no more do I obey their commands. (The same might be said of the psychiatrists.) They fled one night while I slept—picked up their skirts, though do not be misled into thinking they are all female, and tiptoed out from behind my eyelids; it was the only time I can remember their doing anything at all quietly or tactfully—and when I awoke the space in my head was still. Still, it is still. It is still still! Still, there remains one voice, and it is Mob's. Aye, there is vision, in my eyes there is vision, but there are no visions but the vision of Mob, the man who was legion, but whose legions have fled to the hills. It is alone in its head, Mob is, and lonely in this lone place where once legions clambered—to battle, to battle! Aye, I am wounded! Peace. All is not peace, but apace there may come a piece of peace

There was no closing punctuation. No signature.

I suspected I was looking at an actual confession of murder. So why did I feel moved by it?

Frank saw me reading it and walked over to me again.

"You think the killer wrote this, Frank?"

"Might have," he agreed.

"Well," I said, after a moment's reflection, "he must have written it before the murder, because there's no blood on this, and there was definitely blood on his hands when he left the basement! I saw the handprints."

Frank slowly and carefully flipped the board over, revealing the other side to me. It was splattered—very nearly every inch of it covered—with blood.

"Oh, my God," I said, or something to that effect, before I turned away from it. Frank said he was going back to the station and, rather apologetically, offered to drop me off at the foundation on his way.

I took him up on the offer, although I didn't care where he dropped me off. At that moment, I would have gone just about anywhere to get away from that terrible blackboard.

11

Frank let me out in the parking lot, then drove on.

As I crunched across frozen ridges of snow, the breeze crept under my skirt and stroked my thighs with cold fingers. I stepped gratefully into the shelter of our building's lobby. As always, it was dimly lighted and barely heated— in summer it was dimly lighted and barely cooled—our frugal landlord's attempt to cut fuel bills. He, of course, keeps his offices elsewhere; I always imagined them as bright and overheated. Still, on this day, the lobby seemed warm, well, warmer, if not cozy.

When the building was constructed, the architect had foolishly lined the entryway with fake marble, so that on snowy or rainy days you had to tiptoe to the elevators, hugging the wall like a novice skater trying to get off the ice without breaking her neck. There ought to be a law that architects have to live in the buildings they erect for at least a year after they're completed. Not to mention landlords having to live in their properties for a couple of months a year, preferably February and July.

Murder makes some people weep and others throw up. It makes me digress.

As I rode to the sixth floor, I decided my first responsibility was to call MaryDell Paine and tell her that a homicide at the church had probably slain her hall as well. But first I wanted to talk it over with my secretary and my assistant director.

The elevator stopped with its customary jolt. I waited the usual five seconds for the doors to slide open. Conditions weren't always so bad in the building, I mused, but it was nearly eight years old. The last time I complained, the landlord said, "Well, what do you expect from these old places?" This, in a town in which the floors in some houses barely creak after three hundred years.

I was doing it again, digressing.

The twenty paces to my office were carpeted, so at least I didn't have to worry about sliding into home base.

I opened the door. The place was deserted.

"Derek?" I called out as I removed my sodden outer clothing and hung them up to drip in the office closet. My toes felt numb. That was progress, since moments before I hadn't been able to feel them at all. I glanced over at his desk, which he wasn't occupying. It looked atypically neat.

The foundation headquarters may be on the top floor, but it's no penthouse. It's a simple suite of three rooms—a central reception and work area with desks for Derek and for our secretary, Faye Basil; a small conference room to the left as you're facing Faye; and my own small office, which is behind her left shoulder, as she faces visitors.

At that moment, she walked out of my office with a fistful of file folders. She was wearing a three-piece gray suit.

"Faye!" I was all prepared to launch into a melodramatic account of my morning, but it seemed she had her own news to impart, and she beat me to it.

"Jenny, Derek's not here."

It should have been a simple statement of fact, but she said it in the frantic tone she'd use if one of her teenage sons was late with the car at night, drunk, during an ice storm. In other words, her concern seemed excessive. Faye laid the file folders on a corner of her desk without looking at what she was doing. They tumbled to the floor, spilling papers. She didn't even notice, but gestured instead toward Derek's desk.

"He was here. I mean, I guess he was here, but he cleared everything out. And he hasn't been back, and he hasn't even called, and I tried calling his condo, but he wasn't there. . . . Why has he *done* this? I just can't imagine Derek *doing* something like this!"

"Wait a minute." The parts of my brain that weren't frozen were full of images of plastic body bags and the echoes of shrieking women, and I had to clear the screen to comprehend her meaning. As I stepped out of my boots and slipped on the black-leather heels I keep in the closet, I said to her, "I missed that. Tell me again, Faye."

She turned toward me, and now I saw there was also accusation on her face. I couldn't remember Faye ever having been angry at me before, not really angry, at least not any more than exasperated, as any employee feels occasionally toward any boss. The day before, when I had told her about firing Derek, she had received the news with the sorrow a mother might feel. But now it was anger that showed clearly in the unnaturally controlled and precise way she spoke to me.

"I came into work this morning." Her shoulders were rigid. She clasped her hands tightly in front of her, just below the waistband of her skirt. Faye had the rounded stomach that middle age and childbirth bring to women; now her folded hands pressed into it. "Derek wasn't here. Well, that's not odd, I'm usually here before he is. So are you, for that matter. But his desk was all cleaned out, Jenny. Everything's gone!" One hand came loose from her tight grasp and gestured wildly toward Derek's empty desk. She quickly contained it again. "Everything that belonged to him, I mean. His pens and that extra tie he kept in the bottom drawer, and his razor, and that aftershave he used to use when he had a date after work, and that picture of his nieces and nephews, and that kazoo he used to play when he got paid. . . . He's taken everything that's his and left everything that's . . . yours."

She flushed, looked away, then back at me again.

"I mean the foundation's. I'm sorry, I'm just so . . ." But, of course, she wouldn't say "mad at you, Jenny," or "angry" or "frosted" or "pissed off," which was obviously how she felt but she was too much of an old-fashioned lady and a respectful employee to say. And so she finished lamely and told only a partial truth. ". . . upset that he left like this, without even saying good-bye to Marvin and me." Marvin Lastelic was the foundation's part-time accountant. She flushed again. "And to you, too."

I didn't understand it any more than she did.

"But he called me last night, Faye."

I was having a hard time taking it in, particularly on top of everything else. For a moment, I was tempted to inform my secretary—in a restrained and slightly hurt way—that I'd just come from the scene of a murder. But that smacked a little too much of saying, "You think you've had a bad cold? Hell, I've got cancer."

"He called me at home," I repeated. "I'll swear he didn't give me a single hint that he planned to walk out like this."

She firmed her chin, looked me in the eyes, and said, as if to a particularly insensitive child, "Nighttime can be pretty rough when you're all alone, and you're out of a job, and you're not such a young man anymore, and . . ." Tears sprang to her eyes. She turned away from me to stumble over to her desk and sit down. Faye pulled a piece of paper out of a drawer and stuck it in her typewriter. She started typing on it, apparently without seeing that it was a printed contract, already covered with words.

I was astonished by her reaction.

We'd have to work this out, she and I, but later; I wanted to give her a chance to calm down first, so that she wouldn't say things to me in anger that might embarrass us later.

"I'll see if I can locate him, Faye."

The villain of the piece stepped over the spilled folders, and tiptoed into her office. I was tempted to close the door, but I left it open, not wanting to erect any other barriers between us.

12

I crossed the green carpet remnant in my office, walked behind my desk, and sank down in my used brown leather-and-wood swivel chair. The leather made a rat-a-tat-tat sound when I sat down, and the springs complained to me when I leaned forward. I crossed my arms on my desktop and laid my forehead on them.

"Oh, shit," I said wearily to myself.

Like nearly everything else at the foundation, my desk is secondhand, a bulky, chipped old number with a lot of drawers and even more history and character. This morning, the glass that was glued around the edges to the top of my desk smelled faintly of the bleach the building janitorial staff used in their cleaning rags. I turned my face to the side, closed my eyes, and tried to imagine that the light coming in through my windows was summer heat laying a warm, heavy finger on my cheekbone. I tried to imagine that if I suddenly opened my eyes, walked over to the windows, and looked out, I would see green leaves filling the tops of the downtown trees. I imagined breezes, salty air, a flap of wings of a seagull rising from a pier.

I sat up and called Derek's home phone number.

"Hello." It was his answering machine, being flip. "I'm Derek, and you're not. At the tone, tell me who you are, and maybe I'll call you back. Or maybe I won't. Hi, Mom."

It was the same stupid message he had originally put on the machine. Lazy, even in this, he'd never troubled to change it.

I said, trying to keep it light, matching cute for cute: "Hi. This is Jenny. I'm at the office, and you're not. Where are you? Call home, Son. Mom and I miss you."

I waited, hoping he was at home, listening, and that he would pick up the receiver when he heard my voice. When he didn't, I hung up.

"Well, shit," I said again. "Now what do we do?"

I wasn't really that upset. Although this rebellion of his was going to cause me some inconvenience, a part of me rejoiced that he'd shown some spunk: "You can't fire me, Jenny, I quit."

It was then that I noticed that he'd left his "Recreation Hall" file folder on my desk, on top of several of his other records. I reached for it and opened it. Inside were his typed notes from his interviews with the neighbors from the night before. I glanced through them and saw that they confirmed his verbal report—most of the neighbors sounded amenable at best, persuadable at worst. Derek's handwritten notes that he had taken during the interviews, or maybe jotted down immediately afterward, were clipped to the typed copy. The ten pages of stenopad notes in his big, boyish, circling handwriting had turned into one and a half pages of single-spaced typing. I thought back to the evening before: Derek had called me about ten-thirty. Considering the pace at which he usually typed, it had probably taken him about an hour to decipher and to transcribe his own notes. Taking into consideration any breaks he might have taken for coffee, beer, food, other phone calls, or the eleven o'clock news, he probably hadn't ended his workday until midnight or later. If, that is, he had typed the notes at home. It was possible, I supposed, that he had done that job when he came back to the office either last night or very early this morning to clean up and clear out.

While glancing through his handwritten notes, I happened to see that on the last page he'd scribbled with uncharacteristic eagerness: "Good idea, good vibes! Let's go for it, Jenny!" I looked back at the typed version, but didn't find the message there.

Instead of going for it, he'd gone.

I had a sudden image of Derek putting on his ski jacket, getting into his old red Toyota, and driving to the office. It must have still been snowing hard then, visibility must have been terrible, the streets nearly impassable. And yet he had left his warm condominium to come back here, unlock the door to a dark office building, ride up in a cold elevator, enter an empty office, and clear out his desk. I wished the building had a night security guard, so that I might check a log to see what time Derek had signed in and out—as if that knowledge would give me some clue as to the degree and intensity of his perturbation. Had he come over here in the middle of the night, or had he slept on it, dreamed of it, tossed and turned on it, and then resolved at dawn's light to abandon ship?

I didn't get it, and, suddenly, I didn't much like it, either. I resolved to locate Derek, to sit him down and make him tell me what had happened overnight to change him from an eager beaver into a fleeing rat.

I was running out of clichés. Plus, I had other unpleasant news to face.

But before calling MaryDell Paine, I put in a call to Geof at the police station. I wanted to be able to supply MaryDell with as many confirmed facts as possible.

"Hello," I said, when he answered.

"Hi, hon. I guess this is the day the bear eats you."

"I watched them bring out the body."

He sighed. "So I heard. Well, sure. Don't you always?"

I ignored that gratuitous dig. "What do you know?"

"The victim was a man named Rodney Gardner, thirty-one years old. He lived in a house that's for sale across from the church. Do you know which one I mean?"

"Yes."

"Is he the 'fuckin' charmer' you told me about?"

"Yes. He was a jerk, rest in peace."

"He was also self-employed as a carpenter and handyman. He was thirty-one years old and he lived with a twenty-one-year-old woman named Samantha who—"

"Really? She doesn't look over sixteen."

"—who says Gardner saw lights on in the church last night, around one o'clock, and that he put on a coat and went over to see what was going on."

"In a snowstorm? Why didn't he just call the cops?"

"I don't know, Jenny. Maybe he was a dumb jerk. She says she went to bed and that she didn't notice that he didn't come home again. When she got up, she thought he'd gone to a job he was working on. I guess you heard he was slashed and stabbed to death. I hear it was a mess. I've got to tell you, Jenny, they say it looks like somebody went crazy in there. That's the word the detectives are using, crazy."

"I know. Suspects?"

"Did you see the blackboard?"

"Yes."

"Read what was written there?"

"Yes."

"Do you think it was a confession?"

"I don't know. Probably. Maybe."

"You're so opinionated. Well, we're looking for this

Mob person. Do you think that's short for something, Jenny? Moberbly? Moby Dick?''

"Mobster?"

He laughed briefly. "We should ask God. If this Mob gets a reply to his letter, this will be a more important case than it seems. We can build a shrine around the blackboard. Sell bits of the wood to true believers.'' The amusement left his voice, and seriousness descended again. ''We're also looking for the landlord to ask him if the blackboard was clean yesterday. Did you see it, Jenny? Do you remember any writing on it?''

"The side I saw was clean, Geof."

"You do come in handy sometimes."

"You might consider putting me on retainer."

"Or a restrainer?"

"Very funny, cop. What else?"

"Well, so this Mob person is probably the one who was in the building and turned on the lights and killed Rodney Gardner.'' Without pausing, he then said, ''Jenny, I have this feeling that other cops don't discuss their cases in such detail with the Little Woman. I suspect they talk about Little League games and mowing the grass and what's for dinner. Do you think we could try that sometime?''

"Chili."

"What?"

"It's my turn to cook. That's what's for dinner, and it's in a can in the cupboard, so all you'll have to do is warm it in the microwave and find the crackers."

He laughed.

As he had explained the facts of the case to me, an uneasiness had tickled across the back of my skull, but I couldn't identify the source. Instead, I started to say good-bye to him. He stopped me, however, by saying, "Jenny?"

"Yes?"

"You're being calm to the point of blasé. Do you realize

that? It makes me feel kind of . . . sad . . . to think my wife has that much experience with homicide."

"I'm all right, Geof." I spoke, not blithely, but gently and seriously, as he had just spoken to me. "Really, I am. I'm only a very minor witness. To paraphrase a cop we used to know, I'm not the one who's dead. I think that's a very handy perspective. I'm okay, honestly."

After that, I called Mrs. Paine at her home.

But it turned out that MaryDell had already learned of the murder from an in-your-face phone call from Mr. Perry, The Walking Cigar, Yates.

She didn't, however, know about the letter to God that had been scrawled across the blackboard.

". . . written by somebody named Mob," I finished.

"What?" She said it harshly, as if she hadn't really been listening until that moment.

"Mob." I spelled it for her. "Now MaryDell, I don't think we have to give up the idea of putting the recreation hall in that basement. Let's give this a couple of days, see if they arrest anybody. Maybe it will be somebody completely unconnected to mental health." I laughed, cynically, when I heard my own words. "You know what I mean. Anyway, let's see how the neighbors take this, and let's not just assume it's all down the tubes. I'll go ahead and get my proposal ready for the trustees' meeting, and—"

"No." She interrupted in the same harsh tone. "No."

"But—"

"No!"

I would have argued with her, but she hung up on me. I would have been surprised at her reaction, if I hadn't already formed an idea about why she had capitulated so easily.

"Faye?"

I heard her chair wheeling toward the doorway, and then her face appeared, a small, sheepish smile on it.

I smiled back. "I know it's a lot to ask in this weather, but would you let me borrow your car for a couple of hours?"

"That's what my boys say, and then I don't see it again until Sunday," she said, in a chattering way, as if she were nervous or self-conscious. "Sure, Jenny. You know you can borrow anything of mine. Also . . . you can have my apology."

"Thanks, but I only need the car."

I walked into the outer office, stood beside her desk, and took the keys she fished out of her purse and handed to me. When she gave me another smile, along with the keys, I said, "Faye, it's a good thing you're sitting down, because I need to tell you about my morning. . . ."

13

Our parking lot looked as if a strong wind had blown through and swung the vehicles every which way. The neat white parking lanes were obscured by messy white snow, so the drivers had abandoned their cars wherever they slid to a safe stop. Faye's car wasn't hard to find—it was an old gray Volvo station wagon, a heavy tank that tracked well in any weather, and the only car pointed neatly into the curb.

Using her key, which was attached to a ring with a Boy Scout emblem on it, I opened the door on the driver's side. I tucked my coat underneath me, and slid onto the hard, cold front seat alongside a Spiderman comic book, a couple of loose C-cell batteries, an ice scraper, a cassette tape, a quart can of 10-40 weight oil, a metal spout, and a clear plastic box of nails in mixed sizes. To the left of the steering wheel, there was a hand-lettered sign: "Turn off your lights, Mom!" Near the floor, there was a pull-out beverage holder with a Big Slurp soda cup in one hole and a Phillips screwdriver in the other. A Louis L'Amour paperback Western lay on the rim of the cup; I picked up the book and looked in the cup, just to make sure it was empty. It was, save for some small plastic screws that looked stuck to the brown guck at the bottom. I was well equipped if I suddenly had to entertain any teenage boys.

I picked up the cassette and looked at the label: "The Lettermen in Concert." So Faye did get to drive it now and then. Or maybe one of the boys had discovered the magical effect of swoony love ballads on teenage girls.

I turned the key in the ignition. The engine rolled right over. I switched on the defroster and by the time I drove onto the street, it had the windows cleared. I switched the heater to "Floor" and soon hot air was defrosting my toes. If only, I thought, the tanks the U.S. Army purchased worked half as reliably as this one. Somewhere in me, a Swedish gene swelled with pride.

I drove with confidence. Anything that slid into me would have the bigger bruises to show for it.

MaryDell Paine's address was thirty blocks from the murder and on a far different sort of block from the one where the old church basement lay.

As I drove out there, I measured the distance not only in miles but also in the increasing depths of the lawns from curb to porch, in the manicuring of those lawns, and in the increasing size and beauty of the residences. From Tenth Street to Forty-eighth Street, where she lived, the houses grew to brick and clapboard mansions, some antiques, some reproductions of antiques. It took the mailman much longer to walk from his truck to these mailboxes than it did for him to reach the mailboxes on Tenth Street. Beneath the snow, the grass and trees and shrubs on Forty-eighth Street were sucking up chemicals that Tenth Street couldn't afford, perhaps to its ultimate good fortune. The driveways here had already been cleared by snowblowers and hired help, while it would take longer for the residents of Tenth to shovel their snow by hand. The cars in the driveways were different, too—changing from used and American on Tenth, to new and foreign on Forty-eighth.

Let me make it clear that I was not snubbing Forty-eighth Street in my observations: for one thing, it is beautiful; for another, I grew up near it and will probably always live on blocks like it. I'm aware of the differences, that's all; a fact that probably helped to land me in foundation work, which is one of capitalism's safety valves, a seemingly innocuous way to redistribute wealth short of forcing the landholders off their coffee plantations at the point of a rifle butt. The fact that such a system also results in what is euphemistically called "social engineering," has not escaped my notice, or that of Congress, but that, as they say, is another story, or maybe inherent in this one.

I know, I'm doing it again—digressing. But consider the morning I'd had thus far!

I located MaryDell's address and spun my tires up the cleared but icy driveway to park in her small private parking lot. It was roomy enough for four or five cars to park side by side without denting each other's doors. I stepped carefully over the shoveled brick walk that led to the house, which was a vast, three-story clapboard that rambled over a lot and a half. It was immaculately painted in colonial reds, whites, and blues; the flag of the thirteen original colonies fluttered from a brass pole that jutted from the roof. Red silk geraniums bloomed out of season in black cast-iron pots on either side of the double front door. The brass knocker on the door was shaped like an eagle and, when raised, it beat down upon the engraved brass monogram of the house. It was useless, of course; nobody could hear a knock through the solid oak of that front door.

I rang the bell.

It played "Yankee-Doodle."

Not merely the first line of it either, but a whole damn verse and chorus. The last note was dying out when a young black woman in a pink-and-white maid's uniform opened the door, and said, "Yes?" through gritted teeth. I thought her expression of pained annoyance had less to do with me than with the doorbell.

"You could rip out its wires," I suggested.

"I could rip it to spaghetti," she snarled. "Yes?"

"I'm Jenny Cain. To see Mrs. Paine."

The maid glared at me as if I'd made up the unfortunate rhyme on purpose, to torment her further. My serious mission to this house was turning giddy. I was reminded of a survey in which it was demonstrated that the absurd appeals more often to a woman's sense of humor than to a man's. Too true, I thought; it was real hard to imagine Philip Marlowe saying anything as absurd as "I'm Philip Marlowe to see Jean Harlow," and then having to stifle his giggles because of it. The maid allowed me into the foyer, and then departed for the interior while I removed my coat, hat, and gloves and deposited them in a hall closet. The house smelled wonderful—yeasty, like baking rolls, with an underlay of lemony furniture polish. I gazed up the long central stairwell to the second floor and tried to compose myself for the serious interview that lay ahead.

Soon MaryDell filled the hallway, covering the previous smells with the scent of Joy perfume. She wore a green velour jogging suit that made her look like an avocado, and matching clogs, with hose. It seemed a long and eventful time since breakfast; at the sight of her, I had a sudden craving for corn chips and guacamole dip.

"Why, Jenny, what a nice surprise!" she lied.

"I'm sorry to drop in on you like this without any warning, MaryDell," I lied in return, "but we need to talk—"

"If it's about the recreation hall, I already said—"

"It's not, exactly."

"Well, I'm awfully busy this morning—"

"It'll only take a few minutes."

She sighed, resigning herself to the intrusion.

"Come back to the sun porch, Jenny."

I followed her short, stout figure through a myriad of hallways, past assorted Americana. En route, she talked nonstop. It was like following a tour guide through a lesser museum.

"Welcome to the ancestral home, Jenny," she said smoothly. "Five generations of my husband's family have lived in this old barn, and now I'm the lucky one who gets to try to keep it from falling down around our heads. My husband was born here. His mother and her father were not only born here but also died here in their own beds, a fate that probably also awaits us. The central house is circa 1792. Three wings have been added in the last century; the newest wing includes the room to which we are going now. Almost all the furnishings, paintings, and other decorative objects are authentic originals, most of which have required refurbishing by the few remaining handcraftsmen who can still perform the old trades. If you think a plumber's expensive these days, you ought to try calling a coppersmith! Only the furnishings in the sun room are new. You'll have to forgive me that lapse."

Had I detected a note of irony amid the redundancies?

"Anita!" My reluctant hostess called briskly into the kitchen as we passed it. Above the level of the swinging doors, the maid peered up with that same pained expression on her face. A perky little pink-and-white cap sat atop her hair; the cap alone would have been enough to give me a pained expression, but maybe the bobby pins were biting into her scalp as well. "Bring us some tea, will you? And a plate of those breakfast rolls—warm them up for us in the microwave, that's a good girl. Here, Jenny . . ."

"Yes, ma'am."

That was the maid saying that, not I.

We entered a yellow-and-white room with floor-to-ceiling louvered windows. I thought it was pretty optimistic of MaryDell to call it the "sun room," considering the ratio of rain to sun in Poor Fred. Of course, MaryDell had a reputation as a "doer," always trying to change the world into her vision of how it should be. Maybe she thought that if she threw enough sunny colors around, she could change Port Frederick into Port Everglades.

She pointed me into a cushion wicker basket of a chair that put my rear end nearly on the floor and shoved my knees up around my chest. For herself, MaryDell chose a straight-backed wooden chair in which she looked efficient enough to call a meeting to order. I could have moved, but the situation appealed to my sense of the absurd, that renowned female trait I mentioned earlier. I pulled my skirt down over my knees and stayed where I was, gazing up at her from my basket like a baby in a wicker bassinet.

Since she was in a hurry, I didn't waste her time.

"Did you locate your brother, MaryDell?"

"What?" She started, but recovered herself and gave me a meeting-chairman smile. Then she began to talk in an odd, nervous, herky-jerky fashion that was quite unlike her usual smooth, hyperbolic patter. "Oh, yes. Yes, I did, Jenny. It's so kind of you to inquire. I did locate him. Yes, I most certainly did. That was excellent advice you gave me last night; I simply must say it just helped me so much. As it turns out, there wasn't any need for me to be upset at all. I just can't imagine why I was so upset when the solution was just so simple. Why, I called the mission, just as you suggested, and there he was, he was there, all right; he was there perfectly safe. Thank you, Jenny. I'm just so very grateful. It was such a help, really it was, such a help. Ah, Anita! Tea, wonderful! Wonderful tea, wonderful sweet rolls. Here, Jenny, have a—"

"The police will check, MaryDell."

Anita raised her eyes and stared at me over the tray she carried. MaryDell, who had started to lift a teacup from the tray, put her hands back in her lap, as if withdrawing them to safety. In a cold voice, she said, "Thank you, Anita, just leave the tray on the table; I believe that's all we'll be needing now. You may go right on back to the kitchen. There's a good girl. Thank you so much, Anita."

"Yes, ma'am."

We both waited, two gamblers unwilling to blink, until we heard the swinging doors slap back against the kitchen wall.

14

"The police will check what, Jenny?"

"They'll check the mission, MaryDell, to see if your brother really was there." I was trying to leaven the truth with kindness, or at least with a gentle tone of voice, but, damn, the woman annoyed me. I explained: "You know, or perhaps you don't, that they lock the doors of the mission after ten o'clock. No one gets in or out after that, at least not without being noticed. And they don't unlock the doors again until six in the morning. So it will be very easy for the police to find out if Kitt was there. That's what you call him, isn't it? Kitt?"

She nodded. Her lips were tightly compressed, as if they dammed a flood of sentences with which she wanted to drown me. That, and the constant stroking of her fingers on her pant legs, were her only sign of nervousness; otherwise she appeared completely calm, even unconcerned.

"What does he call *himself*, MaryDell?"

Open Sesame. Open MaryDell. The floodgate parted, releasing words of a very different sort from the nicey-niceys with which she usually sugar-coated her speech.

"That's none of your damned business! Who the hell do you think you are coming here to my house, asking me questions that are none of your *damned* business!" Here was a woman who lacked originality, even in her indignation. She made a sudden, visible effort to get herself back under control, drawing her small body up into its meeting-chairman posture. She even managed a forgiving, yet contrite smile. Her next words might have come off a Gracious Lady tape: "I'm so sorry, that was unforgivable of me. I don't know what's wrong with me, Jenny, but I expect that it's simply that I'm upset about the recreation hall, you see, plus I'm very busy this morning. I don't mean to be rude, but really, I'm afraid you came at an especially bad, that is to say, busy time . . ."

"He calls himself Mob," I said firmly. "If I understand it correctly, and you'd know about this better than I, he calls himself that because he thinks he was possessed by a mob of demons. MaryDell, your brother returned to the basement after you showed it to him yesterday; don't you think that's probably what happened? And somehow he got into the building, where he probably intended to spend the night. Now the police are looking for him. Or they would be, if they knew who Mob really was. He's Kitt—what's your family name, MaryDell?"

I waited, though I didn't think she'd answer me.

"Blackstone," she said, after a moment.

"Kitt Blackstone?"

She nodded as if her neck were weighted with stones.

"If you don't want to call the police, MaryDell, I'll do it for you. That's why I came out here, so you wouldn't have to do it and feel like a traitor to your brother. Do you know where he is now?"

Her false calm disintegrated, and she began to cry, but they looked like angry tears, and she sat up very straight to cry them.

"If I couldn't find him last night," she said, enunciating carefully, "how do you think I could possibly find him today, especially today? Call them, damn you, but let me call my husband first. It's the least he deserves. The man deserves some warning before this new humiliation from my brother. I suppose I should thank you, Jenny. But I'll never be grateful to you for what you've done this morning. Never."

"I wouldn't be grateful either," I said.

I pushed myself out of the wicker basket and walked over to a wicker-and-glass table that had a telephone on it. A sunny yellow telephone. I picked it up, carried it over to her, and put it on her lap, as if she sat in a wheelchair. She did seem paralyzed. Her movements, when she punched in the number, were stiff; her words, when she spoke to her husband, sounded as harsh and controlled as notes played on a harpsichord. When she was finished breaking the bad news—it was a very short conversation—I lifted the phone off her lap and called Geof at the police station. He said he would immediately send detectives to interview her.

"MaryDell, I'm sorry."

She nodded, not looking at me.

"Maybe they'll find he didn't have anything to do with it, MaryDell. And in the meantime, we won't give up on the recreation hall. If we can't have that site, we'll look for another—"

"Do you think I care?" she hissed at me, her eyes gone hard, like two black pits. "Why should I care now that Kitt can't use it. It was only for him. It was always for him. I don't give a damn about all those other stupid, dirty, crazy people. Don't mention it to me again—ever. I don't care about it. I don't care about them. I don't care about you. Get out."

I was more than happy to do that, although, I thought, how will I get that report of hers now?

On my way past the kitchen, I looked over the swinging

doors. Anita the maid was seated on a high stool, unmoving, hands folded in her pink lap, staring at nothing, doing nothing. I walked faster, down the hallways, through the foyer, retrieving my coat from the closet, putting it on, opening and closing the front door behind me, trotting back down the brick walk—escaping from this authentic house with its reproduction people.

Before I stepped into Faye's car, I reached into my coat pocket for her keys. I pulled out instead a roughly cut circle of stiff white paper that was probably only about an inch in diameter. Curious, I turned it over and found that it was the back of a black-and-white photograph of the head, shoulders, and upper chest of a young man. He had a pale, pudgy face with an odd, questioning expression. He was squinting into the camera. It looked as if someone had snipped it out of a larger photograph, perhaps for a wallet or a locket. Or maybe to excise it from a larger scene. Or maybe only to give to me. I ran a finger around the edges; they didn't have the sharp, rough feel of a recent cut. They had, instead, the soft dull feel that time imparts. One thing was certain, I hadn't brought it with me. So unless there had been somebody else in Mary-Dell's house, it meant the maid had planted it in my pocket.

"Kitt," I murmured to it, certain of his identity.

He looked so young and so puzzled. What's it all about? he seemed to ask, squinting painfully at me. What does it mean? Why is this happening to me?

I put it back into my pocket to save for Geof, although I didn't imagine that this old photo would be much help in identifying Kitt now. How old had MaryDell said her brother was? Forty-five, forty-six? The boy—man—in the picture didn't look over thirty, if that. Was he already Mob by then, I wondered? When, exactly, did Kitt Blackstone become Mob, the man of many demons? And which one of those demons killed Rodney Gardner?

That was a creepy thought, like sensing monsters in the shadows. I had a sudden impulse to lock the car doors. I told myself not to be foolish, and then I locked them anyway.

The sun had gone behind the clouds, taking the snow's sparkle with it and leaving behind only a flat, gray-white landscape and bitter cold. In the short while I'd been in MaryDell's house, Faye's car had frosted over and chilled like a metal flask in a freezer. The outside temperature was dropping again, as if it were January instead of October. When it's cold in Port Frederick—with those Atlantic "breezes" freezing us in our tracks—it's cold. As we natives say, but quietly so the tourists won't hear, if the salt don't halt ya, the breeze'll freeze ya.

I backed up the Volvo in the big driveway and turned it around so that I could slide down MaryDell's driveway nose first, in first gear.

15

My old friend Marsha Sandy was on my mind, and because of that I swung by her office before returning to my own. Marsha and I had been close friends for so long, and were so open to each other's thoughts and needs, that whenever she came suddenly and persistently into my head, I knew it probably meant she was nearby or thinking about me. If my thoughts of her were strong enough to block out images of murder and mental illness, I was willing to tackle snowy side streets and another half-block trek in the cold to find out why.

It was five minutes to the hour of one o'clock, which meant she was between patients, when I opened the door to her reception area. She almost never ate lunch, a trait that seemed like a character flaw to someone who liked to eat as much and as often as I did. More than once, I had suggested she might want to get counseling for it. Her reply was usually to glance at my hips and smile. As usual, my timing for these intuitive meetings was impeccable. Involuntary but impeccable.

Sure enough, she opened the door to her inner office

just as her receptionist told me that Dr. Sandy didn't have enough time between patients to see me. The patient in question, an anorexic-looking young woman, glared at me over the *People* magazine she was reading, as if daring me to eat up a moment of her rightful share of Marsha's expensive time. If I seemed to be concentrating overmuch on food, it was because I was hungry.

"I've been thinking about you," Marsha said, and smiled.

"Do you have time to tell me why?"

"Four minutes. Come in."

I followed her back into her office, and she shut the door behind us. Marsha waved me to a nubby, many-cushioned couch that was upholstered in pretty, light, peaceful shades of pink, yellow, and green. We sat down at opposite ends of it. I was tempted to remove my shoes and put my legs up on the couch, but I wasn't sure how my feet smelled after sweating under various car heaters.

"Sometime I imagine I'm a fly, Doc," I said.

"What a problem it must be for you finding sunglasses that fit," she replied.

Marsha was groomed to look efficient instead of gorgeous, but her basic beauty still shone through. I wondered how she handled it when her male patients fell in love with her. She probably dismissed the phenomenon by calling it transference, but I thought that theory failed to take into account that most men tended to fall in love with her. Considering the sort of woman she was, I thought that was a highly sane move on their part.

"I'm so proud of you," I said.

"Thanks, Mom."

"What's up?"

"Listen, Jenny, I've heard the news about that murder at the site where you wanted to put the recreation hall for the former mental patients." She was talking fast and succinctly. "And I've been worrying all morning that you'd give up the idea because of it. I want to plead with you not to do that. This town really needs a place like that, and I'd still love to see it in that old basement you described to Joe and me last night." She paused long enough to smile slightly. "The symbolism appeals to me—basements, you know, are dream symbols of deep, subconscious feelings." A hint of frown lines appeared in her smooth forehead. "I have a deep, subconscious feeling that you may be giving up. Are you giving up?"

"Well." I sighed, feeling pressured. "We've probably lost the neighbors' support, public relations have surely gone to hell, and we've also just lost the support of the woman who started the whole thing in the first place. I told you about MaryDell Paine and her schizophrenic brother?"

Marsha nodded.

"Well, Marsha, he's the one the cops are looking for."

She shook her head so hard that wisps of her dark hair flew out of the chignon in which she had restrained them.

"We can't talk about that," she said, disappointing me, because I wanted so badly to gossip about the morning's events, and my small part in them. But then, I knew she didn't have much time, and she had a point to make. In fact, she was saying, "We've got to talk about the recreation hall. Jenny, look at the weather outside! If this is the kind of winter we're going to have, we've got to provide some shelter, we've *got* to, and you're going to do it through the foundation. I feel absolutely inspired by this project of yours, and I want to inspire you."

"Oh, Marsha." I put my hand over my eyes, feeling exhausted.

She stood up, but then bent over to tug at my sleeve.

"You have to go, I've got to see my next patient. But there's somebody I want you to meet. Here." She removed from her skirt pocket a piece of paper that she pressed into my hands. "Here's her name and address.

She's expecting you. She's very sweet and vulnerable. It will be terrible if you don't show up. I'll never forgive you."

"Thanks a *lot.* Stop pulling at me. I'm going."

"Oh, good! Thank you!"

"To the *door,* I mean." I waved the piece of paper in her face. "Is this one of your patients, Marsha?"

"Go see for yourself. Please? Okay?"

As I let her shove me out, I said in a martyred tone, "All right. All right. As there's no phone number on this, I suppose you even told her to expect me at a certain time, too?"

"Whenever you show up. Bye."

As she shooed me away, I groused, "Next time, don't call me, I'll call you." When the outer office door whooshed closed behind me, I looked at my watch. She would make her appointment—it was straight up one o'clock. I was hungry, and damned if I'd let some damned-fool psychiatrist bully me into missing lunch. Her patient—or whoever "Rosalinda N. McInerny" was—might have a psychotic episode if I didn't show up, but I knew I'd have a low-blood-sugar attack if I didn't eat soon. Then we'd both be raving.

The Buoy Bar & Grill—with its crab-and-lobster-salad sandwiches, its curlicue french fries, and its incomparable cole slaw—was near enough to make my mouth water just thinking about it. I walked the three blocks over to it, out of some perverse urge to make the reward sweeter by delaying it. When I got there, however, I found that I couldn't sit down and eat without feeling guilty about the McInerny woman who was waiting for me to show up. Psychiatrists are supposed to be reliable. If your psychiatrist says something is going to happen, it's supposed to happen and you'll probably suffer a relapse, at the very least a crisis of faith, if it doesn't. So what if the psychiatrist made promises before getting permission from all parties? That wasn't McInerny's fault. It was the fault of the psychiatrist's friend, for being such a renowned patsy. I ordered a second sandwich, and potato chips instead of fries (figuring they'd travel better), and more slaw.

"And two large coffees," I instructed.

While I waited for them to put the order together, I used a pay phone to call the office.

"Faye," I said, when she answered. "Do you need your car."

"Oh, no, Jenny, I knew I wouldn't want to go out in this weather, so I brought my lunch today. You can keep it as long as you like. But say, I'm so glad you called in. Jenny, you'll never guess who's back in town and called you this morning!"

"Michael Laurence."

She laughed a little. "Honestly, you're no fun. Well, anyway, he called—oh, he's still just the most charming man, isn't he?—and he left a kind of strange message."

"I'll bet."

"It says, Better Luck Next Time."

"Yes, he certainly is charming."

"I'd just love to see him again. I hope you'll get him to come in to the office to say hello, Jenny." As an afterthought, she added, "If Geof wouldn't mind, I mean." Faye liked my husband well enough, but she had swooned over Michael's more refined handsomeness. Geof's looks had the kind of hard edge that makes mothers nervous; Michael was more the son-in-law of their dreams.

"Any other calls, Faye?"

She reeled off a list of ten or so, concluding with, "Oh, and your husband called, but he asked to talk to Derek."

"Geof did? What did you tell him?"

She stuttered a bit over the awkward subject. "I—I just said, well, I said, Derek wasn't in today. I—I just didn't know what else to say . . ."

"I understand, but if he calls back, go ahead and tell him the truth, Faye, and find out what he wants. Maybe you can help him with it. All right?"

"Okay." She sounded subdued. "Yes."

"I'm going to an appointment that I *think* concerns the recreation hall, Faye. Then I'll drive by Derek's place to see if I can pin him down. I'll see you after that. And thanks again for the car, it's better than a snowmobile."

"It's a beast," she said fondly. "Bye, Jenny."

I got off the phone in time to hear my name called for my order. They had wrapped everything and stuffed it in a big white paper bag. I picked it up and trudged back through the snow to Faye's car, with lunch for two.

I ate my share of the potato chips while I drove.

The address Marsha had given me was 23 North Eighth Street, which would place it near downtown, fairly close to her office and to the Buoy. I turned north on Eighth, at the 100 block, and slowed down, looking for it. I passed an abandoned filling station, a red brick Catholic church with an attached rectory, both of them boarded up, and the west side of our downtown municipal park. Wait a minute, I thought, where was 23? I went around the block and drove more slowly this time. There was no number on the filling station, but I peered above at the various doorsills of the church and rectory until I located an address: 21 North Eighth. The next stop was the park. Huh? I checked for traffic and backed up to make sure I hadn't missed an alleyway or something. No, there was nothing between the rectory and the park. Well, shoot. Thanks, Marsha, old pal, you've given me the wrong darn . . .

"Oh, *shit.*" The truth finally penetrated, dismaying me with its implications and startling me into profanity. "It's the *park.* This woman is waiting for me in the goddamned park. *Damn* you, Marsha Sandy. Oh, *Christ.*"

16

You might think there wouldn't be many people in a park on a day like that, but that would only show how much time you spend indoors in the winter.

I passed kids on sleds, a couple of joggers—good grief—a pair of lovers huddling under a single parka, at least one mother with a stroller, and a few people who seemed to be hustling across the park on their way to somewhere else, somewhere warmer and dryer, no doubt.

I didn't think any of these people were Ms. McInerny.

But diagonally across the park from where I entered it, a person who appeared to be female sat alone at the end of a bench under a dead walnut tree.

Christ, I thought again.

The reason I was so blasphemously upset was that I knew what this meant: it meant she didn't have any place else to go; it meant she spent her days, even her coldest days, in this park, and maybe even her nights, as well. It meant she was one sick lady, living one miserable life. It made me angry, it made me sad, it made me hurry toward her.

I hugged the white paper sack to the chest of my coat. God, it was cold. I was grateful that although I didn't have on slacks, at least the hem of my skirt met the tops of my boots. I was grateful for the cashmere beret that I'd pulled down over my ears, for the extra pair of socks I'd slipped on that morning over my hose, for my lined Isotoner gloves. As I walked toward the woman on the bench, I found myself counting a lot of blessings.

When I reached the bench, I stopped a few feet away and said, "Excuse me. Are you Ms. McInerny?"

She had been studying her mittened hands in her lap, but now she looked up at me. She was a large woman, constructed in circles, like a snowman. Her body was lumpy with overweight and with all the layers of clothing she wore. She was probably in her late thirties, early forties, but her face was unlined. That might have been because the fat beneath the skin smoothed it out, but there was also a dull, passive appearance to it. I'd seen that unnaturally youthful skin before, on women my age and older at the psychiatric hospital where my mother lived. Those women didn't have laugh lines because they rarely laughed; they didn't have frown lines because they were drugged out of their anger. Like this woman, their faces had a hangdog appearance, as if their muscles lacked tone, as if they lacked the ambition to lift those muscles into conversation or expression. She wore no makeup, though her cheeks were chapped red as rouge; she had short, frizzy, light brown hair that escaped in untidy wisps from beneath her cap. The cap was pink, with earflaps that were tied under her fatty chin by a string. It was like meeting in the flesh the woman I had earlier imagined myself to be. What cheek, I thought: How could I, healthy, wealthy, and sane, even pretend to know what life was like for her?

I observed all that during the time it took for my question to register. She nodded. I introduced myself. After nearly as long a pause, she nodded again.

I gestured toward the empty end of the bench.

"Do you mind if I join you?"

She stared where I had pointed, again seemed to have to register the question, nodded. I wiped as much snow off the bench with my gloves as I could, although some of it stuck in icy clumps to the metal. Sighing to myself, I sat down, my white bag crackling.

"I brought lunch," I said. "Will you join me?"

During the pause before she nodded, I reached into the sack and started bringing out the various containers and placing them in the snow on the bench between us.

Her lips came apart slowly, as if they were cold and stiff, or as if she hadn't used them to talk in a long time. In a soft, slow, toneless voice, she asked, "What is it anyway?"

"These are crab salad," I said, pointing at the sandwiches. "That's cole slaw. Potato chips. Coffee. Forks. Napkins. There's plenty for both of us. Please help yourself."

Slowly, carefully, she lifted one of the sandwiches and folded back the brown waxed-paper wrapping. She gazed at it for a few moments before she tried it. After a few bites, during which mayonnaise accumulated around her lips, she said, "It's good." After a few more bites, she said, "Thanks a lot."

"I should have brought chili," I said.

She slowly circled her mouth with her tongue, getting most of the mayonnaise off.

"Do you come here a lot, Ms. McInerny?"

She nodded. The food seemed to speed up her reaction time, or maybe it just warmed her chilled brain.

"But it's so cold," I said.

She stopped chewing, swallowed, and said in a slow

monotone, "It's not so bad today. It'll be real cold in a while." There was a long pause before she added, "I won't be able to come here much longer." Long pause. "It'll be too cold."

"What will you do then?"

She shrugged, a slow rising and falling of her many-layered shoulders. Under a huge brown quilted coat she seemed to be wearing at least two sweaters, a skirt and slacks. On her feet were huge rubber boots lined with dirty white fuzz. She didn't look like a bag lady, however, or even particularly poor, just slightly eccentric. Actually, I should have appeared the more eccentric one, wearing only my coat and a thin wool dress to this snowy picnic in the park.

"Stay in my room," she answered.

"Do you live near here?"

"Not too far." For the first time since I'd arrived, she looked up at me. Her eyes were an unpretty blue; her expression was blankly serious. "I don't mind the snow. But I hate it when it rains. I get so wet." She cocked her head. "Do you like the rain?"

"From the inside," I said, "looking out."

She thought that over, nodded, then suddenly smiled.

We finished our lunches in near-silence, but it was companionable now. I didn't want to press her, but I wanted to know more about her. Evidently, she wanted to know at least a little about me, too, because she said, "I sure thank you for lunch. What's your name again?"

"Jenny. Jenny Cain."

"Do you know Dr. Sandy?"

I nodded. "We're old friends."

"I think she's wonderful. My name's Rosalinda."

"I know. It's beautiful."

"I play the guitar."

"That's wonderful."

She nodded her head. "Yes. I'm supposed to play it every day. Dr. Sandy says it will make me feel better, so I won't be so depressed all the time. But I don't like playing it just by myself. I like to play for other people."

Ah, I thought: there's my opening.

"Rosalinda, if there was a place . . . a nice, warm, friendly place . . . where you could go during the day . . . and be with other people who've been sick, like you . . . and talk to them if you want to . . . or play your guitar if you want to . . . would you go there?"

She frowned in puzzlement. "A hospital, you mean?"

"No, a recreation hall, a place especially for people who have been sick like you have, a place for people who would like to have some place nice to spend some of their time."

"That sounds nice," she said, wistfully.

"Rosalinda, would you go?"

"Go?"

"To a recreation hall like that?"

"How would I get there?"

"By bus, maybe."

"I couldn't do that."

"Why not?"

"I don't know how."

"They'd show you."

"I can't afford to take the bus."

"They'd help you afford it."

"Who?"

"The staff at the recreation hall."

"They wouldn't let me take my guitar on the bus."

"Yes, Rosalinda, they would. Believe me. They would."

"I wouldn't know anybody."

"You'd make friends."

"They wouldn't like me."

"I think they would. Very much."

She glanced slowly at me, then away.

"Rosalinda, would you try it?"

She shrugged her slow shrug. "I don't know."

I decided that was all I could expect. Why, after all, should she commit herself to something she'd never seen or ever heard about before? For the first time, I realized that if we opened a recreation hall, it would have to prove itself to the clients, as well as to the neighbors. We couldn't take anything about it for granted. She seemed relieved when I dropped the subject.

Rosalinda helped me to gather our trash and to stuff it back into the paper sack. I was aware that she watched me as I carried it all to a trash can and dumped it in. When I returned to stand near her, her pudgy fingers were lying in her lap again.

I said, "Thank you for sharing my lunch."

"I am happy to meet you," she replied, with great seriousness. Snow was starting to fall again; small flakes dotted her pink cap, her dark, quilted shoulders, the tops of her mittens and boots. "I think you're the prettiest person that's ever spoken to me in my whole life."

"Thank you." I had to wait a minute before I could speak again. I cleared my throat. "Could I give you a ride back to your room?"

She shook her head.

"Well, good-bye, Rosalinda."

She nodded. "Good-bye, Jenny Friend."

I must have looked puzzled, or something.

"That's what I call people who are nice to me," she explained, her eyes looking straight into mine. I had been wondering if she might be slightly retarded, or if this simpleness was an effect of illness, or drugs. "I have a Mama Friend and a Papa Friend. And Doctor Sandy Friend. I have a Christopher Friend and a Case Worker Friend. Now I have a Jenny Friend. Even if I don't ever see you again, you'll always be my Jenny Friend. Is that all right?''

"Yes," I murmured over the conch shell in my throat. After offering another awkward good-bye, I turned away and walked quickly back to the car.

You win, Marsha, I thought. I'll try.

17

I was so cold by that time that the interior of Faye's Volvo seemed warm by comparison. Slipping into it, I was reminded that before I did anything else I had a promise to keep to her. But I was suddenly so tired that it seemed a great and unnecessary effort to make. Derek was a grown man; surely he didn't need Faye to mother him or me to chase him. I crossed my gloved hands on top of the steering wheel, rested my head on them, and closed my eyes to the sight of the snow falling on the hood of the car.

Damn, what a day. I felt as if I'd taken uppers and downers simultaneously—the uppers shouted "Go for it," while the downers mumbled, "Sleep." I promised my complaining body that I would defrost it and park it after I had completed this errand. Remember how lucky you are, I said to myself. Drive, I said to myself.

I parked on the street in front of the condo complex where Derek lived. I was going to have to get out of that car—just as it was finally getting warm again. I could easily have killed him for causing this noble sacrifice on my part.

Derek's building was at the far end of the empty, covered swimming pool in the center of the complex. I walked into the little vestibule, found his mailbox, with letters inside, and rang the ivory button underneath it. Without waiting for a response, I climbed up to his unit on the second floor and rapped on his door. My fingers were so cold it felt as if I'd knocked with the bare bones of my finger joints. Not only was there no response from his apartment but the whole building seemed soundless, motionless.

After knocking several more times, although I didn't really think he was there, I walked around to the back of the building to check the parking lot. No red Toyota.

Well, at least I could tell Faye I had tried.

Now I wanted to return to the office to make a couple of phone calls that were beginning to seem more urgent to me as activity warmed my blood and melted the ice around my brain.

While making the first call, I took off my left shoe and sat on that foot to warm it.

"Nordic Realty."

"Hi, Michael. It's Jenny. What's the matter? Can't you guys afford a secretary yet? Maybe you'd better not be putting down payments on buildings if you can't even come up with enough money to pay minimum wage to a receptionist."

"Hi, Swede. What's the matter with you? Don't you recognize equality when you hear it? Unlike some executives I could name, I believe in answering my own phone."

I laughed, and felt a rush of remembered fondness for him.

"Speaking of Faye, she says you called."

"Yeah," he said. "Actually, I called to gloat."

I feigned innocence. "Really? Why's that, Michael?"

" 'Why's that, Michael?' " he said mockingly. "Nice

try, Jenny, but you don't convince me. I'm sorry you lost the building for the reason you did, but as tasteless as it may seem, we're celebrating around here. I'll tell you what, though, I was serious about that offer to help you find another site. . . ."

I sat up straighter in my chair. "Celebrating what?"

He laughed, and mocked me again. " 'Celebrating what, Michael?' "

"I'm serious. You shouldn't be celebrating anything yet, because you haven't got it yet—"

"That's not what the landlord said to me when I called him this morning. What the landlord said was, 'Congratulations, Mr. Laurence, you just made yourself a hell of a deal—' "

"I'll call you back," I said, and hung up.

I found George Butts's office phone number among the notes I had taken during our original interview with MaryDell Paine. While I punched in the number and waited, I put my left shoe back on, shook off the right one, and sat on that foot. It was still cold enough to send a chill through the layers of skirt, slip, stockings, and panties.

A woman with a sweet, older-sounding voice answered: "Triple A Management." It was typical of what I had perceived in the old rascal, I thought, to pick a company name whose only relevant purpose was to place him first in the Yellow Pages: AAA Management.

"George Butts, please."

"May I inquire as to who's calling?"

"Ms. Cain, from the Port Frederick Civic Foundation."

"Thank you. Will you hold?"

"Yes."

She was making the enterprise sound like a multifloored monolith, when the reality probably was that she was his wife, taking messages for him at home. The next sound I heard was music from a local radio station. I pictured the phone receiver, lying on its side, placed against a radio speaker. The music hadn't even gone through one syrupy chorus of "Mandy" when she returned, speaking in dulcet tones of regret.

"I'm so sorry, but Mr. Butts isn't in right now."

"Is this Mrs. Butts?"

"Yes, it is."

"Would you take a message for him?"

"Why, certainly."

"Tell George that if he doesn't come to the phone immediately, I will haul him into court for breach of contract. Remind him that the courts consider verbal contracts to be as binding as written ones and that I have a witness."

"Uh, hold on, please."

Same radio song, different chorus.

The next voice I heard was George Butts's, sounding jovial.

"What's this about breach of contract?"

"You gave us until Friday," I said.

"Well, yes, I did," he admitted. "But I figured you folks wouldn't want the old place anymore, not after what happened there last night, not what with the neighbors being so upset and all. Mind you, like I said the other day, don't make me no difference who gets the old place, could be you folks, could be them other guys, but like I said, they got the money in their hands, and all you folks got now is problems, am I right?"

"I'm good at solving problems, George."

He chuckled. "Well, now, you know, I think I'd like to see you solve this one. In fact, maybe you and me ought to get together at the church tonight and see if we can't solve some of our problems."

"I think we can manage this over the phone, George."

You old lecher, I thought, and with your wife right there in the house, too.

"Tell you what, then," he said. "I'm a fair man. If I said you could have until Friday, then, by God, I'll give you until Friday morning—"

"Noon, George. You said noon."

"Right, noon. But by twelve-oh-one this Friday afternoon, I'm going to be takin' somebody's check."

"You're all heart, George."

"I kinda hope you win," he said, and chuckled again. "It'd be a pleasure doin' business with you. You're smart. And, besides, you're prettier than that real estate fella."

Still chuckling, old George hung up.

Actually, it was debatable whether I was prettier than Michael Laurence. I called him back at the realty office, and once again, he answered the phone.

"It's not over 'til the fat man sings," I said.

"What are you talking about, Jenny?"

"The other day, George Butts promised me that we'd have until Friday to make an offer on his basement, Michael. I just phoned him to remind him of that fact. He's still willing to wait until then, so I would advise you not to count your apartment building until the foundation's laid."

"Why are you always so unpleasant to me?" he said.

"Why do you always ask for it?" I replied, and slammed down the phone. I then spent a few moments staring at the phone, feeling acutely embarrassed. Why did I *do* that? Why *was* I so unpleasant to him? He was a perfectly nice man, and he was only out to make a buck like any other developer. Yes, maybe it was a buck to be made at the expense of needier people, but he hadn't known that when he got the idea. Ease off, Cain, I thought. And don't be an ass. Call him back and apologize.

I reached for the phone but drew back my hand.

I couldn't do it. I wanted to do it, I really did, but I was afraid he'd say something to set me off again.

There was a sound of typing from the outer office.

God, I hoped that Faye hadn't been listening—she'd always idolized him, and my behavior would have done nothing toward removing the clay from my feet. Hung up on him. Jeez, Cain.

I felt a sudden, overwhelming urge to call my husband and touch home base.

"Hi, honey," I said, when he came on the line.

"Where's Derek, Jenny?"

"Derek? Oh, well, Faye was being tactful, Geof. She didn't want to tell you that Derek seems to have said the hell with it, and flown the coop. When we arrived this morning, he had already gone. I guess he came in before the office opened and cleaned out his belongings."

There was silence at his end of the line for a moment, before he said, "He's not at home either."

"No," I agreed. "At least he wasn't as of about an hour ago. What do you want with him anyway?"

"Why didn't you tell me he had a key to the old church basement?"

The back of my scalp crawled, just as it had earlier that day, only now I knew why. "I forgot, but so what? It was a church, a lot of people must have old keys to it. I mean, Geof, you can't possibly think that Derek had anything to do with that murder. Do you?"

"You told me he was on that block last night."

"Well, yes, but—"

"What time was that?"

"Uh, well, he called me about ten-thirty, when he got home, so—"

"How do you know he called from home?"

"I guess I don't, actually—"

"Did he say anything about going into the basement?"

"No. Why would he do that? No, of course not."

"Maybe he went in to look around again; that wouldn't be so unusual, not if you're considering buying it."

"Well, I guess it wouldn't. But, Geof—"

"I'm sorry, I'm not being clear. I'm not accusing Derek of anything, Jenny. I'm worried about him. He had a key, he was in the neighborhood. There was a killing. And now he's missing. The back door was jimmied, which is probably how the killer got in. But Derek might have used *his* key to get in the front door. We're wondering if he saw something, or heard something, maybe even walked in on it. It was a particularly bloody and violent murder, and . . ."

He paused, but I didn't fill the silence. I was too upset to speak.

"I'm sorry," he said again. "You don't need these details. I'll shut up. Listen, Jenny, maybe Derek woke up in the middle of the night, got pissed off at you for firing him, and decided to clear out of town temporarily. It's probably only coincidence that he's gone. I just want to find him to be sure of that. So if he calls you, or if he contacts Faye, you tell him to call us. All right?"

"Of course."

"Can you think of any place he might be? With parents? Brothers or sisters? Friends? A favorite place to get away from it all?"

"Faye will know. I'll switch you."

"Thank you. I'm sorry about this."

"Break this gently to Faye, will you? Hold on."

"All right, but come back on the line when she gets off, will you? I have something else to tell you."

Great, I thought.

I called out to Faye to pick up the phone, and then I sat rigidly at my desk, clutching the edge of it with my fingers, watching the back of her head as she absorbed this latest police bulletin. When she had finished the conversation, she wheeled her swivel chair around and stared in at me. Faye looked as if she had just been told that one of her own sons had been in an automobile accident, his condition unknown. I picked up the receiver again and punched down the button to put Geof back on my extension.

"Okay," I said, "what's the other good news?"

"In the course of questioning Mrs. Paine," Geof said, "the detectives asked for the name of her brother's psychiatrist. She gave them quite a list because it seems he's been through a number of institutions and doctors. Would you like to guess who the most recent one was?"

"You're going to tell me it's Marsha, aren't you?"

"That's right."

No wonder she'd said, "We can't talk about that now," when I had told her the police were looking for Mob. Poor Marsh, I thought: she must have been feeling a tremendous conflict of interests.

"Are you going to talk to her?" I asked him.

"Yes, I thought I'd better do it personally. I've already set up a meeting with her after her last appointment, five-thirty, her house."

"May I join you?"

"Yes, if you want to."

We said good-bye to one another and hung up.

I looked at Faye, to find that she was sitting at her desk, quietly crying.

"Faye," I said, "we'll find him."

It was an idle boast, of course, in the same category with "Everything's going to be all right," and "Don't worry, I'll take care of it." She looked as if she wanted to believe me, but didn't, which was an entirely appropriate and realistic attitude on her part. If anyone found Derek, it would be the police; either that, or he'd just show up on his own, wondering what all the fuss was about.

Outside our windows, the day was getting grayer and the snow was falling harder, making it likely that many businesses would close early. I decided we should join them.

"Do you want to go home, Faye?"

She nodded, soundlessly, and then swiveled out of my sight. Soon I heard the small shuffling, clicking, and clattering sounds of a secretary closing her desk for the night. I clicked open my own briefcase and swept Derek's file and my own notes into it. Then I walked over to the windows, pulled down the shades, and drew the curtains across them. Thin, cool light seeped around the curled edges of the blinds, framing and illuminating the curtains from behind. I bowed my head for a moment in my darkened office. It wasn't exactly a prayer; it was a respite. Then I gathered my briefcase and purse, walked out of my office, reached back for the light switch, shut the door, and waited beside Faye's desk for her to finish closing up for the day.

She worked silently. It looked as if I was the bad guy again. The way she was thinking was that if I hadn't fired him, he wouldn't have tried so hard to please me last night, and then he wouldn't have gotten into the danger he might be in. Ergo: all my fault.

Ordinarily, Faye and I would have confessed our fears and tried to comfort each other, but the only comfort she'd take from me now was news that Derek was safe at home. She was usually more fair-minded than this; I didn't know what had gotten into her—unless her motherly instincts were simply overwhelmed by her concern for Derek.

Finally, she sighed and pushed herself back from her desk.

"Ready?" I said.

She nodded.

"Will you drop me at my car?"

Faye nodded again, so I stopped trying to get her to talk to me. Eventually, she'd figure out that her anger at me was unreasonable. I had not caused Derek's problems. In the meantime, however, I was the principal who'd kept her child after school, causing him to walk home late, after dark, when perverts waited on street corners. I didn't feel like trying to defend myself. When she got over blaming me, she'd come around again. In silence, we gathered our purses, coats, hats, put on our boots, held open doors for each other, descended in the elevator, walked to her Volvo, and got in. Faye drove. I gave her directions to my car, and, silently, she followed them. She pulled up in the snow beside my Accord, and I got out of the Volvo. Before shutting the car door, I looked back in at her. She nodded again. What could I say? "Oh, grow up" occurred to me, but I bit my tongue on it.

Adapting to her language, I nodded back.

Then I stepped out of the way, slammed the door, and waited for her to drive off. When she didn't, I realized she was waiting to see if I got my car started safely. Of course, I thought, with a sudden rush of affection for her, mothers worry about the safety of even their most maddening children. Feeling obedient, and maybe a little comforted, I climbed into my own car, started it, then waved triumphantly, foolishly, at her. She nodded—of course—and drove out of the school parking lot. I stared after her, thinking that mothers can be pretty maddening themselves sometimes.

I drove home and slept for the rest of the afternoon.

18

At five o'clock I woke up, with just enough time to dress, heat and gobble a few bites of chili to sustain me, and then drive over to meet Geof at Marsha's home. When she let me in, he was already there, waiting in her den. As Marsha and I walked past the kitchen door, there was Joe Fabian again, apron and all, washing still more dishes. He glanced up, grinned, and waved a soapy hand at me.

"What did you do," I asked her sotto voce, "hire him?"

She crooked her left arm through my right one and leaned in toward my ear. "We were going to take a few days off, to go somewhere together, but I couldn't rearrange my schedule. So he took some of his vacation time anyway, and he's staying here with me. We're playing house."

"Don't tell me," I said. "He's the mommy and you're the daddy. He stays home and cooks while you go to work every day. Sounds a little kinky to me, Marsh."

"I can't get him to do my laundry, though."

"Good for him," I said.

She squeezed my arm before letting go of mē.

Geof and I sat together on her sofa for an hour while Marsha sat on the floor in front of us—cross-legged—telling us about her patient Kitt Blackstone.

"I would have come to you, Geof," she said, "but I had to think a bit about the ethics of this situation. I called a few of my colleagues this afternoon—hell, I even called one of my old medical school professors—to ask them how they handle situations that put the law in conflict with confidentiality. My final decision is this:

"I do not personally believe that anyone in this community is at risk from Mob, but because of the nature of his illness, I cannot be absolutely sure of that. I will, therefore, talk to you about the aspects of his case that *I* think"—and here, she looked hard at Geof, as if to underscore it—"directly impinge upon your case. I will not open my files to you. I will not talk about any other aspects of his history or treatment. You may subpoena me if you like, but I will not voluntarily go any further than I am about to do this afternoon. All right?"

He smiled a little and shrugged.

"No commitments, huh?" Marsha asked, and she smiled back at him. "All right. Then save us some time. Tell me what you already know about him."

Geof nodded. "He began showing signs of mental illness when he was about sixteen. According to his sister, Kitt suddenly changed from a bright, popular kid to a strange, angry, withdrawn boy who began to flunk out of school. At first, his parents blamed his friends, but they were all bright, popular kids, too. Then his parents suspected drugs, but they couldn't find any evidence of them. They even thought it might be the influence of rock and roll, but they couldn't blame it on that for long. They took him to a doctor, and then another doctor, and finally to a shrink, and to make his sister's long story short, he was finally institutionalized, for the first time, at the age of seventeen.

"Since then, his life has been a series of trips back and forth between his sister's house and hospitals, with periods in between when he evidently just wanders, nobody knows where. Sometimes he's fairly lucid, most of the time he isn't. His official diagnosis is paranoid schizophrenia, which, as I understand it, is a chronic condition. Mrs. Paine told the detectives that he was finally beginning to show some improvement, under your care. She didn't know exactly why, but something was beginning to work, and that's why he got released from the hospital. She was angry at you about that, by the way. Do you know that?"

Marsha nodded to confirm it.

"She thinks you let him out too soon."

"I took a chance," Marsha admitted. "You see, the reason he was beginning to improve was not because I performed any kind of analytical miracle on him, but simply because I was lucky enough to get his medications balanced, probably for the first time. Kitt is on an anti-psychotic medicine that quiets the voices that speak to him and holds down the hallucinations, and that makes simply all the difference in the world in his ability to function. He'd been on the medicine before, you understand, but the problem was that it has a side effect that makes some patients extraordinarily restless. They tell me it's awful, and I believe them. So I had worked to balance that drug with another drug that alleviates that side effect. And it was working. He felt better. He was getting better. And I thought he was ready for another try at outpatient treatment again. That's why I signed his release from the hospital."

The problem and the risk, she told us, was that he had to take his medicines properly. His continued recovery—his sanity—depended on it. If he failed to do so, even once, there was the possibility that his psychotic symptoms would commence again, making it difficult for him to have enough of a grasp on reality to remember to take any medicines at all. Or he might take the antipsychotic medicine, but forget to take the pill for the side effect. Then he'd get the side effect, which would discourage him from taking the antipsychotic medicine, which would then make him crazy again. In that sense, it could be a vicious circle. If he got sick again, the voices that spoke to him might even tell him not to take the medicines.

"And he would obey them," she told us.

"Do you think something like this has happened?" I asked.

"Yes," she said, "because he has missed his last two appointments with me, something he never does when the voices shut up. The voices don't like me, you understand, because they know I represent their doom."

"You talk about them as if they're real," Geof said.

"Oh, they are very real to Kitt," Marsha told him. They both suddenly looked sidelong at me, as if including me in the dialogue, but their gesture was more than courtesy, it was a silent, shared concern that said: How's she taking this, is this too painful for her? It was often like that for me when people got to discussing mental illness; they worried that they were being tactless because of my mother. In response, I always feigned careless objectivity, as I did now. Probably not fooled, Marsha glanced back at Geof, who was probably also not fooled, and continued, "The voices are as real and as loud and as powerful as any voice any of us has ever heard, and they are relentless; they are a constant chorus in his mind. Plus you have to understand that Kitt's particular voices are biblical in nature, which lends them even more authority."

"Why biblical?" I asked.

She shrugged. "Who knows. I don't. They just appeared—actually, they've been whispering to him since he was a small boy, although nobody ever realized it until he got officially sick—and they were demonic from the start. I think the biblical influence may have increased over time, because at some point he began to read the Bible as a means of trying to understand and appease them. Eventually, he read it fanatically, almost every waking moment, because the act of obsessively concentrating on it was the only means he had of trying to shut them up. Of course, the problem was, they directed him to read all the passages about demons, over and over, again and again.

"He eventually came to believe that they were the various demons mentioned in the New Testament. When he is sick, he believes that only Jesus Christ can drive them out. Unfortunately"—she smiled sadly—"Christ has never 'spoken' to him. Kitt, of course, believed that was only because he was himself so evil that Christ turned his face away. That's what the demon voices told him, anyway. But when he's taking his medicine properly, he's rational, and he's able to accept that the voices are due to some physiological imbalance that we can, to a large extent, although with some side effects, control with medication."

"Is he a split personality?" Geof asked.

"No," she said, "that's not what schizophrenia means. It's true that he does call himself Mob when he's sick, and sometimes he gets deep enough into his illness to confuse himself with the person in the story. It is also true that he might seem like two different people to you, if you knew him, because when he's having a psychotic episode, believe me, he's quite a different person from when he's relatively sane. He can be quiet and docile, but he can also be a little frightening. In spite of that, 'Mob' is more like his personal metaphor. Mob is not a separate personality, as such."

"You say he can be frightening," Geof said. "Do you mean violent? Have these voices ever directed him to hurt somebody?"

"No," Marsha said firmly. "I mean, I've known him to get furiously angry, and even to throw things—but who hasn't? But he's never hurt anyone else, at least not to my knowledge. The voices *have* many times directed him to harm himself. They have tried to talk him into suicide countless times, and they have nearly succeeded on several occasions. But no, they seem to be inner- and not outer-directed. That's why I find it so difficult to believe that Kitt is responsible for this crime."

"But . . ." Geof said, letting it dangle.

Marsha's head dropped for a moment before she looked back up at him with a discouraged expression.

"Well, you're right, of course. With mental illness, there is almost always a 'yes, but.' The voices *could* alter their message. He *might* even begin to hear different voices. It's possible. Frankly, I don't think it's probable, given his long and consistent history with those demons, but I have to admit to you that it is possible."

"Where do you think he is, Marsha?" Geof said.

She looked directly at him. "I do not know."

"Would you tell me if you did?"

She looked over at me. "I do not know that, either. I'm thinking about it, though. Believe me, I've been thinking about that very question a lot today."

He didn't press her further, and I kept my nose out of it.

"Will you stay for dinner?" she asked us.

But Geof needed to return to the station, and I didn't want to interrupt her probably all-too-brief idyll with Joe Fabian, so we declined, asking for a rain check.

Out on the street, by our cars, Geof leaned over to kiss me.

"You taste like chili," he said.

"What will you do for dinner?"

"I'll pick up a sandwich, and then I'll eat some chili when I get home. Where are you going now?"

"I don't know," I said. "Home, I guess."

"The prints on the church door have been identified as Kitt Blackstone's, Jenny. He's been picked up a few times before, on minor charges, mostly having to do with vagrancy and disturbing the peace."

"Why didn't you tell Marsha that?"

"She knows his record, and she knows he was there."

"Geof, I really don't think she'd hide him."

"I know you don't." He kissed me again, then lifted his head and squinted at me with a speculative gaze. "And crackers."

19

I discovered that I felt too restless to go home.

Instead, I meandered in my car, aimlessly following the streets that were clearest of snow and ice. Straight ahead onto Benjamin Franklin Avenue. Right onto Twenty-second. Down four blocks, left onto James A. Madison Boulevard. Across three blocks, left onto Seventeenth. Down five blocks, and right onto Adams, across one block, left onto . . .

Tenth Street.

Well, well. Now wasn't this a coincidence. . . .

I parked in the first cleared spot I encountered, which was directly in front of Perry Yates's neat brown saltbox house, and then I trudged out into the weather once more.

My destination was the house next to Yates's.

I accept only a minimal salary from the foundation, which I thought I might actually try to earn that evening—since I hadn't earned much of it that day—by shuffling up a few front walks, climbing a number of front steps, ringing some doorbells, and polling as many residents as I found at home.

To the first person who opened a door, and to everyone after that, I said something along the lines of "Our foundation will decide tomorrow whether to purchase the old church basement for use as a recreation hall for former mental patients. In any project we take on, the feelings and opinions of the neighbors are very important to us. We'll do this only if it's okay with most of you; we don't want to force any project down your throat. So, considering what happened last night, how do you feel about the idea today?"

They didn't think very much of it anymore.

But another truth that also came out of this third batch of interviews was that they didn't want the noise, dirt, and bother that the construction of Michael's apartment complex would bring, either. They had liked the idea that MaryDell's group would clean up the old church, pretty up the property, and let the improvements go at that. That prospect, it turned out, had appeared to them preferable to bulldozers, dust, hammers, power saws, and blocked traffic. Before the murder, that is.

"Hell," one crusty, voluble old homeowner said to me, after his wife had invited me into their tiny house for a very welcome and hot cup of tea, "we don't want all them apartment people! Perry Yates talks about turning that old empty lot into a parking lot, but now I ask you, if you got a parking lot, what are you going to park in it. Cars, that's what. Pickup trucks. Motorcycles. It's gonna be noisy. It's gonna be crowded, we ain't gonna be able to find a place to park on our own street when all their friends start pilin' in here. And you can bet them apartments ain't gonna be no nice little places for families or retired people—no way. Never is, these days. Gonna be the only ones can afford 'em gonna be young punks livin' there in them apartments and workin' gals, drinkin' beer and partyin' all night. No thank you. I'll take them quiet crazy people anytime over Perry Yates's improvements! Besides, I hear most of them crazy people won't be·havin' their own cars, so we won't be havin' a lot of extry traffic on the street.''

But he was a tough old bird; the others were not so sanguine about the murder on their block. I was disappointed, for the sake of the project, but I could hardly blame them.

Finally, I stood on the stoop of yet another gray saltbox house, one with a bright red door and a blue doorknob.

Marianne Miller opened the door much more cautiously this afternoon than she had this morning.

"Oh, Jenny," she said when she recognized me, and then she urged me to "please come in."

I had been so upset myself that morning that I hadn't noticed that her blue eyes had blue circles under them. I saw them now. Her small, pretty mouth was pinched and trembling a little, maybe with exhaustion, maybe with tension or fear. She seemed to have changed since this morning, but then, I supposed she'd had a rough day. Two kids, trying to work, and having a murder next door would certainly have worn *me* slick, I decided.

"I'll take that," Marianne said, as I removed my coat in her tiny foyer. She held out her hands for my hat and gloves as well. I thought she would stash them on the hooks that were attached to the wall in the foyer, but she stuffed the hat and gloves inside the coat in a distracted, fumbling sort of way. She draped my coat over her arms and carried it with her as she preceded me into the living room, as if she'd forgotten about it. I followed her, observing her slender shoulders covered by a red plaid shirt, and her trim hips and legs in their blue jeans. And I finally thought of the one thing that I knew about Derek that the cops didn't, that Faye didn't, that nobody else did, in fact: he'd been attracted to this woman.

20

I followed her into a scene of cheerful chaos that I seemed to be seeing for the first time, which just goes to show how distracted I'd been that morning. In the living room, I stepped carefully between a potter's wheel and a Fisher-Price toy barn, and sat on a cushion that she hurriedly cleared for me on a ratty old sofa near the bay window where we had stood, watching the cops arrive.

Still holding my coat, Marianne lifted a rattan rocking chair over the floor strewn with toys, kicked some of them out of the way with one foot, set the chair down near me, and sat in it. She folded my coat onto her lap. Her fingers began to fiddle absently with my lapels, as if the coat were a security blanket and the lapels were the silk binding. It was odd. I nearly said, "Don't you want to get that coat out of your way?" But the obvious truth was that she didn't, and since I didn't really care if she wrinkled the coat—it needed to go to the cleaners anyway—I let her have a go at it.

"Jenny, have they found the guy who did it?"

"I don't think so, Marianne."

She looked as if she might cry. "It scares me so much."

The noise level in her house was such that I might have thought she was running a nursery school if I hadn't known there were only the two girls. She offhandedly introduced them to me as Blake—a pretty, blond five-year-old and Chesley—an adorable redheaded toddler. Whenever either of the girls raced by, their mother grabbed them, pulled them onto her lap—on top of my coat—and hugged them until their protests and fidgeting forced her to release them again.

She acted as if she could hardly bear to let them out of her sight or her grasp.

"How do you get any work done?" I asked.

"Oh, *this* work gets done." She pointed vaguely at a bright, clever abstract oil painting that hung on the wall to my right. "I get the important stuff done. I'm not sure *how;* I mean if you ask me in five years how I managed to produce anything worth selling during this period of my life, I probably won't be able to tell you, but somehow it gets done. Of course, I don't sleep a lot, and I haven't read a book in three years, and I wouldn't recognize a date if he bit me. But mostly it's the other stuff that never gets done like the *housework,* or the bills that don't get paid on time, and I don't expect I've balanced my checkbook in three months, and, God, I never return phone calls like I ought to—it's a wonder I have any friends left— and I forget to put out the trash, and it piles up . . . well, it's stuff like that, that's what I can't seem to get done. It used to make my husband crazy. Gosh, it makes me crazy sometimes. Maybe I'm raising crazy kids . . ." She stared around her living room. "I mean, wouldn't it make you crazy, if you lived like this?"

"Yes," I had to agree.

"I'll bet you don't have any kids, though."

"Nope," I also agreed.

She sighed and stroked my lapels as though they were

a cat's back. "You get up in the morning, you have a leisurely cup of coffee, right?"

"Yes, more or less."

"Saturday, you want to sleep late, you can. At night, you want to watch prime-time TV, no problem; you want to curl up with a good book, no big deal, you just do it. Talk on the phone any time you want to, take your time in the shower, go to the bathroom by yourself—"

"It's that bad, is it?"

Chesley skipped by and her mother grabbed her, hugged her fiercely, and then released her.

"It would almost be worth getting married again," she admitted, and then her voice turned bitter. "Except just because you have a man around the house doesn't guarantee he'll be any help."

When the child was out of the room, Marianne asked me, in a tight voice, "Do they know who did it?"

"I don't really know," I hedged, like a good police spouse. But then, I thought, that's not fair to her; she needs to be able to protect herself and her kids. "Well, they are looking for a suspect, a man whose name is Kitt Blackstone, but who calls himself Mob—"

"Mob?" She looked incredulous. "They can't possibly mean Mob. I *know* Mob. Well, I mean I guess I know him as well as anybody could, but I do know he's a gentle soul. Well, okay, maybe not gentle, exactly, but Mob wouldn't kill anybody. Why in the world do they think that?"

I was incredulous now. "Because he was there last night, Marianne, in the basement, and he left a sort of confession. How in the world do you know him?"

"Oh, he used to hang around here," she said, almost casually. "Around the neighborhood, I mean. Asking for coffee or doughnuts and stuff. There was one old lady who fed him regularly, and they used to let him sleep in the church sometimes."

"Good grief," I said. "Did you tell the police this?"

She widened her eyes. "Well, no. Why would I? They didn't say anything to me about Mob. They just asked me if I saw or heard anything, which I hadn't. Oh, Jenny, if they're looking for Mob, they're looking for the wrong person—I don't care what sort of confession he's supposed to have written. Mob was always writing stuff! He was always leaving notices on trees and funny, crazy little messages in our mailboxes. It wasn't any of it real, it was all just his imagination! Jenny, if the police are looking for Mob, that means the real killer is getting away. Oh God. Right next door," she whispered fearfully. "It happened right next door while my babies were asleep. What if he'd broken in here, what if he'd—"

"Do the children understand what happened?"

She shook her head until her ponytail swung behind her shoulders, but her words partially belied the motion. "No! Well, sort of, I mean, they kind of know what dead is, and they see killings all the time on TV, but it isn't real to them. I'm so scared they'll have nightmares about it tonight, and what will I say to them? God, how will I sleep, what if he comes back to this block, how can I protect them all by myself?"

"Marianne, the reason I'm here again is that I'm looking for my assistant director, Derek Jones. He was on this block, conducting interviews last night. You didn't happen to see him, did you?"

"Derek?" she said, with a sudden, quick smile that gave me the answer. This woman seemed to know all the missing people in Port Frederick.

"Was he here?"

She nodded and blushed—an old-fashioned reaction to a new-fashioned question. "He said he had a couple of other questions to ask me, and well, I'd already put the kids to bed, so I invited him in for a cup of coffee. Well, actually, we had a couple of beers, is what we had, I hope you don't mind, I mean, it was after hours, and all—"

"I'm not a cop, Marianne."

She smiled nervously. "Yeah, but you're his boss. He says you're a great boss. Well, anyway, we talked about the project a little, and—" She stopped and then amazed me by blushing furiously and glancing down at her hands. When she looked up, it was to smile shyly and to say, "He's very nice, isn't he?"

I smiled, nodded. But how in the world could I now, with any tact—and even in this new-fashioned world—ask her how long he had stayed with her, or when he had left her house?

"You don't think Derek noticed anything next door, do you, Marianne?"

"No!" She shuddered a little and rubbed my coat lapel furiously between the thumb and fingers of her right hand. "I don't think there was anything for us to notice! The cops told me they thought it happened after midnight, and I was asleep by then, and Derek had gone home a long time before that. And I guess poor Rod was stabbed, so it's not as if there was any gunshot to hear, or anything—"

"You didn't hear any screaming, or—"

"No." She swallowed convulsively. "Oh, poor Rod. He was a real dumb bum; I suppose that's terrible to say, but, really, I never could stand him, he was always smirking at me, like I should be interested in him or something—"

She stopped cold and seemed to turn a little pale.

"What? What, Marianne?"

"Nothing." She gave a little shake. When she looked at me, her glance slid quickly away. "It's just . . . it's just that I didn't even like him to be around the children; he was just so greasy and smirky and kind of filthy in every way, you know? Nothing like Derek. It was so nice to be around somebody as nice as he is; I mean, he's so nice and clean-cut and intelligent and funny and— Did you say you're looking for him, Jenny?''

I nodded.

"Why?"

I hedged again. "He didn't come in to work today."

"Really?" She started to smile, then hid it.

"If you hear from him," I said, "would you ask him to call me, please?"

"Sure. He said he'd call me. But I don't imagine I'll hear from him." But she blushed saying it, thus divulging just how much she hoped to hear from Derek again. I didn't seem to have planted any additional fears in her mind. That, she didn't need, what with worrying about murderers and about whether her new acquaintance would call her. I, on the other hand, was already worried about her not hearing from him. It was a matter of principle with Derek always to call a woman if he said he would and never to leave her dangling, wondering what she'd done wrong. Derek had an understanding of power—from the powerless person's point of view—that most men didn't. It was one of the perceptions that had drawn him into social work. That sense of the responsibility of sexual power had been one of the things I'd expected least from him and then had learned to admire most about him.

I noticed that in his absence I was sainting him—and people only become saints after they're dead. This past tense business had to stop. I concentrated for a moment on some of Derek's faults—procrastination, laziness, lack of initiative, irresponsibility of other sorts—and sure enough, he came infuriatingly alive to me again.

"Marianne, I may not be a cop, but I'm married to one," I told her.

"I know," she said, and then grinned.

That was another one of Derek's failings: he gossiped about me altogether too much!

"Well," I said, "if they've made an arrest, I'll hear about it and call you. All right?"

"Thank you." It sounded heartfelt.

"I'd better go." I got up from the couch and tried to glance tactfully at my coat. It was now thoroughly crumpled in her lap. But when she handed it to me, she seemed unaware of any lapse of etiquette on her part. When I slipped it on, it smelled of the patchouli fragrance that she wore. She walked me to the door.

"I wish you didn't have to go so soon," she said fretfully.

When I stepped outside, she closed and locked the door quickly.

Late afternoon had slid into an early night. Compared with the bright, lively mess of her little house, Tenth Street suddenly seemed very dark, cold, and quiet.

21

It was time to go home. I should have gone home. I figured that I had finally earned it. But beyond the darkened church basement and the empty lot beside it, lights glowed in the shabby little saltbox house where Grace Montgomery lived. If Marianne Miller was frightened, the crazy old pig lady was probably terrified—and all alone with her dementia.

Sure, I thought as I stood on the snowy sidewalk pondering the prospect of visiting her, she might scream at me, she might be way beyond reaching, she might not even open her door to me this time. I should forget it and go home. But would it kill me to try? Would it kill me to try to offer her the same small comfort that I had promised Marianne—that I'd call her as soon as the police made an arrest? Besides, it would only take a few more minutes.

I pulled my collar up more snugly around my throat, secured my purse strap over my left shoulder, stuck my gloved hands in my coat pockets, and bent my head into the blowing snow like a cow.

"Moo," I said, and struck out cross country.

The church basement was a black, snow-covered hump, its front door barricaded by police bulletins that I sensed, more than saw, in the darkness under the eaves. The lot next door was a white square on a checkerboard. But the snow had turned Mrs. Montgomery's place into a gingerbread house, quaint, small, and pretty. The fact that she had apparently turned on all her lights to scare the demons away only made her house look all the more, and ironically, cozy.

She surprised me by admitting me at once.

"Quick!" she whispered urgently and tugged at my arms with her crippled hands. "Come inside. He's out there. You mustn't be out there alone. Quick! Shut the door. Lock it, lock it! Draw the curtain! He can't see us through the curtain. But he knows we're here. He's out there in the snow. Did you see him? I know what he looks like. The devil drives a red car. Is it locked? Did you get them all locked! Come in, come in. Here, you sit there— he can't see us in the middle of the room. My piggies will protect us. They have eyes everywhere. Pigs are fierce, they'll fight you to the death; my pigs will kill him if he tries to hurt us. My, you're a pretty thing. He likes pretty things. And ugly things like Rodney Gardner. And ugly old things like me. Tea. I have tea. Drink some tea—"

The fact was that neither of us had moved an inch away from the front door after I had closed and locked it. She stood as if imprisoned in her aluminum walker, her eyes wild and staring all around her house. Her words poured out like tea from the nonexistent tea kettle. I touched her arm. "Mrs. Montgomery—"

She flinched, then raised her walker, and began to clump away from me. I stayed where I was, made awkward and unsure and a little frightened by the sheer nuttiness of her behavior. I talked a good game, but the reality of being confronted by dementia was more than I knew how to handle.

She circled slowly, painfully, in her walker until she faced me again.

"Stay with me, girlie! My pigs will protect you. He'll leave in the morning. The devil is afraid of the light. All we have to do is wait out the night. Turn on the lights. He's afraid of my piggies. He knows they're my protection. They'll protect you, too. Have some more tea. I'll bake some cookies. I'll take a bath. You can sleep on the roof. It's nice out, you'll be warm on the roof, and you can see everything from up there, and you can tell us when he's coming. He's coming. He's coming. He's coming."

"Mrs. Montgomery, do you have a doctor?"

"Doctor doctor."

"What is your doctor's name?"

"He is a surgeon with a knife. He operated on that nasty Rodney Gardner, didn't he? Slash slash. Slice slice. Blood blood." She began to cackle with gleeful laughter. "As my father used to say, it couldn't happen to a nicer boy! I told them this would happen! Perry told them! But nobody listened, oh no, nobody listens to an old woman and a nice young boy—"

"I want to call someone to come and stay with you. Mrs. Montgomery!" She was still babbling, while I tried to get her attention. "Do you have a daughter or a son? Any relatives here in town? A friend, someone to help you?"

Instead of answering me, she lowered herself into a chair, picked up a little pig figurine, and began to stroke it and croon to it: "Sooie. Sooie. Sooie."

I crouched down beside her walker.

"Mrs. Montgomery? Grace? Can you hear what I'm saying?"

"Sooie," she crooned, "sooie."

"What does the devil look like, Mrs. Montgomery?"

"Sooie!" she cried in alarm. "Sooie, sooie!"

"It's all right," I said apologetically. I began to stroke

137

her hands as they stroked the silly pink porcelain pig. "It's all right, it's all right."

When she had calmed a little, I risked taking the time to shake my arms out of my coat and to let it fall to the filthy floor around me. The room was stifling. I looked around then until I found a pig that was painted a pepperoni red—they came in all colors and sizes—and I picked it up and held it in front of her.

"What a pretty red pig." I spoke softly. Her eyes moved from the pig in her hands to the one in mine. "Pretty, pretty red piggie."

"Sooie, piggie," she said.

"Was the devil's car red like this?"

She shook her head. Her hands began to stroke the pig again. Quickly I found another piglet, one that was painted an orangy, pimento red.

"Was it red like this?"

"No, no." She was getting upset again.

I held out a cherry red pig to her. "Like this?"

"Red devil!" she shrieked and pointed to my pig. "Evil, evil!"

I put the cherry red pig behind my back, out of her sight. My heart was beating faster as I said, "Who was in the car, Grace?"

"The devil, the devil!"

"When did you see it, Grace?"

She looked at me with eyes that suddenly looked clear and sly with awareness. She leaned toward me and whispered, her breath foul with neglect, "The devil hates the dark. Comes the sun, the devil flees!"

"You saw it just before sunrise? Is that right, Grace?"

I'd gone too far. I felt like a torturer, merciless. She stared at me, wild-eyed, and began to pant like a dog that needs water. I was afraid she'd hyperventilate. Quickly I switched off the nearest lights, dimming the rooms to a more peaceful level of illumination. Then I grabbed yet another pig—this one a fat pink china sow with five piglets attached to her china teats. I began to stroke it and croon to it. "Sooie," I sang, feeling absolutely ridiculous, and "Pretty pigs," I whispered to the old lady, "such sweet, pretty little piggies. Sooie, sooie." Gradually, her breathing became more normal, and she calmed down, until finally she looked at me with what seemed to be a little peace in her eyes. Not exactly sanity, perhaps, but a little peace.

"It's late," I said softly. "Time for piggies to sleep?"

She nodded, then kept on nodding, until her own eyes began to open and close in rhythm to her rocking: back, close; forward, open; back, close; forward, open. I whispered an offer to help her to bed, but she didn't respond. Her head fell softly back against the chair, which stopped rocking, and her eyes closed. The old crippled fingers ceased their stroking of the pig in her lap. When I was sure she slept, I struggled back to my feet. My knees cracked in protest. I put "my" pig back where I'd found it, making a face of distaste at it.

I wandered—carefully—through her sty of a house again, dodging the pigs that dangled so bizarrely from above. Curious as to how she'd affixed them up there, I peered above my head to examine one of them. She (?) had tied a noose of plain wrapping string around the pig's neck, then knotted the other end of the string onto a decorating hook that was plugged into the ceiling. The various pigs hung down at different lengths that were probably above her head, but not all above mine. Though I tried to avoid the lower animals, still I bumped into several of them, which then clinked into other pigs. The effect was nightmarish.

I was looking for a telephone and for the book of personal phone numbers that I hoped to find beside it.

Her phone, it turned out, was a wall fixture (sticky to my touch) located in the hallway opposite the bathroom.

Sure enough, her book of telephone numbers was beside it, a big black plastic notebook with what looked like forty years of numbers scratched out and written over. The older numbers were written in a small, fairly legible hand; the newer numbers were a large, unreadable scrawl. I looked first under the "M's" and got lucky: there was an Anita Montgomery listed there—in a medium-sized, but still readable notation—and a Madelaine Montgomery. I tried Anita first, hoping she was a daughter, niece, or cousin who might actually give a damn.

"Anita Montgomery?" I inquired, when a woman answered.

"Yes" came the suspicious reply.

"I'm trying to reach a relative of Mrs. Grace Montgomery. Are you a friend or a relative of hers?"

"I'm her great-niece." The voice was no less suspicious and sounded, if anything, even more reserved. "By marriage. Who's this? Has something happened to Aunt Grace?"

I introduced myself and explained the predicament.

"Shit," the woman said wearily. "Dammit."

"Will you come over?" I was not prepared to take no for an answer, an attitude she may have perceived because she said, "Yes. Oh, hell, sure. Yes." She hung up without thanking me, but then, it wasn't as if I had done her a favor.

22

She arrived forty-five minutes later, a big, blowsy woman carrying an overnight case that she lugged back down the tiny hallway to her aunt's bedroom. When she came back into the living room, she gave me the sort of look that apes direct toward zoo visitors: full of resentment and disdain.

"She'll sleep like that all night," Anita Montgomery said, in a full, loud voice that would have awakened nearly anyone but the old woman. "You might as well go. I'm going to bed myself. I brought my own sheets; I'm damned if I'll sleep in her filthy ones." She batted a dangling pig out of her way. "Can you believe anybody lives like this?"

For a moment, because of that question, we were survivors in the same lifeboat.

"You've stayed with her before?"

She nodded heavily and said with emphasis, "I've done this before."

"It wasn't only the way she was acting," I admitted to her, "it was also the idea of her being alone tonight. The suspect in that murder is still at large, you know."

"Oh, hell." With an explosive oomph, the niece-in-law lowered herself into one of the faded chintz armchairs. "I could tell the damn cops who done that, and he ain't no danger to Aunt Grace."

She had my attention.

"There was this crazy guy, this nut, who used to go to our church—we all used to belong to that church used to be next door, the one where that guy got killed this morning—anyway, this nut, he must of fell off the same tree as Aunt Grace. Couple of damn Brazil nuts, they was. He claimed he heard these voices from the Bible—devils, like—and Aunt Grace, she believed every word he said; they was always whispering away in the kitchen about them damn devils. Used to give me the willies."

She glanced down at the scrapbook that lay on the table at her elbow and then looked meaningfully at me.

"She show you this thing?"

I nodded.

"Creepy, ain't it? Well, this nut, he used to come over all the time and cut and paste 'em for her—"

"But he's—"

She raised her chin and flared her nostrils like a haughty pig. "I know. He's nuts, she's nuts, and they're cuttin' out articles about other nuts. You tell me."

So it was Mob, I thought, who used those dainty scissors.

"I know my Bible," Anita Montgomery said, "and I know you shouldn't ought to be talking to them devils. When I heard them talking that devil-talk, I used to start saying the Twenty-third Psalm as quick and loud as I could. . . ." She raised her chin, and then her voice, to a shout that caused the pigs dangling nearest her to quiver in the air. *"LordismyshepherdIshallnotwanthemakethmeliedowninstillpasturesheanointethmysoul—"*

Grace Montgomery stirred, as if she'd been nudged in the ribs, but she didn't wake.

In the middle of the niece's shouting, I stood up. I'd had it. That was it. Enough. Get me out of here. I grabbed my coat and put it on during *yeatholwalkthroughthevalley-ofdeathhisrodandhisstafftheycomfortme—*

I held both of my hands up in front of me: Stop.

"You leaving?" She looked surprised.

"Yes."

She turned her stolid gaze toward the sleeping woman and said casually, "This time I'm putting her away. No ifs, ands, or buts. I don't care what my Jim says—" She looked up at me. "—that's my husband." Her expression was defensive. "This time, I don't care what anybody says. It's not as if *he* takes care of her. Hell no. *He's* never the one who picks her up and cleans her up, you bet. She's not *my* family, for damn's sake. Why should I do it? Nobody in her family gives a damn, so why should I? Why should I always get stuck with her? She's going in the loony bin this time, and that's where she belongs. Crazy old lady. Never said a kind word to me in her life, never did a kind thing for nobody, I don't know why I'm even trying to help her like I do. She don't deserve it."

"Good night," I said.

She turned the corners of her mouth down in disgust.

I let myself out of the house. Released myself, was more like it. Escaped. Fled. Bolted.

Outside, I inhaled the clean, cold air as if I'd been holding my breath under water, thrusting through wavering, distorted leagues of dark water to the surface of an ocean.

I let the air out again in a rush that created a frosty cloud in front of my face.

The night was full of comparisons. This time, compared with Mrs. Montgomery's home, the outside air smelled wonderfully clean. The biting cold felt as fresh as new sheets—and I felt as if I could sleep in them for a week.

Across the street, there were no lights showing in the windows of Rodney Gardner's house. Either his young widow was gone, or she wasn't afraid of the dark. The "For Sale" sign was nearly invisible.

I walked back toward my car. The single streetlight at this end of the block was haloed in snow. My body cast its own long, thin shadow on the whiteness. Feeling a little spooked—this was a block on which a murder had just occurred, after all—I walked faster. As I was unlocking my car, a man's voice called to me from the porch of the corner house.

"Why don't you give up?"

I was so startled that when I whirled around, I dropped my keys in the snow at my feet. I couldn't make out the face of the man who was standing in the darkness on his porch, but I recognized the resonant voice of Perry Yates. One of the neighbors I visited must have called him to tell him I was on the block. He didn't shout at me. He didn't have to. His words carried clearly in the cold, thin air, like a preacher's in a deadly still sanctuary.

"Rod Gardner wouldn't be dead if you folks hadn't come around," the voice accused. I had no reply to his charge; just possibly it was true. The words were creepy, coming from a faceless man in the dark of the porch. He said, "Anytime you put maniacs in with normal folks, you're gonna get trouble. Anybody knows that. Even MaryDell Paine. She tell you about her brother's history? Did she? Maybe you should have asked. Maybe if you'd asked, instead of just taking her word for things, Rod Gardner would still be alive. You, and people like you, you're responsible for this terrible thing. Now there's a young widow, and soon there'll be a poor little fatherless child. I'm telling you right now to get off our block."

I stood silently in the snow, not wanting to listen to him, but also not wanting to get down on my hands and knees in front of him and grovel in the snow for my keys.

There was silence then. Maybe he was hoping I'd fight back, but I was only hoping he'd go inside. When he did,

I didn't see his movement in the dark, but only heard the front door quietly close. As soon as I heard that, I got down to look for my keys, trying to tell myself that the only reason my fingers were shaking was because of the cold. I found them fairly quickly and drove away, trying not to sound as if I were in any kind of a hurry.

23

Geof was asleep when I got home.

Still wearing my camel wool dress, but barefoot, I crossed the gray carpet in our bedroom to sit on the edge of his side of our bed. I hated this ultramodern bed that two previous wives and a few girlfriends had slept in, just as I hated our bare, white-walled bedroom and our angular, cold-hearted house. It wasn't so much that I was jealous of its history—although, to be honest, I was a little— as it was that nothing of us seemed to stick to it. We walked through, we came and went, ate, slept, and made love, but for all the impression we left on the house, we might as well have been renting it. On this night, however, after the crazy, crowded chaos of Marianne Miller's and Grace Montgomery's houses, our own bare, aggressively sleek bedroom was, for once, a relief to me.

Of *course*, I was digressing. It was a wonder I wasn't hallucinating.

I looked at my sleeping husband and felt immediately warmed and comforted. Lovely man. Intelligent, well-intentioned, humorous, handsome, loving man. Lightly snoring. Smelling of Safeguard soap and herbal shampoo and of his male self. Sleeping so sweetly.

I showed no mercy.

"Wake up, Geof." I touched him lightly at his temple, with one finger. "I'm sorry." I touched him there again. "You have to wake up." I pressed four fingers into his bare upper arm, feeling the give of large, slack muscles. "Come on, honey." I scratched his earlobe with my fore-finger. "Wake up, wake up." I stroked his cheek with the back of my hand. "Ow!"

The hand that was buried in sheets suddenly shot out and grabbed my hand. Before I could retreat, he stuck my fingers in his mouth and bit them.

"I'm sorry!" I laughed and tried to tug my hand away.

"You'd better be." Geof kept hold of my hand as he rolled over on his back. He closed his eyes again and mumbled, "You'd better tell me the house is on fire. Is the house on fire?"

"Yes, and there are burglars downstairs."

"Oh, well." He opened his eyes, yawned, looked at me. "All right. That's all right, then. Why are you so late?"

"Why are you in bed so early?"

"I had hopes." He grinned weakly at me, looking dopey with sleep. "I was waiting. Like the naked housewife waiting for her hubby at the front door. Only I fell asleep."

"Where's the cellophane?"

"What? Oh." He began to laugh.

"I do have good reasons for waking you up, Geof."

"You don't need one." He looked down at his lap, which was covered by a white sheet. "I'm providing one." His fingers released mine and began to walk up my right leg, starting at my knee.

"Your legs are cold," he said.

I stopped his hand, under my dress, at mid-thigh.

"Momento, Señor."

"Que?"

"I'm late because I went back to Tenth Street to find out how the neighbors feel now about the idea of the recreation hall—only I found out some other things."

He sighed, withdrew his fingers from under my skirt, and folded both his hands circumspectly in his lap. As naked police lieutenants go, I suppose he managed to look fairly alert and efficient.

"Such as?" he asked.

"First, have you located Derek? Or Mob?"

"No. I'm sorry, Jenny."

My chest constricted, and I experienced a moment of stark, panicky fear for my missing colleague. I found myself talking faster, as if that would help the police to find him sooner.

"Geof, when Derek and I met Marianne Miller, the young woman who is the neighbor just to the south of the church basement, Derek was attracted to her. When I went back tonight, I remembered that, and so I stopped by her house to ask her if she saw him last night. She says she did. She says he came in for a couple of beers, and that he left about nine-thirty. She says that Derek told her he had to get home to type up his interviews. Does that help you at all, Geof?"

His smile was brief but kind. "To tell you the truth, we already knew that, Jenny. The detectives asked the immediate neighbors about their activities last night, and she mentioned Derek."

"Did she tell them that she knew Mob and that he used to hang around the neighborhood, cadging food?"

"She didn't, but others did."

"Oh."

He patted my hand. "What else have you got?"

"Either something or nothing."

"Is this multiple choice?"

I smiled, which was the point of his joke.

"I also saw the neighbor on the other side of the church, a Mrs. Grace Montgomery—"

"The pigs."

"Right. She's completely nutty. But in the middle of a lot of other nonsense she said something about the devil driving a red car—"

Geof's grasp of my hand tightened, then relaxed.

"—and that she knew what the devil looked like, and that the devil was afraid of the light. All I got out of her after that was that the car was a cherry red and that she saw somebody driving it just before, or maybe right around, sunrise. Now I'm probably putting one and one together and getting three, but I will remind you that Derek's Toyota is a bright cherry red. Maybe Marianne Miller told a little white lie. Maybe Derek didn't leave her house until the next morning—before the kids woke up."

"Did she describe the person in the car?"

"No."

"Man or woman?"

I shrugged. "Sorry. Does this help?"

"I don't know. But I do thank you, Officer."

"Was it worth waking up for?"

He studied me for a moment, seemed to sense that I was over my brief anxiety attack, and clamped a hand over my knee. "We can make it worthwhile." Momentarily, his conscience overtook him. "But not if you're too tired, or if you're feeling too bad about Derek. It's up to you."

I did feel leaden with worry and fatigue, but I lifted the sheet off my husband's lap anyway.

"How can you think so clearly when there's no blood left in your head?" I inquired.

"That's it," the lieutenant declared as he grabbed me and pulled me down on top of him. "She has just waived all rights. Frisk her, boys."

* * *

It was hours later, but still sometime in the night, that I woke him up again. I had shot up in bed myself, feeling unaccountably disturbed by an innocuous dream about photo albums. When I connected it to the photograph in my coat pocket, I got out of bed, pulled a robe around me, and padded downstairs to retrieve it. I was staring at it as I walked back upstairs, pondering whether this was worth waking Geof over, when it occurred to me that Kitt is sometimes a nickname for Christopher. That decided me. I shed the robe and crawled back under the covers, but I also turned my bedside lamp on low beam.

"Honey," I said, shaking him a little. "Wake up."

He did, quickly, blinking at the light.

"What's wrong this time?" Geof said.

"Look at this picture." I handed it to him.

He frowned and squinted at it, until his sleep-fogged vision cleared. "So?"

"I think it's Mob when he was a younger man. Somebody put it in my coat pocket while I was visiting MaryDell Paine this morning. Will it help?"

He shook his head and handed the picture back to me. "No, too old. The detectives got a recent one from his sister. Who gave this to you?"

"The maid, I think, don't ask me why."

"Maybe we'd better talk to the maid, then."

"Good luck, she's a shade taciturn."

He gazed speculatively at me. "Then maybe you'd better talk to her first. Simple curiosity, of course. You're merely wondering if she gave you the photo, who it's of, and why she'd do a thing like that. Wouldn't hurt to ask. And it wouldn't put her on guard—or endanger her job—the way it might if we were to ask her. You want to try?"

"Sure, why not."

"I can think of a lot of reasons why not," he said dryly, "and if they happen to occur to you, feel free to change your mind about doing this. The truth is, I shouldn't get you involved in a case—"

"I'm—"

"Already involved, I know. It's practically a way of life with us, isn't it? Listen, if you get anything useful out of her, I'll fix dinner one extra night next week."

"Two nights."

"Hey, it's not *that* risky."

"Okay, one dinner and one vacuuming."

"Are you kidding? Listen, at those prices, I'll talk to the maid myself." But he laughed. "All right, all right, you tough negotiator, you. I'll fix the two goddamned dinners. But one of them's going to be your leftover chili that I put in the freezer tonight."

"Not fair!"

"Okay, I'll add a salad. Listen, it was good chili."

"Well, I'm sorry you had to eat it alone."

"I think maybe chili is one of those foods that's better eaten alone." He smiled at me. "All those beans. Now, may I go back to sleep?"

"No," I told him, apologetically. "There's something else. I met a woman today, a patient of Marsha's, who mentioned having a friend named Christopher. I'm wondering now if that might be Kitt Blackstone?"

"Why should it be?" he asked, reasonably enough.

"It's possible, that's all."

"They're both crazy, you mean?"

"Well, yes, but more than that—they've probably both been institutionalized, and I suspect they've both spent a lot of time on the streets. I think they could have met, so what I'm saying is, maybe she could help you to find him."

"What's her name and how do I find *her?*"

"Her name is Rosalinda N. McInerny. Try the phone book, Cop, and if you don't find her there, call Marsha Sandy, and ask her for Rosalinda's address. If Marsha goes all doctor/client privilege on you, then go look at the benches in the city park, because that's where she spends her time.''

"Jesus."

"My sentiments exactly."

"Is that it? Don't you have any leads on any other crimes?"

I laughed. "I'm working on a B&E, but I don't have anything for you yet." I turned off my light, then scooched closer to him, and whispered, "If you're not too sleepy, I'd kind of like to commit another bit of assault upon your body. Whatdaya say, Copper?"

He reached rather aggressively for me.

"Oh, *mon capitaine*," I teased him.

"For a snitch, you're remarkably cooperative," he observed a moment later.

It should have helped me sleep, but I was too wide-awake by then. As I lay beside Geof, my worries about Derek grew into full-fledged fears that pressed at me in the dark until I felt sick with them.

24

In the morning, I rolled over and went back to sleep for another half hour after the alarm sounded, which meant that Geof was already gone by the time I arrived downstairs.

He'd left a note, with my phone messages from last night: "I forgot, Marsha Sandy called, call her back"; "Council for the Blind wants to pick up our old clothes next Friday"; *"Time* magazine wants you to renew your subscription"; "Your sister called, nothing important"; "Your boyfriend called a couple of times, hung up when I answered."

Damn, I thought, smiling at that last message, and here I've told him never to call me at home.

But I remained jumpy, a state of mind that coffee didn't help. I knew I was overtired. I knew I'd best keep a tight rein on my emotions, and be wary of trusting my own judgment that day.

The first thing I did at the office was to call Marsha to assure her that I would continue the crusade for a recreation hall on Tenth Street. My rationale for overriding the neighbors was that by the time we closed the deal, the murderer would probably have been apprehended, and the fear would have diminished. I spent most of the rest of the morning preparing for the board meeting the next day and worrying about Derek.

Faye wasn't much help; she was so concerned about him that it was all she could do to staple the minutes of the last meeting together, and finally she even gave up on that. Typing was beyond her capacity that morning, and answering the phone and pretending to be cheerful caused her voice to tremble so much that I started picking up all the calls myself.

At one point, I asked her to file the original copy of the minutes and the meeting agenda. Later, when I asked her to pull them out again to insert an addendum, she couldn't find them. We looked under "B" for Board, "T" for Trustees, "F" for Foundation, and even "M" for meeting. On a hunch, I found them under "D" for Derek. That's when I finally said:

"Faye, we have to talk."

She was sniffling into a tissue and didn't look up.

"Come into my office, please," I requested.

I didn't want to do this now; we were both too strung out, and it seemed to me that it was unwise for either of us to have a confrontation of any sort with anybody that day. But finding the board minutes under "D" for Derek signaled the full extent of her distress, if nothing else, so I decided to risk it.

She followed me and sat down in Derek's usual chair, but kept her nose in the tissue and still didn't look up at me. Faye, who was normally a rather youthful-looking fifty-two, appeared all of that and more this morning. Her usually neat hair—which was short and a natural-looking brown—appeared unbrushed. Lately, she'd been wearing suits and high heels, but today she had gone back to wearing her old uniform, which was a simple skirt, blouse, and flat-heeled shoes. Maybe the suit had signified ambition, and maybe she had decided that ambition was dangerous. Derek had been assistant director, and look where it got him. She'd been barely civil to me all morning.

I began bluntly.

"I am not the enemy, Faye."

That startled her into looking at me.

"Oh, Jenny, I don't—"

"I think that at some level, you're blaming me because Derek is missing. You are probably thinking that if I hadn't fired him, he wouldn't be gone, and, of course, you're right about that, Faye."

"I—"

"If you were the boss, would you have fired him?"

She blinked and her mouth tightened. "That's not fair."

"Sure it is." I spoke sharply in spite of myself. "So, would you have fired him, Faye? Knowing his work record? Knowing about his performance evaluations? Knowing what the job demands and what he supplied? And if not, why not?"

"I'd have given him another chance!"

"How many chances, Faye?"

"I don't know." She shrugged irritably, angrily. "As many as he needed!"

"Even when he continually failed to do jobs right, or on time, so that the work fell on you?"

"Yes!"

"Even when they fell repeatedly on your secretary?"

"My . . . ?" That seemed to put it in a new slant for her, but she rallied anyway. "Yes, if she didn't mind!"

"How nice for her," I said, sarcastically. I felt my temper slipping away from me and tried to clamp it down again. "In other words, Faye, you didn't mind it that Derek's failings caused more work for you."

"No." But she was too honest to maintain that line for long. "Well, I didn't mind much. I understood—"

"What? That he was incompetent, or that he was lazy?"

"Jenny! He's missing! He might be dead!"

"And it's all my fault," I said, flattening out each word.

She looked shocked, as if she had been brought face to face with the really terrible thing that she had, at heart, been silently accusing me of, but she still wasn't ready to admit it. Instead, she stood up and said, in what for Faye was a truly nasty tone of voice, "Everything in the world doesn't revolve around *you*, Jenny!"

She stomped out of my office then, leaving me staring, openmouthed, at her stiff back. Good grief. Talk about misjudging a situation, talk about using the wrong approach—Faye wasn't angry at me because she blamed me for Derek's disappearance . . . she was mortified at herself, for the "sin" of coveting Derek's job!

It all made sense now—the upscale dressing she'd been doing, the willingness to take on whatever jobs Derek dropped, and now the guilt when it seemed that because of his misfortune she might actually get her wish. And it was true—she was doing most of his job anyway, and I had been thinking of promoting her instead of hiring somebody new to replace Derek. Poor Faye.

I got up quickly from my desk and practically ran to hers to say, "Faye, I'm sorry," to say anything to paper over our argument, so that no irreparable space opened up between us before we had a chance to figure out a way to salvage things. I didn't want her to quit, and, heaven knows, I didn't want her to step over some line of attitude or behavior that might force me to let her go. But I got there just as the outer door to the foundation offices was slamming shut behind her. The closet door hung open, revealing an empty hanger—that was still swinging—where her coat had been.

Tired, I sank down in Faye's swivel chair.

"Gentlemen," I rehearsed saying to my bosses at the board meeting tomorrow, "it seems we've suffered a little attrition on the staff this week. . . .

"Of course none of it is my fault, gentlemen."

Oh, hell, no, of course not.

It was while sitting at Faye's desk, pondering the impenetrables of management—of people, that is—that I remembered to check on Mrs. Montgomery. I was curious to know how she'd made it through the night and what the family would do with her now. Actually, my better judgment told me *not* to call, to let it alone, in fact. But my better judgment didn't seem to be in good working order that day, so I opposed it.

After looking up Mrs. Montgomery's number in the phone book, I dialed. I let her phone ring ten times before I hung up. Maybe they'd already taken her to a hospital to be committed, or at least to be examined. I felt myself smiling a little cynically: to have her head examined. We all ought to have our heads examined now and then, starting with me this very day. I looked up the niece's number again and dialed it.

"Hello," a lumbering, sleepy female voice said.

"Anita?"

She grumbled an affirmative.

"This is Jenny Cain, the woman who was at your aunt's house last night. I apologize if I've gotten you out of bed. I'm just calling to see how she's doing. Did you have a long night with her?"

"You wouldn't have any idea," she said in a disgusted but more wide-awake tone of voice. "The old bitch woke up not half an hour after you left, shrieking and carrying on, and when I tried to calm her down, she just batted at me like I was hornets or something. I couldn't get near her. So I called my husband—he's her nephew, after all, ain't me that's related to her—but he couldn't be bothered, oh no, not her own flesh and blood. So I figured what the hell, if he don't care, why should I break my back trying to help the old bitch? I was just gettin' a bunch of black-and-blue marks from it, and no thanks from her, you can bet your life on that, so I just said the hell with you, old lady, and I came on home. Only it was one in the morning by that time, and then my husband and me, we had to fight about it when I got home, and I never got to bed until about, I don't know, what time is it anyhow?''

"Eleven-thirty. You left her alone?"

"The old bitch near drove me out!" she shouted.

"She doesn't answer her phone, Anita."

"That's because she's too damn crazy to hear it," she shot back. "Probably thinks it's church bells or something, or the damn bats bangin' in her belfry. Listen, she ain't my care. I don't want nobody botherin' me about her again. I'm tired, thanks to you and her. I'm going back to bed. Good-bye."

I quickly moved the receiver away from my ear so that my eardrums would survive when she slammed down the phone.

"I've got to get out of here," I said aloud.

For one thing, I hadn't had lunch, and for another, driving over to check on Grace Montgomery was the responsible thing to do. It would also give me just the excuse I needed to join the other rats who had abandoned ship.

25

The snow had stopped, but the most recent cold front stayed with us. In fact, the white-gray sky looked as if it might dissolve at any moment, and the air smelled like more snow to come. Poor Fred natives know that the best defense against the weather is to ignore it, but it's usually February before we manage to do that, and then only because we're so numb we no longer give a damn.

Regardless of the weather, there were four "Things To Do" on my mental list: eat; check on the pig lady; talk to MaryDell's maid; and somehow get a copy of that detailed report that MaryDell said her committee had compiled. I definitely needed that report—and five copies of it—for the board meeting tomorrow or there'd be no real estate transaction on Friday.

Accordingly, keeping first things first, I headed my car toward the Sunnyside Up & Cup to get the breakfast I had missed by sleeping late.

"Hi, Jenny," the hostess greeted me.

"Hi, Marge. Put me in a back corner, will you? Put

me where nobody will see me and want to sit down and have a little chat. I'm feeling antisocial this morning."

She nodded as if she understood the feeling well and said, "I'll put you behind the kitchen door, facing the back wall. Nobody ever wants to sit there."

"Perfect."

I ordered an omelet with two kinds of cheese, green peppers, red peppers, onions, mushrooms, black olives, and chopped ham, along with hash browns, biscuits, orange juice, and coffee.

"How do you stay so skinny?" the waitress asked me.

"I worry a lot," I replied.

While waiting for my order, I considered various plans of attack on MaryDell and her maid. A frontal attack was one possibility. I could just call and say, "MaryDell, I need that report . . . and by the way, I'd like to talk to your maid." To which she'd reply, "I told you, that project is dead . . . and why do you want to talk to my maid?" So that was out.

The waitress appeared with my coffee. "Cream?"

"Please."

I could skip the general and attack the troops, that was another possibility, which might mean calling every member of her committee until I found one who hadn't gotten the word and who had a copy and was willing to lend it to me. That prospect seemed a little iffy, however, particularly since MaryDell wasn't exactly known for recruiting independent thinkers to her committees. She was definitely a general who liked her soldiers to respect the chain of command, so all I'd be likely to get in response to such a request was, "Oh, you'd better ask MaryDell about that."

The waitress brought cream and my orange juice.

"Marge couldn't find you a better view than this?"

"Hello, wall," I said, and she laughed.

Okay, skip the report for a minute, I thought. What about the maid? Maybe I could find out her name and call her at home tonight. Fine, except how was I going to discover her name, without asking MaryDell? It wouldn't be any good to call people I knew to be friends of the Paines: they might know her first name, but it wasn't likely they'd know her last.

"Here you go, Jenny."

The waitress placed my food in front of me.

I attacked it with vigor.

As I swiped the last bit of melted cheese off my plate with my last bit of biscuit, the answer came to me. And if I was reading the situation correctly, I'd be able to talk to the maid *and* get the report at the same time. My brain felt alive again. It must have been all that good, old-fashioned, nutritious grease that did it.

I didn't even mind the cold now. It actually seemed invigorating. I started my car with that virtuous feeling of "mission" that now and then overcomes me. The food and coffee had acted like amphetamines on me, filling me with energy and optimism: Derek would be fine, the murderer would be found, and the recreation hall would open to great fanfare in a few weeks.

"Your fuel is low," the computer in my car informed me.

"No way," I retorted. "I am gassed, man, and ready to roll."

It did strike me that I was being a shade manic, but it beat the bone-dragging exhaustion I'd felt before eating. I slid into the first corner I came to, and fishtailed around it, murmuring "whee" under my breath. Before I put into action my plan of attack for conquering MaryDell and her maid, I would stop by Tenth Street to check on the old lady. If she was still in bad shape, I'd try calling the other

"Montgomery" in her address book. Somebody was going to have to put Grace under a doctor's care, but I didn't think it should have to be me.

I parked in front of her house and walked up to her door with a fairly springy step.

"Mrs. Montgomery?" I called loudly as I knocked.

I rang the doorbell repeatedly and knocked again several times. It didn't seem possible that she could have gone anywhere, so I thought she might be asleep, or hiding among her pigs and delusions, within her little house. Unwilling to give up without checking on her condition, I tromped around to the back. When I knocked on that door, my knuckles pushed it open. Startled, I let my knuckles continue to push it all the way back to the wall. This was not good. This, I did not like.

A clear view of her kitchen was before me.

The house was as warm as ever, as dirty as ever, but quiet.

"Grace?" I called out.

It was only the thought that she might be ill, or might have fallen, and need help that propelled me into the house against the good sense that screamed GETTHEHELLOUT-OFHERE in my head. My feet and knees tingled with a cowardly desire to race over to Marianne Miller's house again.

I stepped through the kitchen, listening hard, my knees suddenly so weak I felt as if they were wading through thick water.

"Grace?"

I waded into the hallway and looked into her bedroom. Nobody home but us pigs. I pushed back the door to her bathroom, looked in, and did a double take. Her tub was half-filled with water, in which maybe a couple of dozen little porcelain pigs floated. I stepped closer and peered down at them. A few had swallowed too much water through their snouts or the holes in their bellies, and had sunk to the bottom, drowned. Was she so crazy that she took baths with her pigs? Did she play with them in the tub, like a child with his rubber duckies? On the bathmat, one of her true-crime scrapbooks lay open to a double page: on the left side, there was pasted the most recent article about the murder of Rod Gardner; the facing page was blank.

That blank page gave me a chill that even the overheated house couldn't warm.

I walked back out into the hall, dodging the dangling pigs.

"Grace?"

I turned the corner into the living room and collided with her.

She was hanging from the ceiling.

I shrieked like a stuck air-raid siren. I batted her body and the myriad pigs away from me and stumbled back down the hall, through the kitchen, out the back door, down the steps, into the backyard. I was screaming, and I kept on screaming. JesusJesusohJesus.

I ran down the alley to the back of the house next door and hammered. Nobody answered.

I raced to the next house. Nothing.

By the time I reached the third back door, I was screaming "Fire" at the top of my lungs, hoping somebody would hear me and call 911. There was nobody home at the third house, either. I thought desperately, Doesn't anybody stay home anymore? When I bolted for the next house, I suddenly realized it was the corner house. Perry Yates's brown saltbox. I stopped, not quite so panicky that I couldn't hate the idea of going to him for help. But I was now closer to his house than to any other; it would be inexcusable of me to take the time to run somewhere else.

At first, it didn't seem as if anybody was home at Yates's house, either, and I ran from his back porch to try the houses on the other side of the street. Hell, this was getting ridiculous, I thought wildly—I could have gotten help faster by getting in my car and driving to the police station!

"What do you want?"

I turned around again, to find him standing in his doorway, staring at me. He stepped out on his porch. I was not so out of breath myself that I didn't notice that he was, too. He was wearing a brown parka, brown work pants, and snowy galoshes.

"I can't even shovel my own front walk without interference from you people," he said. "I could hear you yelling all the way down the street. What kind of trouble are you causing now?"

"Your phone," I said, pushing past him. "Where is it?"

"Hey, get out of my house!"

I turned on him viciously. "You'll be pleased to know there's been another murder on this block, Yates. *Now* may I use your phone to call the cops?"

"There." He pointed. "On that table."

I punched in the number. Yates walked in and stood over me. In a stilted, angry tone, he said, "You've got a lot of nerve saying that to me." But when I glanced at him, I saw that his eyes were sending another message, a triumphant one, which was: "I told you so." He didn't ask me who had died but stood close by, listening to my hurried conversation with the first cop who answered the phone.

"Poor Grace," he intoned when I hung up.

I brushed past him again and went out front to stand on the sidewalk to wait for the detectives. I couldn't stand to be in the same room with him. And if the killer came after me, he'd have to do it outside, in public, in broad daylight. Stalwart, that's me. My knees caved in, and I collapsed ingloriously to the sidewalk. That pathetic old woman—

her worst nightmares had come true and at the hands of the one ''crazy person'' she trusted. I sat on that ice and sobbed like a frightened, sorry child until the first police car rounded the corner. When I saw them, I stood up on my waxed-paper knees. I took off a glove and wiped at my cheeks with cold fingers.

26

Since he had been promoted, Geof didn't often make house calls, but he arrived with all four tires sliding for this one. The first thing he said to me when he joined me on the sidewalk in the snow was, "Honest to God, Jenny."

"We've got to stop meeting like this," I said humbly.

"I thought we had," he retorted. "Are you all right?"

"Oh, I'm always all right," I said, half-disgusted. I greeted the other detectives I knew: "Hello again, Frank."

"Jenny."

"Hello, Ailey."

My old nemesis, Ailey Mason, smiled slightly and said, "I think this is where I came in." Like Geof, he'd married recently, and the change had improved him. He was still a pompous young ass, but he was a happier ass now and a little mellower as a consequence. I thought his bride must be slipping molasses in with his oats.

I was allowed to leave soon after I told them everything I had seen, said, touched, and done in the vicinity of Grace Montgomery's house.

With a nod to me, Frank and Ailey walked off together to assist the investigation.

"Jenny," Geof said, "are you sure that Ms. Miller said she knew Mob? You're sure she told you that he used to hang around this neighborhood?"

"Of course I'm sure. Why?"

"Because none of the neighbors recognized him from the photograph the officers took around this morning. If he panhandled regularly, you'd think they'd remember him. So I'm wondering if she's got him confused with somebody else, or maybe she did know him but from somewhere else."

"What did she say about the pictures?"

"She hasn't been at home to ask."

I shrugged. "I don't know."

He dug into his inside coat pocket and came out with a piece of paper that was folded into quarters. He unfolded it and handed it to me, saying, "Here's a copy of the photograph his sister gave us, Jenny. We're passing these out around town, so you might as well have one, too."

I took it, staring at the visage of the bearded, wild-haired man who stared suspiciously back at me. The young man in the other photograph had looked a little hurt, unhappy, and puzzled; the older man in this one looked out-and-out crazy and not a little dangerous. According to the small print, he was six feet two inches tall and weighed between 190 and 210 pounds, and when last seen he had brown hair, brown eyes, and a graying brown beard. This was somebody you'd definitely notice—and probably try to avoid—if you spotted him on the street.

"I'll watch out for him, Geof."

"In more ways than one, if you please," he said. "Do you think he saw you, Jenny?"

"I have no idea, but what difference would it make anyway? I didn't see *him.*"

"You're assuming he thinks logically."

"Oh. Right."

"What are you going to do about the recreation hall now?"

"I'm going to go ahead and make my pitch at the board meeting tomorrow and then leave it to the trustees to decide. It would certainly help if you'd catch this guy, Lieutenant."

"We're doing out best, Citizen Caine." He leaned over to kiss my lips.

"I love you," we said at exactly the same time.

"Jinx, you owe me a Coke," we said, also at exactly the same time. Without knowing in advance that I was going to do it, I suddenly found myself leaning against his chest. Our arms went around each other, and I started crying again. Geof comforted me by stroking my hair and repeatedly kissing the top of my head. After a few minutes of that unseemly public display, the police lieutenant escorted me back to my car. I waved at him. He waved back at me. Jeez, I thought, as I drove off, thank goodness I married a cop who doesn't embarrass easily.

I drove home to change clothes before launching my next mission, which was to interview MaryDell Paine's maid and to get a copy of that report.

Although I might be able to accomplish it dressed as I was, there was a fair chance that I'd be stuck out in the cold in my car for a while, so I wanted to put on more and warmer clothing, just in case. While I had stood at the curb with Geof, I had discussed with him what I planned to do. He hadn't objected, particularly since police officers were guarding the front and rear entrances to the Paine house just in case MaryDell's brother showed up there. "But, please," he'd begged, "don't find any more dead bodies, all right?" I told him that had never been my life's ambition in the first place.

I was a little worried about my timing, though. For one

thing, I only had this afternoon and this evening to get my hands on that report in order to have it for the board meeting tomorrow morning. For another, I didn't know what hours the maid worked. She might leave before I got to her. Even if she lived in, this might be her day off. There were any number of unknown factors that might foil this "Detective 101" course plan of mine, including the possibility that I might not be able to stand the cold for very long.

At home, I removed my dress and slip, but left on my bra and panty hose. I pulled long thermal underwear over them, then added long wool socks. Then I slipped on a pair of thick wool harem pants, gathered by elastic at the ankles, and a tightly knit wool ski sweater that had, in the past, managed to keep me warm even on icy mountain slopes in Vermont. I started downstairs, but the phone rang, and I trotted back into the bedroom to answer it.

"Hello?"

When nobody answered, I said "Hello" again, then hung up. Must have been a wrong number, I decided, since the only heavy breathing had been mine. I was too young to be so winded. I should enroll in a spa. The problem with that, though, was that aerobics always seemed to me like God's way of explaining boredom. And if I wanted to lift weights, I could have children.

In the kitchen, I fixed a pot of coffee. While it perked, I put together a crunchy peanut-butter-and-raspberry-jam sandwich on thick wheat bread and wrapped it in a plastic bag. I put that, along with a banana and a small bag of Fritos, into a brown paper sack, to which I added three double-fudge brownies. That gave me all the food groups: crunchy, salty, sticky, and sweet. The phone rang again.

"Hello," I said.

This time whoever it was hung up on me first. I hate it when people do that; if they get a wrong number, the least they can do is apologize for bothering you.

The percolator gave its final, weak little burble, telling me the coffee was ready. It was Geof who had talked me into going back to an old-fashioned aluminum percolator, by avowing that it got and kept coffee much hotter than any drip system could. He was right. I filled a thermos with the aromatic, steaming brew.

Now I was almost ready for camp. But what would a wise camper need for those long, boring stretches between archery and canoeing? Notepaper and pen—I stuck those in the paper sack along with the food—and a good book. I ran back upstairs and retrieved from my bedside table *Too Close to the Edge*, which was proving to be a terrific police procedural by Susan Dunlap. I figured it was just the thing to inspire me—maybe even give me a few tips—for the snooping job that lay ahead. I also put carefully into the bag an envelope in which I stuck the "before" and "after" pictures of Kitt Blackstone.

I carried my provisions into the hallway, where I ended up having to sit down on the floor to pull on my boots with the sheepskin lining. Finally, I pushed my fattened arms into a ski jacket that was lined with dyed black rabbit fur (about which I always felt guilty, although why about the rabbits and not about the sheep?) and elasticized below my butt, clamped on sheepskin earmuffs, and covered my head with a red wool stocking cap.

Before putting on gloves, I looked up MaryDell Paine's phone number and called it.

The maid answered: "Paine residence."

"Hello," I said in a chirpy voice. "I'm calling on behalf of the Veterans of Foreign Wars. May I speak to Mrs. Paine, please?"

"I'll see if she can come to the phone."

That was all I needed to know, so I hung up.

I put on ski gloves, picked up my car keys, thermos, and paper bag, and left the house. I was as bulky as Frankenstein's monster and walked just about like him, too. Clump, clump, clump.

Also, I was sweating.

"Come, Igor," I said, and shut the door behind me.

It was four o'clock, and I was not feeling nearly as cheerful as I was pretending to be. But being of good cheer can also, in certain circumstances, serve as a useful diversion. I didn't go so far as to whistle while I worked, but I tried like hell to forget for a while what I had seen and heard in Grace Montgomery's house that horrible afternoon.

27

I cruised past MaryDell Paine's house once to count the cars in her parking lot, not that that would tell me whether she was still at home. Her car—whatever it was—was probably locked into one of the stalls in their four-car garage. But when I spotted an old rusty Oldsmobile parked there, one that had also been parked there during my last visit, I felt pretty sure the maid was inside.

I drove around the block and parked in front of a minimansion owned by some former friends of my parents. They might send out the houseman to question my presence, but once he reported that it was only a Cain sitting out there, they'd merely shake their heads and attribute my aberrant behavior to the fact that everybody knew that all the Cains were crazy. I'd never liked them anyway, not even in the days when they used to come over to play poker and drink martinis with my folks. He'd always tweaked my cheeks hard enough to hurt, and she'd always sat on her massive butt while my mother ran back and forth from the kitchen to the den with drinks and sandwiches. Let 'em cluck. The hell with 'em.

I let my engine run for a few minutes, delaying the moment when I would have to switch it off and the car would cool down.

My plan wasn't very sophisticated—I was simply waiting for the lady of the house to leave. What I figured was that a Super Volunteer, Overcommitted Person like MaryDell was bound to have more committee meetings scheduled than the Pope. And if I knew my Dedicated Civic Person, she wouldn't let a little thing like her brother being missing and wanted for murder get in the way of her responsibility to chair the Committee to Paint the This or the League to Build the That. If she didn't have any meetings to go to this afternoon, surely she would tonight. The weather wouldn't matter; a mere blizzard rarely canceled anything for very long in Poor Fred.

There was one other car, or rather a van, parked on the block, with "Mitchum Drywall Contractors" painted across both sides. Cheezit, the cops. I wanted to drive over, roll down a window, and ask them if Mrs. Paine had left the house in the last few minutes, but I knew they wouldn't appreciate the attention. On the other hand, if Geof hadn't found time to tell them of my mission, they might come wandering over to inquire about me. It struck me as kind of funny—them sitting over there watching for somebody to arrive; me sitting down here waiting for somebody else to leave.

We gotcha covered, MaryDell, I thought.

Evidently, Geof had informed them, because nobody bothered me.

At five o'clock I turned on the engine again and ate the banana while the car warmed up. I decided to save the coffee for the periods between heat. At five-twenty, I turned on the engine again and ate half of the peanut butter sandwich and one of the double-fudge brownies. At five thirty-five, even after another quarter-cup of coffee, and even though I was trying very hard to wait at least another twenty minutes—to warm up the engine, if not to eat—I chickened out again. Both the afternoon and the car were getting darker and colder. I had tried to read my mystery while there was still enough light, but it was too good; I was afraid that if I got engrossed in it, I might miss seeing MaryDell arrive or leave. God, I hoped it was leave. I was already feeling like a popsicle, and if she was away now, and then came home, and I had to wait still longer for her to leave, I'd probably give up. It was obvious to me that I wasn't cut out for surveillance work, especially not in below-freezing weather.

A newish, pale yellow Cadillac Eldorado sedately rounded the corner down the street and headed my way. It slowed at the entrance to the Paines' driveway before turning in and going up the drive. It was MaryDell herself, in a mink coat and matching mink turban. From my distance, it looked like a small, plump woodland creature was behind the wheel.

"Oh, frozen buffalo shit," I said in disgust. The fact that each word blew frostily into the air only deepened my sense of self-pity.

Even though it had only been five minutes since I last warmed up the car, I switched on the engine again and then ate the rest of the sandwich and the Fritos. It is not easy to eat Fritos while wearing ski gloves, but don't good things often come at the cost of some effort? I was starting in on the second brownie when the yellow Cadillac with the mink at the wheel came barreling down the drive again, slid nearly all the way across the street, backed up with a ferocious spinning of its wheels, and spun off at a good clip down the street. I'd always heard that minks were testy creatures; well, who could blame them? Or maybe MaryDell was late for a meeting, I surmised.

"Okay, Little Liza." I sighed. "Cross that ice."

I got out of my car, slogged up MaryDell's front steps—which, surprisingly, had not yet been cleared of the latest snow—and rang the doorbell. The maid answered right after Yankee Doodle came to town and just before he stuck the feather in his cap.

If the maid recognized me, she didn't let on.

"Is MaryDell home?"

"She just left."

"Did she leave a package for me?"

She frowned. "What package?"

"It's a report. She might have put it in a manila envelope, or a binder of some sort." I continued, with truth if not with candor. "She was supposed to get it to me for an important meeting that's being held tomorrow."

"I don't know anything about it."

"Darn. I've really got to have that thing. . . . Do you think she might have left it in her office? Could I look for it there? I'll bet she meant to leave it out for me, but she was in a hurry and she just forgot."

"She was in a hurry all right," the maid said dryly.

"I'm freezing," I said, finally telling a complete truth. "Could I come in?"

With a grudging air, she admitted me, shutting the door behind us.

"Is it warm in here?"

She pulled her head back, like a chicken. "Can't you tell?"

"Not yet." I looked her in the eyes and said in my best authoritative executive voice, "I can see that she didn't leave it on the hall table. I've really got to have that report. Where's her office? I'll take a quick peek there."

She looked exasperated, but then merely shrugged and surrendered the fort easily. "I guess it's okay. Come on back here, then."

I followed her down the hall, past the kitchen, past the sun porch, and on into a corner of the house that was more a nook than an office. It was barely big enough for a small, built-in desk with two telephones, a swivel chair, and three

file cabinets jammed in against the desk. It surprised me—
I'd expected something more elegant and official. I knew
that many, maybe even most, women who do volunteer
work feel uneasy about granting themselves the dignity of
a full-fledged office in which to conduct their business,
but I had not expected such insecurity from MaryDell.

Her desktop was not particularly neat, but the papers
on it were sufficiently revealed so that I could see there
was no report pertaining to a recreation hall for former
mental patients.

The maid was standing at my shoulder.

I turned boldly to the first file cabinet to my left. I
pulled out the file labeled ''R-S,'' expecting a brown hand
to clamp over mine.

She didn't stop me.

I quickly found the file I was looking for, in the first
place I looked, under ''Recreation Hall.'' Easy. Feeling
cocky, I turned to the maid and said, ''Does she have a
copier?''

She jerked her head, bidding me to follow her.

The copier, it turned out, was in the kitchen, in a hallway leading to the garage. The maid had stopped following me around and had returned to her kitchen work. While
I ran the copying machine, I reflected on my act, which
seemed to me to be about on a moral par with breaking
and entering. Was I justifying my means to suit my ends?
Yes, I decided with no great pride, I guess so. I made only
one copy—as if that were some sort of penance—and returned the original to MaryDell's file. With the copy tucked
into my coat, I clomped back into the kitchen.

''May I talk to you?''

Anita looked up, suspiciously, from the pot she was
stirring, and her former truculence reappeared. ''What
for?''

''You did me a favor yesterday—''

''What favor?'' she asked, scornfully.

"You gave me the picture of Kitt Blackstone."

Her eyes shifted away from mine, back to the contents of her pot, but at least she didn't deny it. "Yeah, so what?"

"Well, I just wondered why, that's all."

"What d'you mean, why?"

I wished that she would look at me again, so that I could smile at her and display a few friendly teeth. "Mrs. Paine gave the cops a more recent picture of him, so I just wondered why you gave me *that* one."

"Good God Almighty." Her head jerked up. Although she sounded angry, the quick glance she shot at me looked frightened. "I didn't know she give them a picture. Just forget I give the other damn thing to you, just forget it!"

She was stirring faster now and bits of thick creamy sauce slopped over onto the stove top.

"Oh, hell!" she said furiously. With quick, nervous motions, she turned off the gas under the pot and wiped her hands on her apron. She glared at me and said, "All right!"

She walked, almost ran, over to a closed door, which she opened to reveal what was probably her "maid's room." I saw beyond her back a neatly made single bed, an armchair, a potted plant, and a dresser. She got down on her knees in front of the dresser, pulled open the bottom drawer, and lifted off items of clothing until she found what she was looking for. As she walked back toward me, clasping the object to her chest, I saw that it was a photo album.

"Here!" She thrust it at me and stood watching me as I leafed through it. She had her hands pressed over her heart, as if to still its beating.

What I saw were family photos, in which I recognized MaryDell and her tall, beefy husband, along with many of their friends or relatives whom I didn't know. What many of the photographs had in common, outside of repeated faces, were small holes cut in them. They were holes where another face or another figure should have been.

"Did she cut him out?" I asked.

"He did," she said, and her eyes narrowed again.

"He?"

"Mr. Paine. He got mad one time, at all the money they was spending on Mr. Kitt, and he took him some scissors and just cut that boy clean out of every picture in the house. Said if Mr. Kitt ever come around again, he'd cut his real head off his real shoulders, too."

"Why, Anita? Why'd he hate him that much?"

"It was the money, like I said." She eyed me, looking scornful and disgusted. "Plus, you got to understand what it's like having a crazy person around all the time—Mr. Kitt, he was dirty, he smelled, he yelled and cussed and stole things, he got violent sometimes, like they say, and he cost Mr. Paine lots of money in doctors and stuff."

"What do you mean violent?"

"I mean *crazy!*" she yelled at me. "I mean throwing stuff around and breaking it, that's what I mean! Expensive stuff. Nice stuff. He didn't care what he broke!"

"How did Mr. Paine feel about his wife helping Kitt?"

"Hated it," she said, more quietly. "He hates anybody doing anything to help Mr. Kitt. Mr. Paine, he thinks Mr. Kitt ought to pull himself up. One time Mr. Paine, he sabotaged a job that Mrs. Paine had got lined up for Mr. Kitt, just because Mr. Paine, he thought Mr. Kitt ought to have got it for himself."

"When did he cut these pictures out?"

"I don't know. Maybe six, seven years ago."

"So you thought there wouldn't be a picture to give to the police?"

She didn't reply, which I took for assent. I pulled out of my pocket the copy of the more recent picture of Kitt Blackstone and handed it to her.

"Then where do you think Mrs. Paine got that picture of him?"

She drew back her head in that chicken movement again and shoved the picture back at me.

"That ain't Mr. Kitt," she said disdainfully, as if glad to catch me in some error. "Not unless he's got him one of them hair transplants. Mr. Kitt's been near bald since I can remember. And he's got kind of a sweet face. He *ain't* sweet, he's crazy, but he's got that kind of face, like a nice kid, even if he is forty-something years old. He sure don't look nothing like this."

"Do you know who this man is?"

She shook her head and shrugged.

"But this is weird," I said.

"You ought to try workin' here," she said dryly.

"I still don't really understand why you gave it to me."

She smiled, a cold and malicious smirk that nearly hid her fear.

"Maybe I like to put them to a little trouble now and then, like they's always puttin' me," she snapped. "And maybe doing something like this beats puttin' rat poison in their"—she sneered—"*coq au vin*. And maybe I just wanted to, that's all, it ain't none of your business why I do what I do."

I put the folded paper back in my coat pocket and slipped my gloves back on. "Why did you keep that little picture of Kitt, Anita? Were you fond of him?"

"Him?" She stared incredulously at me. "He's *crazy.*"

"Why, then?"

She shook her head, as if I were very stupid.

"They can afford to throw away things. Even nice things. Real nice things. It's a sin what they throw away." She cocked an eyebrow, and a touch of dryness crept into her anger again. "You find interesting things when you empty wastebaskets in somebody else's house. So I hold on to 'em. 'Cause you never know when they might come in handy.''

"Do you know where he is, Anita?"

"Mr. Kitt?" She laughed, an unpleasant, cynical cackle. *"He* don't even know where he is half the time, so how should I know?"

Too much time had passed, enough for at least a short meeting to convene, be conducted, and close. I started for the kitchen door, and she followed me.

In the front hallway, with my hand on the doorknob, I started to tell her not to bother informing her employers about my visit. But as I turned to face her, my glance was caught by a sudden movement at the top of the front stairs.

"What are you doing here, Jenny?" MaryDell called out. She started down the stairs toward us.

"MaryDell?" I replied, dumbly.

Anita whirled around as if her strings had been jerked.

"Mrs. Paine," she said in an angry, panic-stricken voice. "I didn't hear you come back, ma'am, I thought you was gone. . . ."

"I haven't been out of the house, Anita."

"Then who was that left in your car, Mrs. Paine?"

I waited tensely for her answer, and when it came, I bolted out the front door, running and sliding down the lawn toward the police van.

"Nobody, Anita," she'd answered. "Nobody took my car. You must have imagined it."

28

The cops in the van saw me coming and opened the back door to me. I climbed in, saying breathlessly, "That was Mob! That wasn't Mrs. Paine—that was Kitt Blackstone driving that yellow Cadillac!"

"Aw, shit!" exclaimed the officer who'd opened the door to me. He slammed the door shut, and we were moving before I'd had a chance to catch my balance. Besides the plainclothes officer in the back of the van, there was the driver, who was turning the wheel with one hand and holding the speaker to his radio in the other, barking information to the dispatcher. Both officers looked very young to me; I didn't recognize them or know their names, but this was not the moment for introductions.

We swerved around a corner, and I stumbled, then fell onto the carpeted floor. After righting myself, I leaned against a metal wall of the van, though that didn't keep me from swaying violently, side to side, with the rocking and rolling movements of the vehicle. The driver was giving the dispatcher the Caddy's license number. The other officer, after checking quickly to see if I was okay, had slipped up into the front passenger's seat, displaying an agility to rival an acrobat's. Left behind in the bare rear of the van, I looked around: this was no fancy surveillance vehicle, with cameras, monitors, radios, or telescopic lenses; this was just a plain old van used for plain old hiding and peeking. At least it was warm, thanks to a little portable heater attached to the wall directly opposite me. But the violent herky-jerky movements of the van, combined with the hot air blowing in my face, made me feel nauseated. I prayed that I would not distinguish myself by throwing up.

There were small surveillance windows in the walls, but we were going too fast, and I was bouncing around too much to be able to look out of them. It was all I could do, in fact, to stay upright and to keep from hitting my head repeatedly against the side of the van. The officer in the passenger's seat kept glancing back at me with a sick, half-smile of guilt and worry on his face. "We should have let you out!" he shouted back at me once. And then a few minutes later, "The Lieutenant's gonna kill us if you get hurt!" And finally, "Jesus, here we go! Hang on, Ms. Cain!"

Here we go where? I thought wildly.

The van came to a sudden, sliding halt that sent me tumbling across the carpet. I slammed into the back of the driver's seat. Involuntarily, I cried out at the pain of it, then cursed myself for a sissy. But the shoulder was the same one I'd hurt a few years before in a lobster pound. I heard the men grabbing shotguns and throwing open their doors. "Stay down!" they both hissed at me. I didn't have any choice; I had to stay down because my shoulder was now lodged between the driver's seat and the four-speed gear-shift mechanism. Blasts of cold air suddenly came at me in stereo from the two open front doors. No lights came on in the van when the doors opened; the cops must have fixed it so they wouldn't. It was good and dark outside by then and bitterly cold.

"I will never do anything like this again," I swore to myself at that moment. I wasn't hearing any noise from outside the van, which both reassured and terrified me. At least there hadn't been any gunshots. Where in hell were we? And what was going on out there? Could I risk a look out?

With as little movement as I could manage, I extracted myself from the van's grasp and then inched over a bit until I could see out the passenger door. Under the bottom edge of it, I saw—thanks to the natural illumination of the moon on the snow—a Michelin tire with a Caddy insignia on the wheel cover. My heart went into its reggae mode, and I froze, unable to work up the courage either to move closer in order to see more, or to move completely out of what might be a line of fire. I felt sick again and found myself mentally paraphrasing the officer's words with an "Aw, dammit." I was never, never going to get myself into anything like this again. Never. Never.

I was listening as intently as if a bear were in the woods and my life depended on hearing his approach, but I still didn't hear anything informative.

When that kept up for several more minutes, I decided I must be all alone on the scene. But the scene of what? Moving quietly and cautiously, I raised myself to my knees, then bobbed my head up until I could just see out the window. Quickly I jerked my head down. But nobody had shot at it. I risked another peek. All I saw was the yellow Caddy—or at least, *a* yellow Caddy—which was nose-deep in a snowbank in the front yard of a modest frame house. The driver's door hung wide open; the interior light cast a throw rug of yellow onto the snow.

One of the cops, I saw now, was circling west, slowly and carefully, keeping to the trees where possible. His mate was duplicating his efforts, to the east. I wondered why they couldn't just follow footprints in the snow, until I saw that the snow all around us was well trampled by a good many more than one set of feet. Soon, the officers disappeared from my view along the night-darkened street. I couldn't remember if I'd heard them radio in this location, so I didn't know whether to expect reinforcements anytime soon.

After a few more silent, cold moments, I alighted as quietly as I could from the van, closed the door a bit, and stood behind it. Smart, Cain, I thought: now they can only shoot your ankles or your head. Still, it was dark, and I was standing in shadow.

It seemed we were in a lower-middle-class neighborhood where, if people were curious about us, they were certainly hiding their interest well. A couple of dogs barked, including a chained one close by that kept barking and lunging. I felt a moment of irrelevant fury at the owner who would keep his animal outside on a night so bitter. But apart from the dogs, there were no sounds or signs of life. No curtains moved in the windows, no doors opened a crack, all was silent and—except for the occasional streetlight, porch light, and interior lamp—dark. The dog on the chain barked ever more frantically, until I became afraid that he would strangle himself on the chain that bound him; the other dog down the block echoed in high-pitched, hysterical yips.

A back-porch light flew on in the house where the chained dog was going berserk, and a rough male voice yelled at the dog to "shut the fuck up." In the illumination of the porch light, I saw that the animal was a beautiful malamute that was barking and lunging at its own doghouse. Suddenly, I realized why—another dog had stolen into it. I watched as the second mutt—a great, furry creature, as big as a St. Bernard—dashed out of the doghouse and raced toward the dark at the back of the yard. Just as it reached the shadows, the dog got up on its hind legs and ran.

I was too surprised for a moment to react, but then I screamed: "There he is! It's Mob!"

Both officers came running, listened to my impassioned, shouted instructions, and then vaulted the fence and disappeared into the dark backyard. I waited tensely, stamping my feet and clapping my hands against the sides of my legs to try to keep my blood circulating.

But when the two young officers returned—exhausted and sucking air—all they had to show for their desperate hunt was the pelt of the ''dog'' they were chasing. It was a soft, warm, luxurious mink coat. The driver held it out to me. I stroked it briefly with my gloved hands and felt a totally unexpected surge of gladness—which I hid from the officers—that the coat was limp and empty.

How would he stay warm now? I wondered.

In the hours that followed, roadblocks and a house-to-house search ensued, but Kitt Blackstone eluded them. He had disappeared as completely as if he had turned into one of the phantoms in his mind. This time, his sister wasn't given any opportunity to hide and shelter him or to mislead the police. The photograph she had originally given them, of the bearded, wild-eyed man, was a picture of an actor playing a role in a play she had helped to produce at our local theater—one of her many volunteer jobs. MaryDell Paine's career as a respected civic leader was over, at least for a while. Eventually, people will forgive hardworking volunteers almost anything, even harboring fugitives and impeding the police. Eventually, they'd say, ''Well, he was her brother, after all, what was she supposed to do, turn him in?'' To which my husband would have replied, furiously, ''Yes.''

But for now, Kitt Blackstone was gone again, giving the citizens of Port Frederick the terrifying feeling of having a raving monster on the loose.

29

At the trustees' meeting the next day, I skirted over the fact that Derek was missing—a fact the police didn't want publicized—and that Faye had not returned, either to work or to apologize.

"Flu bug," I lied to my five elderly bosses.

They seemed to accept that with sweet trust.

By describing them as sweet and elderly, I do not mean to imply that they are dumb and docile but, rather, that I'm fond of them and that they all happen to be around seventy years old. That does not make them feeble. God knows, they're not feeble.

For that Thursday morning meeting, I had also called in Marsha Sandy and her friend Joe Fabian, whose hometown job was that of county mental-health director. Together at one end of the long conference table we faced: Jack Fenton, chairman of the board of First City Bank; Edwin Ottilini, founding partner in the law firm of Owens, Owens and Ottilini and also chairman of this board; Roy Leland, chairman emeritus of United Grocers; and Pete Falwell, retired president of Port Frederick Fisheries.

"I've never heard of this project before," Roy Leland immediately objected. "Where'd it come from, all of a sudden?"

"I'm sure Jennifer will explain everything," Mr. Ottilini said dryly, with a slight and knowing smile directed toward me. He was the oldest, the most formal, but possibly also the kindest and most shrewd of them all.

"I want you to know right off the bat, Jennifer," Jack Fenton said, in the strong, fair way he has of expressing himself, "that I won't vote for this if we have to force it down the neighbors' throats."

"If it comes to that, we won't, Jack," I promised.

"What if one of the clients goes nuts?" Roy demanded. He is a man as broad as he is blunt. "What if he sets the goddamn place on fire, and somebody sues us?"

"The insurance information is in the packet in front of you, Roy," I said, a shade too soothingly, evidently, because it made Jack Fenton and Mr. Ottilini smile. Roy, however, merely harrumphed and calmed down.

"What's the damned hurry anyway?" Pete Falwell asked.

"Look outside, Pete," Jack advised him, and then I explained about the competition and about the singular advantages of the site.

They finally let me make my formal presentation, but they were far from convinced by the time I had finished. It was the unseemly—to them—need to hurry and the attitudes of the neighbors that bothered them in varying degrees. I wasn't even sure we had a majority after Marsha mesmerized them and Joe browbeat them.

But then I said, "Gentlemen, it's all very well for us to sit here talking dryly about this problem, this project. We're all sane"—I smiled at them; they all smiled back at me—"one hopes. We're well dressed, well fed. We're warm. We have someplace to go after this meeting and to our homes after that. We have family and friends, we have good intentions, and you certainly have good business sense."

I smiled at them again; a couple of them unconsciously nodded back at me. Good, I thought, two votes.

"But what you don't have," I continued, "unless some of you are harboring secrets from the rest of us, is a personal knowledge of what it is like to be on the streets, a little crazy, homeless, and hopeless."

My trustees, except for Mr. Ottilini, stirred a bit restlessly. This was getting a shade sentimental for Pete's, Roy's, and even Jack's taste, I could see. Jack was the only Democrat among the trustees, but I knew that even he had a limited appetite for sob stories. I sensed their recoil, and so I stood up straighter and put a brisk, businesslike note into my voice.

"I wouldn't ask you to buy a car without seeing it," I said. "I wouldn't sell you a suit until you had it on. And I won't ask you to help someone you've never met."

That was Marsha's cue, the one we'd cooked up over the phone that morning. She, in turn, glanced meaningfully at Joe Fabian. He got up and walked over to the door that connected the conference room to my office. He opened that door and disappeared for a moment. When he came back in, he was leading by the hand our secret weapon: Rosalinda N. McInerny.

The trustees, those old-fashioned gentlemen, pushed back their chairs and stood up in their places. They didn't sit down again until Rosalinda was settled in the chair Joe pulled out for her, between him and Marsha.

I was watching Rosalinda's face: there was panic there. Were we helping her, or using her? I wondered.

"Gentlemen," Marsha said in a matter-of-fact voice, taking over from me, as we had also planned, "I'd like you to meet one of my patients, Rosalinda McInerny. She already knows who you are and what you're trying to decide."

From across the table, Jack Fenton shot me an amused glance that said, "Uh-huh. I'm on to you." Only someone who knew Mr. Ottilini very well would have caught the wisp of a smile at the corners of his thin, dry lips.

"I have asked Rosalinda to tell you a little about her history," Marsha was saying, "and she has bravely agreed to do that." She turned to the woman, and her voice was low, gentle, and soothing. "Do you feel like doing that now, Rosa?"

A whisper: "Okay."

"This is hard for her," Marsha informed us, stating the obvious. "It's possible that I shouldn't even have asked her to do it. But she says that if I'll ask her questions, she'll try to answer them as well as she can. All right?"

Marsha seemed to be appealing to everyone there, and we nodded. I suspected that they were all feeling as tense and uneasy as I was. This might backfire.

"Rosa," Marsha said, "when did you first get sick?"

After a pause, a whisper: "When I was twenty-one."

"How many times have you been in the hospital since then, Rosa?"

A long pause, and then: "Thirty times."

"How many hospitals have you been in?"

Rosalinda picked at her skirt and then looked up. In her soft, almost childish voice, she said, "Uh, I'm not sure. I don't exactly remember. I think it's maybe six or seven?"

"I think that's right," Marsha said gently. "Maybe even eight or nine. And what's the average length of time that you've spent out of a hospital since you were twenty-one, Rosa, could you tell them that?"

Rosalinda whispered something to Marsha, who whispered something back.

"Six months," Rosalinda said. "I get real sick, and then I go into the hospital for a few months, and then I get out for about six months, and I get real sick again, and I go back in again. I think one time I was out for almost eight months. That was nice.''

"How long have you been out of the hospital this time?" Marsha asked her.

"Three months," she said, with unmistakable pride.

"It is a clear cycle, you see," Marsha told the trustees. "And one of the keys to breaking the hold of the illness is to crack that cycle. Her illness, with which I would rather not label her here, is of such a nature that it seems to build in severity, all the while plunging her into deeper and deeper despair. Rosalinda, as you see her today, is at a peak of functioning and well-being—"

Pete Falwell looked simply stunned at that statement.

"—and we are trying hard to break the old pattern, so that she can progress instead of decline. But, gentlemen, it is very hard to progress, when the only bright spots in your days are your visits to your state-paid psychiatrist and your visits from your social worker. I'll tell you the truth. Rosalinda and I have talked at some length about this idea for a recreation hall, and she's not at all sure about it. But I know, and I think she understands, that her hesitancy is a symptom of her disease. That disease makes her despair of ever having the confidence to go anywhere, of ever having the ability to speak to people, and of anyone ever loving her.'' Marsha cast a loving glance at her patient. "With my support, Rosalinda would attend such a recreation hall. And if it is managed in the way that is promised, she will be encouraged there. She will begin to feel comfortable, liked, and needed. She will have some place that is important to her to go to, and there will be a much greater chance that we will break the pattern that binds her.

"Gentlemen, in my practice, I see many others who are like Rosalinda, at least in their chronic suffering. I won't beg you to provide this recreation hall, and neither would they. They have, most of them, too much pride to do that. But I will tell you that"—she paused, as if searching for the right words, and then smiled wryly at us—"it would help. It would certainly be a big help."

She smiled at Rosalinda. "Is there anything you'd like to add to this?"

Rosalinda thought a minute, but shook her head.

"Thank you, Miss . . . Rosalinda," Mr. Ottilini said.

She ducked her head, then looked up and smiled shyly at me. "Thank you," I mouthed back at her, and she smiled more broadly.

Joe ushered her back out of the conference room. The trustees rose to their feet and stayed there until the door closed on Rosalinda.

There was a general clearing of throats and shuffling of chairs as everybody sat down again.

Mr. Ottilini inquired, "Do we need any more discussion on this issue?"

The other board members shook their heads.

"Do I hear a motion?"

"Move," said Jack.

"Second," said Roy.

"Opposed?" inquired Mr. Ottilini.

No one was.

"Jennifer," Pete Falwell interjected, "if you talk to Mike Laurence, tell him we're sorry that he's the one we're beating out of this thing. But, hell, he used to be one of us; if anybody ought to understand our position, he should. Right, Roy?"

"Right," the big man said.

I didn't disabuse them of that notion.

"All right, Ms. Cain," the chairman said, by way of instructions to me. And that was that. We moved on to the next order of business.

I didn't hang around in the conference room to chat with the trustees after the meeting, as I usually did. I was eager to get to my office to let our visitors know the outcome of the vote on the recreation hall.

"*Yes,*" I announced, as I walked in and faced Marsha, Joe, and Rosalinda.

Marsha looked enormously relieved, Joe seemed to relax a little, but Rosalinda didn't change her basic expression of pleasant, passive puzzlement. After I had thanked each of them, I ushered them into the outer office and then out into the hall.

Two police officers were waiting there.

"Ms. McInerny?" one of them inquired of Rosalinda.

30

Later, when I called Geof to protest, he said, "I'm sorry, Jenny, but we hadn't been able to locate her. She wasn't at her apartment, but she was never in the park, either. So when you mentioned this morning that she was going to be your surprise witness at the trustees' meeting, I thought of sending over a couple of officers to question her about Kitt Blackstone."

"You didn't tell me. You let me set a trap for her."

"Jenny, this is a murder case."

"And all's fair, I suppose."

"Hell, yes."

Of course, he was right; of course, he had done the right thing; of course, I had to admit it. But even after I hung up, I was still feeling the sting of Joe Fabian's anger when he had first assumed it was I who had betrayed them. And I knew I'd never forget the whimpering, clinging terror into which Rosalinda had disintegrated when the cops tried to question her. Not that it had done them much good.

"Ms. McInerny," they'd said, "do you know the

whereabouts of a man by the name of Kitt Blackstone, who is also known as Mob?''

She'd brought her hands together in front of her heart and clasped them beseechingly, and she had started to cry in short, panicky little whimpers, like a newly weaned puppy. The officers were only doing what they were supposed to do; I knew they didn't mean to cause the harm or the scene they did. But within seconds, they had Joe Fabian shouting at them to leave ''Ms. McInerny alone,'' while Marsha embraced the sobbing woman and tried desperately to calm her. It didn't work. Soon, Rosalinda was calling, ''Mob! Mob!'' like a child beseeching Superman to fly in and rescue her.

It was clear, however, that the Friend Christopher she had mentioned to me was, indeed, the Mob for whom the police were searching. But it was also clear that even if she knew where he was, she wasn't capable of telling them. The poor cops, after trying to ask the same question in several different ways, finally subsided into standing by helplessly, staring at her, and looking thoroughly baffled. They didn't even protest when Marsha and Joe hustled Rosalinda into an elevator. It was clear to all of us that they weren't going to get any help from Rosalinda, at least not then, and possibly not ever.

The cops took the next elevator down.

I walked back into the foundation offices, just as my trustees began emerging from the conference room. Thank God they were all old enough to be hard of hearing, I thought.

''Jenny,'' Roy Leland hailed me. He approached, strutting belly first as always. ''Now, listen, don't let that landlord have it all his own way. Don't give him everything he's asking for, force him down on the terms. I could come along, I can rearrange my schedule—''

''I'll manage, thanks anyway, Roy.''

''Well, all right, but—''

"Jenny," broke in Jack Fenton, "I wish you'd send our best wishes along to Faye and Derek. If you think they're going to be sick much longer I'll have my secretary order some flowers—"

"That's sweet, Jack, but I expect they'll be back tomorrow, or Monday at the latest."

"All right, but—"

"Come along, Jack," Edwin Ottilini said. "And Roy, Pete. Let us now return to our own businesses, and let Jenny get back to doing so well what she allows us to think we do—which is to run this place." He tipped his felt hat toward me. "Good-bye, my dear."

I was embarrassed. "You give me too much credit."

"Don't be silly," Jack Fenton, the banker, corrected me in a fondly stern manner. "This bunch has never granted 'too much' credit to anyone. Isn't that right, Edwin?"

"*You* certainly never have, Jack." The old attorney wheezed out a dry laugh as he departed. The other three followed him, rumbling together about interest rates, college tuitions, and golf handicaps.

"Bye, boys," I murmured as the door closed behind them.

I remained standing for about a second, and then I slumped down to the carpet, where I stretched out on my back and simply lay there in my suit, heels, and all. If anybody had walked in at that moment, I might have found it very difficult to explain myself, although the reason was as simple as exhaustion. I closed my eyes and felt myself going limp.

There are beds made for this, I reminded myself.

So I struggled up and drove home. It was four-thirty in the afternoon. I slept until the next morning, my dead slumber interrupted only once, by a telephone call at three o'clock in the morning.

Geof was in bed next to me by then, and he picked up the receiver but quickly replaced it.

"Whoozit?" I mumbled at him.

"Hung up," he said.

I was asleep before he had a chance to curse.

I dragged around the house the next morning like a bear coming out of hibernation—stumbling, bumping into things, grumbling to myself, feeling hungry enough to eat a tourist. It was Friday, always my favorite day to make deals because people are eager to get things over with, to get their business settled so they can begin enjoying their weekend. On Mondays, they don't want to give away anything, but with each succeeding day in the week, they're a little more anxious to close that deal, make that quota, earn that commission. By Friday afternoon, they're ready to make the sale, along with concessions. "Oh hell," they'll say, "let's do it." To which my reply is, "Fine. Sign here."

George Butts, the landlord, had promised me until noon to make my offer on the basement, and I took nearly all of that time just to come awake. Gradually, my hollow-feeling limbs filled with blood again, and my brain cells started cooperating in an effort resembling intelligent thought.

By eleven-fifteen, I was ready to buy real estate.

31

Tenth Street was a quiet, sunny, cheerful place on this morning, even taking into account its general shabbiness and the snow on the ground.

I parked directly in front of the basement.

When I had called Butts that morning, he had offered to meet me at his office, but I wanted to visit the basement again before slapping a check in his palm. The truth, which I didn't confess to him, was that I wanted to see if I felt any different about this building because a murder had occurred in it. Perhaps it would seem dark and depressing to me now, maybe it would spook me; at worst, it might feel more like a grave than a basement. If its effect on me was unpleasant, I was afraid it might seriously affect the former mental patients. Their sensitivities and paranoias would surely be more vulnerable to atmosphere than mine.

So it was with some feeling of trepidation and suppressed hope that I navigated the path to the double front doors, and pushed them open.

The lights were on throughout, almost as if somebody

else had been spooked. But the effect, I was glad to see, was a happy one. The place was somewhat cleaner than when I had seen it last, too. That's a macabre happy effect of homicide—it results in a good washing down afterward at the scene.

I walked to the door of the large meeting room, which must have been horribly bloody very recently, and discovered that I didn't feel any horror. A curiosity, yes, and the head-shaking wonderment that sudden death brings to the spectators on the sidelines, but nothing much more than that. I hadn't really known him. I hadn't liked what little I had known. Perhaps it was callous to care so little, but I discovered that I was more interested in the living who might inhabit this place for a long time to come than in the dead man who'd been here briefly.

I walked off in search of the landlord. That old lecher was probably the only thing I had to fear in this place; he had struck me as being grabby in every sense of the word.

I found him in the kitchen.

"Morning, pretty lady," he said jovially, and pointed me toward a chair at one end of a large, rectangular wooden table. "Thought we might conduct our business right here."

I smiled. "Fine with me. And, by the way, feel free to call me Ms. Cain."

He grinned. Old George may have been horny, but he was not slow.

Murder didn't seem to have brought the price down.

I laid out my offer on behalf of the foundation.

I expected him to be primed with an automatic counteroffer from Michael Laurence's construction firm, but I was ready for that. Sure enough, Butts leaned back in his chair, hooked his thumbs through his belt loops, and grinned at me. "Well, now. My other buyer, he called me just this morning after I spoke to you, and told me he'd come up a full thousand over your first offer.''

I looked across at him and smiled knowingly until he laughed. He didn't know it, but he and I were the only players in the game now, and we certainly weren't going to play it by Michael's rules. Michael knew what Butts didn't, which was that as a representative of the foundation I could keep topping Michael's thousand-dollar raises until he folded. And that if I had to, I'd sweeten it with my own money and write it off as a charitable deduction. I certainly wasn't about to let Butts know that, either. It was only Michael's bluff, anyway, his last shot at me. But I wouldn't let him goad me into an unnecessary spending war that wasted foundation funds. Or my own. There were other, quicker ways to skin this old bobcat who was leering across the table at me.

"What are his terms, Mr. Butts?"

"Five percent down, a third of the remainder on closing, a third in six months, the final third in a year."

"Twenty percent down," I countered. "The rest on closing."

He gazed at me a moment, looking frankly appreciative and not, I think, of my beauty. "All of it? Cash?"

"Yes."

I was gambling on two things: that Michael's fledgling firm couldn't match those terms; that Butts would be more interested in getting money in his pocket now than in keeping his fingers crossed that it would trickle in over the next twelve months or more. And it was Friday.

He leaned forward and, with the forefinger of his right hand, he tapped one of my hands, as if to make a point—or to close the deal.

"Well, now," he rumbled in a self-satisfied voice, "I think you folks just bought yourself a basement."

It took me a moment to comprehend that he had not tried to boost my offer any closer to his asking price.

Granted, my terms were good, but I was still surprised that he basically took my first offer. Had I come in too high? Were my terms too good? In my rush to beat the winter weather—and Michael—had I squandered foundation funds?

"Subject to appraisal, and so forth," I warned, moving my hand away.

"Oh, hell." He leaned back, and blithely waved the question away. "Sure."

Feeling a little less confident now, I took out a foundation check and my pen. *No,* I thought as I signed the check, this *is* a good deal for the foundation. I was positive it was. Old George was greedy, that was all; he obviously wanted to grab some fast cash. I was able to grin as I handed the check to him.

"It's a pleasure doing business with you, George."

"Likewise." He smirked. "I'll walk you out."

Since that was exactly what I was afraid of, I kept my guard up all the way to the front hall. He tried to guide me out with his hand on my back, but I walked faster. He tried to grab my elbow, but I jerked it away, ostensibly to dig for my keys in my purse. Finally, exasperated, I turned toward him in the foyer and stuck out my right hand.

"Good-*bye,* George."

He took my hand, but then tried to tug me into the meeting hall where the killing had taken place. He was a strong man and a determined one.

"I had it cleaned up real nice," he said. "Let me show you—"

At that point, when I was actually beginning to get a little nervous, I pulled out my best weapon:

"Cut it out, Mr. Butts. Remember, I can always have that check canceled."

We looked at each other with perfect understanding. Instantly, his grasp turned into a legitimate handshake. I quickly pulled my hand out of his. I was no longer finding him either amusing or harmless. In fact, I was greatly relieved when he backed away and promptly left by the back entrance.

I started to go out the front door.

But then, with Butts gone, I changed my mind: one more look at the place, I decided, and then I'd leave.

I stood in the hallway thinking: Here . . . they'll place a reception desk, with maybe one of the clients to attend it . . . a bathroom for the men, one for the women . . . they'll probably be in charge of keeping their own recreation hall clean, and I bet they'll do a good job of it . . . meetings in here, and food service . . . could put in a piano, maybe a coffee bar . . . down here, the director, maybe a counselor, or would it be a social worker? Too bad there's not more office space, but you can't have everything . . . back door . . .

I pushed it open and leaned out to look in the alley, partly to see if Butts had really left. He had. I breathed deeply, and felt myself relaxing in spite of the cold. Nothing had really happened, I reminded myself, so don't go making a big deal out of it. He wasn't going to rape you, for God's sake. Old George was just after whatever he could get. Determined not to let him get the best of me in any way, I forced my thoughts back to the recreation hall.

A little space for staff parking, that's good. . . .

Had Rod Gardner's killer gone in and out this way? Had he run down the alley behind the houses? No, I remembered that the police thought not, since all the bloody footprints—Mob's footprints?—led out into the front yard. But the police had made a mess of any prints there might have been out here in back. This door had been jimmied; the front one had been left ajar.

I ducked back into the basement and walked quickly back to the front door. All right, I thought, as I made sure it was locked behind me when I left, so it spooks me a little, so I have an overactive imagination, big deal. But more important, I thought, pushing images of murder away from me, how would Rosalinda feel if she were leaving this place today, after spending a few hours with her friends?

In her place, I thought I felt contentment. It warmed me as I walked back out into the cold.

32

Rodney Gardner's widow was backing down her driveway in front of me as I pulled away from the curb. She was driving a classic green MG with the top down. A lamp stuck up out of the seat beside her, and two other lamps without shades protruded behind her. Either she didn't look behind her or the lamps blocked her rearview mirror, because she pulled right out in front of me so that I had to slam on my brakes. My car fishtailed on a slab of ice while my heart performed the same maneuver in my chest. At the sound of all the screeching, she turned to look in my direction. She grinned insolently, waved, completed her turn out into the street, and proceeded on down Tenth Street at a sporty clip.

Absentmindedness I can forgive, especially in a new widow. It was the "screw you" grin she had given me that goaded me into speeding after her. Anyway, she was heading downtown, which was my destination, too. When I turned at the corner, there were only two cars between us, but she was now going slowly enough that they grew impatient and went around her, leaving me right behind the

MGB. She speeded up again. When she glanced back in the rearview mirror once, I found myself looking directly in her eyes. For an instant, there was something taunting in them, as if she was laughing at me. I told myself I was imagining it, but as I followed her, left down Jefferson, I had the definite feeling of being led somewhere. My initial anger at her rudeness slipped away, but I still felt annoyed, and uneasy, for some reason. Where was she taking me?

By the time she, and then I, turned right onto Fourth Street, it was clear she was luring me along for some kind of ride. Whenever cars came between us, she slowed until I caught up; whenever she turned, she carefully signaled, waiting to speed up until I'd made the turn, too.

What the hell?

In the middle of Fourth Street—which was one of a cluster of gentrified streets that were mostly populated by single people, childless couples, and well-to-do retirees—she turned left into a brick-paved driveway. I pulled over to the curb across the street and let my engine idle while I watched her pull in beside a red car. All right, I thought, show me. I wished I could remember her name. Susan? Saddie? Sallie? Sammie. That was it.

She parked, got out of her car, and began to haul one of the small lamps out of the backseat. Now I could see what she wore: a tight-weave orange sweater dress that clung to her pregnant belly like marmalade to a roll, black tights, and high-heeled black leather boots. No coat. No hat over her tousled, fallen-angel hair. The lady was tough, I thought; she didn't hurry, she didn't look as if she felt cold. She did, however, look down the driveway directly at me, and one side of her pretty mouth curled up.

What, I asked myself, is your game?

I rolled down my window, grinned at her, and waved.

It didn't faze her. She merely tossed her curls as if to say, so what? and picked her sexy little way across the snow to the front door of the elegant brick condominium. Somebody inside opened the door, let her in, and the door closed behind her. And that was that.

That was *what?* I put my car back into drive and slowly moved away, wondering what she was trying to pull or to show me. Because that's the feeling I had had, that she was triumphantly showing off something to me. But what? Her new condo? And why me?

I drove another block before it hit me: She *had* shown it to me—I just hadn't recognized it. I accelerated back to her block. This time, I pulled right into her driveway. I got out of my car. I walked up to stand behind her MG. It was a beauty, all right, a real classic, but it wasn't the car of interest at the moment. It was the red car—the red *Toyota* beside it that riveted me.

The Toyota had a "Ski Stowe" bumper sticker, and the license plate was framed in metal that said, "I'd rather be skiing." It was Derek's car.

I abandoned all dignity then—I didn't give a damn if she taunted, flaunted, vaunted, or even why—and ran to the front door and rang the bell repeatedly, like a crazy woman. Please, I thought desperately, I don't care why you're here, just be here!

The door opened to reveal Derek, who looked absolutely stunned to see me there.

I slumped against the doorjamb. "You're safe."

"Jenny," he said, in a low, surprised voice, and then fell silent. Behind him, the pregnant blonde was leaning against a wall, her hands pressed behind her back, grinning that half-grin at me. Derek didn't ask me to come in.

"We've been worried about you," I said, stumbling over my words. Why was he looking at me so strangely, and what in hell was he doing here, in this elegant condo, with this slatternly girl? I wanted to ask him that; I wanted to pull him out the door with me, and tuck him safely into my car, and drive him home, and lock his door for him.

But I didn't do any of that; I just stood and stared back at him. Finally, I asked, "Are you all right?"

He blinked, then nodded. "Yeah."

"Derek, the police want to talk to you."

He looked back over his shoulder at the girl and then at me. I thought I had never seen him look so discouraged, so unhappy, but all he said was, "I guess you'll tell them I'm here." Derek sounded so resigned, so lifeless.

"I'll have to," I said.

He nodded. "Tell Geof I'll call him." And then Derek closed the door in my face. Gently, but nonetheless in my face.

There wasn't anything I could do but leave, which I did, feeling as if I could cry from relief but also from a deep sadness that welled up whenever I thought of Derek's blue eyes. They were now the dull eyes of a dead leprechaun. The old Derek would have laughed at the very idea— "Leprechauns can't die, Jenny!"—but this new Derek looked like a very mortal man with no laughter left in him. I thought: The good news, Faye, is that Derek's alive; the bad news is that he isn't.

33

The Nordic Realty building, where I stopped on my way to the office, looked even more alpine this afternoon, like a warming house on a ski slope. I felt as if I should prop some skis against the porch railing and stick my poles in the snow in the front yard. Instead, I merely knocked snow off my boots and walked inside.

"Congratulations." Michael Laurence looked up from where he sat at the reception desk in the outer office. He wore a black-and-red-checked Pendleton shirt over a black cotton turtleneck, a combination that set off his dark, romantic coloring. He looked like a logger, I thought; no, I amended, he looked like the Eastern-educated son of the owner of a logging camp—who was looking at the person who lit the match that started the fire that burned him out. "The Swede wins again. Did you come to gloat?"

"Hello," I said. "No. I'm sorry we couldn't both win."

"Uh-huh."

"Well, I am. Jack Fenton and the rest of the board send their regrets, as well." I took off my coat and hung it on a coat tree. "But they expect that you, of all people, will understand."

"Right," he said.

I settled uninvited into a Western-style chair that was angled into a corner of the room with a triangular table and a matching chair. There was a telephone on the table. I pointed to it. "May I use this?"

He gave me a quizzical look, but nodded.

I phoned the police station and left word with Ailey Mason about where to find Derek, and then I called the office. I hoped, for many reasons, that Faye had chosen to work today. When she answered the phone, I was relieved. I told her Derek was alive and, at least compared to her probable fantasies, well. Her initial stiffness dissolved into embarrassment and apologies, but I didn't want to deal with them or with her at the moment. As tactfully as possible, I put her off until the next day. When I hung up, Michael was doodling on paper with a pen, appearing uninterested in my conversations. I knew he would be too stubborn to ask any questions.

"Are you busy?" I inquired.

"As a matter of fact, no." He looked up. "Now that we're not going to be developing Tenth Street, I have some free time I didn't expect to have. So no, I'm not busy."

"It's only one building, Michael."

"It's the one we wanted to start with."

"So renovate around it. We'll spruce it up. We'll consult with you. We'll try to coordinate with your renovation designs for the rest of the neighborhood. Don't give up, Michael."

He squinted at me as if I were a speck on his horizon.

"You kill me," he said, and then, with a furious sort of frustration, "Why that building? Why—out of all the buildings in this godforsaken town that I should have stayed out of once I left it—why that one?"

"Because it was presented to us as the best site by a

group of people who had put tremendous effort into the search," I said. But what I was really thinking was, Yeah, *why* that one? Although what I told him was true, I wondered for the first time if there might not be more to it than that. How did MaryDell Paine's committee come to pick the very building, the very *odd* building, where her crazy brother used to go to church?

I didn't discuss that with Michael, but said instead, "You never used to give up so easily." His involuntary grimace made me instantly regret the observation; it had been excruciatingly tactless. I rushed to make verbal amends: "I'm sorry, I mean . . . listen, so you don't get the first building you wanted . . . what else is on your wish list? What was your next purchase going to be?"

He took a while to decide to answer me. "Well, after the basement, we were going after some of the properties that are in better repair. We wanted to get them while they're still fairly reasonable, and we wanted to start with properties that wouldn't require that much outlay to renovate. They'd be quick showplaces for us."

"Which ones, for instance?"

"You are still a cheerleader, Jenny," he said, with a tone of nastiness that I chose to ignore. "Go team, right? Okay, my next approach was to the guy in the brown house on the south corner—"

"Perry Yates?"

"Yes."

No wonder Yates was so opposed to us, I thought.

"He has a couple of other properties around there," Michael said. "We thought we'd try for all of them and that would give us a good start on the project. But hell, I don't know, now, I just don't think your project fits in with ours. . . ."

"You scared of a few crazy people?"

"Maybe," he said bluntly.

"Did you buy the house across the street from the church, Michael?"

"I told you, we haven't bought any other properties, Jenny. And I also told you we were going to start with the better ones, not the old rattraps like that one. You don't listen to me. Hell, you never did pay any attention to me."

I ignored that. "Who bought it, do you know?"

"No."

"Could you find out?"

He regarded me with displeasure. "You do not lack for nerve, Swede." But he wheeled his chair up to the computer on the desk and punched the keyboard. I walked over to stand behind him, reading the multilist information over his shoulder. The name of the buyer wasn't there.

"Do you remember the name of the real estate company on the 'For Sale' sign?" he asked.

"I'm not sure there was a name," I said. "It may have just been one of those generic 'For Sale' signs."

"Well, then it was probably a private transaction, and we wouldn't have it listed here. Whoever bought it probably got a better deal than the sellers did . . . that neighborhood is ripe for gentrification, and everybody in the business knows it." He glanced over his shoulder to give me a sour look.

"There are other *buildings*, Michael."

"What else do you want to know?"

"Look up something around Fourth Street, will you?"

"What do you mean, something?"

"Oh, one of those new condos; see if there's anything listed with maybe three, four bedrooms, two-story, completely renovated—"

"You and the cop moving?"

"We're looking," I said vaguely. "What do you have?"

He rolled through the neighborhoods on his monitor, finally stopping at a screen full of expensive condos. *"We* don't have anything listed over there, yet. *We* were hoping to renovate our own neighborhood and offer our own quarter-million-dollar condos.''

"That's what they're selling for?" I asked, ignoring his sarcasm.

"See for yourself," he said, pointing at the screen.

The Fourth Street condos were, indeed, selling for all of that, and more. What had Derek done, I wondered, sold his own modest condo, pooled resources with Sammie Gardner, and then purchased one of those costly beauties? If so, he had moved even faster than I had in getting the church basement. If he'd moved that fast while he worked for me, I wouldn't have had to fire him.

"Interesting," I said.

Without warning, Michael wheeled around to face me in his chair. He grabbed my wrists and pulled me down into a hard, angry kiss. When I regained my balance and got some leverage, I pushed myself away from him.

From a safe distance, I regarded him.

"You asked for that," he said.

"I didn't."

He looked down at his hands; he was flushed and breathing hard. So was I, and I felt sick to my stomach. After Butts, this was too much. Maybe it *was* my fault. I walked over to the coat tree to get my coat and put it on.

"Goddamn it," he said in a low voice.

I looked back at him. I wanted to say, Stop this, this is silly, but then, I wasn't the one suffering from unrequited whatever-it-was. It wasn't my place to tell him how he ought to feel. A hundred other sentences formed in my brain, and backed up in my mouth. But I had a history of always saying to Michael the very things he didn't want to hear and of doing exactly what he hoped I wouldn't. I was tempted to at least say, "I'm sorry," but I wasn't sure I had anything to be sorry about. And besides, even that used to annoy him. So, for once I kept my mouth shut. Feeling awkward and frustrated, I walked out the door and closed it quietly behind me. It did occur to me to be very grateful that I hadn't married him any of those times I had had the chance. I hoped that one of these days he'd figure out that he ought to be equally grateful.

Feeling shaky, I walked back to my car.

It had been a long time since I'd had to spurn the advances of two men in the same day. I did not consider it a compliment. It filled me with self-doubt. Was I putting out signals I didn't intend?

I had a strong urge to see Geof, but the middle of the afternoon, in the middle of two homicide cases, wasn't a good time to interrupt his work. I thought of Marsha, but she'd be with a client now. My other friends would be at work, and my sister wasn't exactly my choice of company on any given day. I knew what was wrong with me: I was feeling lonely because two old friends—Derek and Michael—were seeming long ago and far away from me. On an impulse, I drove by the downtown municipal park to see if Rosalinda was sitting on her bench, but she wasn't there.

You can't just drive around all afternoon, feeling sorry for yourself, I decided; you ought to get to work on some other foundation business. This thought gave me the excuse I needed to visit another old friend. She wouldn't be at work; she was long retired from teaching. But she had never retired from the knack of making people feel better.

34

My old sixth-grade teacher, Miss Lucille Grant, lived in a one-bedroom apartment on the second floor of a brick fourplex in a shabbily genteel part of town. She was over eighty now, a big, plain, heavy woman who lived alone, but for the frequent company of former pupils like me. We seemed to regard Miss Grant—or Miss Lucille as we called her in our thoughts—as a beloved, elderly aunt who'd loved, scolded, and influenced us as few others had in our lives.

Over English Breakfast tea and real scones with clotted cream, I related to her the story of Mob ("Poor fellow," she said); of Michael ("So handsome, but so badly spoiled," she said of that former pupil); of Derek ("Oh my," she said, "oh dear, that's very bad"); and Rodney Gardner ("Bound for a bad end"); of the old church basement ("What a fine idea!"); of the pregnant girl ("Poor little baby"); of the artist with the two girls; of the Walking Cigar who looked like Wayne Newton ("Is that a rock-and-roll singer, dear?"); and of poor old Grace Montgomery ("Fear and hatred breed their own kind").

I talked, and she listened. I talked, and she poured. I talked, and she spread plum jam on another scone for me. I talked about my trustees (which made her smile); about Marsha Sandy and her boyfriend ("He's not from here, is he?" she asked); and about Rosalinda ("Poor child," she said). I told her about my problems with Faye; about MaryDell Paine and her husband who cut his brother-in-law's head out of pictures (*"Just* like him!" she said of that former pupil); and about surly maids and barking dogs. I talked, and she let me, until I ran out of words and felt better.

"Jennifer, dear," she said when I'd finished, "walk over to that bookcase, please . . . yes, that's the one . . . and get out my King James version of the Bible, will you?"

"Yes, ma'am."

I found it and laid it on her lap.

Miss Grant began leafing through the index, murmuring as she searched, "There are two or three different versions, although I believe they are sufficiently similar so that it doesn't matter which one . . ."

She found the reference she sought and thumbed backward to . . . "All right. Mark five, verses three through twenty. Oh my, no, this won't do, the King James calls him 'Legion,' and I believe you told me that he calls himself 'Mob.' " She closed the Bible decisively and held it out to me. "Put this back, dear, and fetch me the Good News Bible. I'm sorry to say we'll have to read that version instead." I did as I was told—just as we had all fetched and carried for her in the sixth grade—while she fretted aloud about the "sad lack of poetry and majesty" in the Good News Bible. But when she had it in her hands, she thumbed through its index, saying in a schoolteacher-ish voice, "How shall we look it up, Jennifer? Under parables? Insanity? Jesus? Mob? Demons? Oh yes, all right . . . here it is under miracles . . . 'driving out demons' . . . we'll use Mark again."

She leaned forward once more to read to me, and I leaned back again to listen. I closed my eyes and was once more in the schoolroom, listening to this vibrant teacher with the magical storyteller's way about her. . . .

"Jesus and his disciples arrived on the other side of Lake Galilee, in the territory of Gerasa," she read, giving it the entrancing feeling of "once upon a time." "As soon as Jesus got out of the boat, he was met by a man who came out of the burial caves there. This man had an evil spirit in him . . ."

With my eyes still closed, I smiled, because her voice had descended dramatically on the word "caves," and she had put a chilling vibrato into "evil spirit." If I had been eleven years old, I'm sure I would have hugged my arms, shivered, and giggled softly to my friends.

". . . and lived among the tombs."

She gave those words equal weight, like Lived-Among-The-Dead. I smiled to myself again.

"Nobody could keep him tied with chains any more; many times his feet and his hands had been tied, but every time he broke the chains and smashed the irons on his feet."

Smashed, she said.

"He was too strong for anyone to control him. Day and night he wandered among the tombs and through the hills, screaming and cutting himself with stones."

I wasn't smiling anymore; I was imagining a bleeding, screaming maniac, haunting the tombs like a crazed beast. "I am wounded," the confession on the blackboard had said, but had he meant physically, psychologically, emotionally, or, maybe, spiritually? Had Kitt bled from cuts to his body or to his soul? I was seeing the townspeople, my own townspeople, gazing with frightened eyes at the hills where he roamed, this walking nightmare of a man. On his face, I imposed a distorted version of the photograph of MaryDell Paine's younger brother. It gave my vision a terrifying immediacy.

"He was some distance away when he saw Jesus; so he ran, fell on his knees before him, and screamed in a loud voice, 'Jesus, Son of the Most High God! What do you want with me? For God's sake, I beg you, don't punish me!' (He said this because Jesus was saying, 'Evil spirit, come out of this man!')

"So Jesus asked him, 'What is your name!'

"The man answered, 'My name is "Mob"—there are so many of us!' And he kept begging Jesus not to send the evil spirits out of that region.

"There was a large herd of pigs near by, feeding on a hillside. So the spirits begged Jesus, 'Send us to the pigs, and let us go into them.'

"He let them go, and the evil spirits went out of the man and entered the pigs. The whole herd—about two thousand pigs in all—rushed down the side of the cliff into the lake and was drowned.

"The men who had been taking care of the pigs ran away and spread the news in the town and among the farms. People went out to see what had happened, and when they came to Jesus, they saw the man who used to have the mob of demons in him. He was sitting there, clothed and in his right mind; and they were all afraid. Those who had seen it told the people what had happened to the man with the demons, and about the pigs.

"So they asked Jesus to leave their territory."

Miss Grant shook her head sadly at the frailty of humans.

"As Jesus was getting into the boat, the man who had had the demons begged him, 'Let me go with you!'

"But Jesus would not let him. Instead, he told him, 'Go back home to your family and tell them how much the Lord has done for you and how kind he has been to you.'

"So the man left and went all through the Ten Towns,

telling what Jesus had done for him. And all who heard it were amazed.''

Before I opened my eyes, I thought: And they lived happily ever after. When I glanced up at Miss Grant, she was paging backward through the New Testament.

"According to Luke," she said, when she found her reference point, "the poor man called himself Mob because . . . 'many demons had gone into him. The demons begged Jesus not to send them into the abyss.' '' When she looked up at me, there was compassion in her blue eyes. "I suspect he was a paranoid schizophrenic with severe psychosis, don't you, dear? And really, wasn't it a favor to him that Jesus drove the demons out entirely rather than giving him drugs? So only the pigs suffered the side effects.''

"You," I said fondly, "are putting me on."

She smiled. "I am struck by the coincidence of the man named Mob, and the pigs in the water in the old lady's bathtub. Aren't you, dear?"

I stared at her. "No. Yes. Does it mean something?"

"Well, if it does," she said with a sweet, firm confidence that was familiar to me, "I'm sure you'll think of something, Jennifer, dear."

I was reminded of how, in the sixth grade, we used to ask Miss Grant questions. More often than not, her reply was: "I think you can figure that out for yourself." And so, of course, we were forced, actually, to think, always a painful process. When we brought our pitiful results to her, she would either say, "Let's think about that a little more, shall we?" Or, "How very clever of you!" And so we never learned if she had known the answer all along.

I rose, kissed her soft cheek, and thanked her. Just before I left, I got down to the foundation business I'd had in mind when I arrived: "Miss Grant, ever since Michael Laurence left town, we've had a vacancy on our board of trustees. Would you let me suggest your name for nomination?''

"I think I might enjoy that," she admitted, with a smile that was nearly mischievous. "I know all those boys."

And that, to my extreme pleasure, took care of that. She was the one female in town whom none of my old-fashioned "boys" would dare to oppose. I credited myself with brilliant inspiration.

Then I trotted along to "think about that"—the coincidence of the pigs—"a little more." After seeing Miss Lucille, I felt—there's no other word for it—cleansed.

35

I grabbed a very late lunch at the Buoy.

Then I called the artist, Marianne Miller, to ask if I might drop by to see her again. She told me that if I didn't mind visiting while she mixed paints and while the girls raced about, it was fine with her. "But I really don't want to disturb you while you're working," I said. To which she laughed wearily and replied, "Disturb? In this house? You don't throw blocks, do you?"

"No," I admitted, smiling at the phone.

"You don't scream at your sister, do you?"

"Well, at least not at your house."

"You don't kill people, do you?"

She asked that with a panicky little catch to the words, almost a sob. I said, "I'm about five minutes away. I'll be right over."

"Thank you," she said, as if she meant it, and hung up.

When I arrived, expecting the usual chaos, I was surprised to walk into a quiet house. She'd put the girls down for their afternoon naps. "Normally, I'd be working now," she said with a nervous twist of her hands, "but today I just can't. . . ." She glanced back over her shoulder, as if looking through the wall of her house toward the church basement and Grace Montgomery's house. "Did you hear what happened to Mrs. Montgomery?" When I told her I had, without elaborating, she wrung her hands some more and said, "Oh God. There was this awful screaming. I told the police I heard a woman screaming, and I just can't bear to think that might have been Mrs. Montgomery, that she might have suffered that much. . . ."

"That was somebody else," I said quickly. "Do you mind if we sit down?"

"Oh God, no, I mean, sure, of course . . ."

She let me hang up my coat this time and used her own hands to wring and stroke, instead. Once more, we walked into her living room, and I sat on the couch, while she pulled up the rocking chair. I didn't want to tell her where I'd found Derek, but I did want to get some information from her about the woman I'd found him with. The task, therefore, was to question her, without letting her know why.

"It looks like we'll buy the church," I began.

"What? Oh, good. I'm glad, really."

"I'm going to send letters to the neighbors to keep all of you informed about what we're doing. Do you think there's any point in sending one to Rodney Gardner's widow?"

She tensed suddenly and focused on me as if she'd just seen a wasp on my nose. "To Sammie?" Her mouth seemed to curl with involuntary distaste. "Yeah, send her a letter . . . the exploding kind, with a bomb in it!" Her expression of distaste altered, seeming now to focus on herself. "Gosh, I shouldn't say things like that, she's pregnant, I wouldn't want to hurt the baby. But . . ." She leaned back in the chair, flopped her arms wearily over the sides, and sighed. "Oh hell, don't bother with her.

She's moving. Besides," she added, witheringly, "I doubt if she can read."

"You don't like her," I said with deliberate understatement.

"Hah." She clamped her teeth, then barely opened them to say, "I hate her. I've got a friend who says I should be grateful to Sammie Gardner, may she roast in hell, because she was the final straw that broke up my rotten marriage. But how am I supposed to be grateful to a slut that called over here for my husband all the time and talked to my girls in that sexy, mocking way she's got, so they were asking me questions about Daddy and That Lady. Bitch. *Bitch.*"

"Did Rodney know?"

She shrugged, heavily. "For all I know, Rodney *watched.* He was just that kind of nasty person. *They* were just that kind. He was always coming on to me, so maybe he wanted to make it a quartet, heck, I don't know, it was so sickening. . . ."

"Does she still see him?" I asked.

"Who? Perry?" Marianne didn't seem to notice the surprise with which I registered that name. "Heck, I don't know, aren't I supposed to be the last to know? Or, I guess that's the wife, isn't it, and I'm no wife anymore. Thank goodness. Thank *God.*"

"You were married to Perry Yates?" I asked, disbelieving.

This time she caught my surprise, and she laughed bitterly. "I know. I'm nuts. But I was used to dating flaky artists, you know, and he seemed so kind of serious and stable, like he'd be good for me. Good for me! That's a laugh. The best I can say about Perry is that I got my girls through him. And the bastard even tried to take them away from me. If I hadn't given up all my rights to everything we owned, including this house, he'd have gotten them, too. Bastard."

"It must be hard, having him right down the street."

She shivered. "It's awful. I hate it."

"Did he do that on purpose?"

"You bet he did." But she grimaced. "Aw, I don't know. The truth is, Perry doesn't have any sensitivity to other people's feelings, it's like this handicap, like he's crippled only he's not in a wheelchair. When I'm really into hating him, I think he moved in down there just to make my life more miserable, but the truth is, he doesn't think enough about me to care whether he makes me happy or miserable. I expect he just moved there because he already owned it, and he needed a place to stay. Believe me, it wouldn't have occurred to him to move tactfully out of the neighborhood!"

"Does he still own this house?"

She nodded grimly.

"But how could he have taken the girls from you?"

She put the fingers of her right hand over her mouth and rubbed it. Her eyes focused on her feet as she murmured, "He's just that way. He gets away with things. He just would have, that's all."

Probably because he had something over you, I thought. But what? Whatever it was gave him enough leverage to keep this house. Was this one of the properties that Michael had been planning to purchase from Yates? Would her ex-husband kick out his own children if the money were right? Somehow, I suspected that Perry Yates would do just that. A cynical voice inside me said: No wonder she had seemed so tolerant of the proposal for the recreation hall and even so tolerant of an alleged murderer—it might have seemed to her that almost anything would be better than Michael's project that might lead to her losing her home.

"Have you heard from Derek?"

I nodded.

"I thought maybe he'd call me." Her face clouded over,

but she tried to smile at me, making an effort to appear nonchalant. "Men."

"Some men," I agreed. Maybe she'd hear from somebody, somewhere, about Sammie Gardner's latest conquest, but that particular bit of bad news wouldn't come from me. "I'd better go, Marianne, so you can get some work done if you want to. Thanks for letting me drop by again."

"Anytime." But she looked puzzled, as if she had just noticed that my purpose in coming to see her again wasn't at all clear to her. "Did you just come to tell me you bought the basement?"

"Yes," I said. Liars, as Geof was forever telling me, hang themselves by talking too much. I retrieved my coat and left her house quickly, before my tongue tied a noose.

I returned to the office, where Faye and I worked steadily and quietly together through the rest of the afternoon. She apologized to me, saying, "I feel like a fool." I was frank with her; I told her that the way she had acted—especially in stomping out of the office and then in not even showing up the day of the board meeting—was unacceptable. I told her that I thought I understood why she had acted as she did, but that I wasn't ready to respond to it yet. In the meantime, I was glad to have her back, I was glad Derek was found, and if she didn't have any objections, could we please get some work done? I was as pompous as a prime minister, and that last bit—about getting some work done—was sheer petulance, of course. But she wasn't in any position to call me on it, and I wasn't in any mood to apologize to her. For anything. By the close of the workday, we had reestablished a sort of companionable relationship, but it wasn't all smoothed over. My feathers had been good and ruffled. I wasn't sure I even wanted to keep her on the staff, much less move her into Derek's job.

36

That evening, Geof and I shared the unusual experience of eating dinner together, at the same time, in our own house. He called to let me know he was on his way and then showed up just as I was setting out the place mats. It was long after dark.

"Hello!" I said, looking across the dining room table at him. "Who are you, Stranger?"

He pretended to reach for his back pocket. "I have some identification on me."

"I'll bet you do."

He laughed and walked over to kiss me.

"Good steak," he commented later.

"Nice wine," I told him, after a few sips of the California burgundy he'd brought home with him for this special occasion: dinner together.

"Well," Geof said, stabbing his salad, "Derek kept his promise to you and called to tell me where he was living. So I went over there personally, to talk to him." He forked in a mouthful of the cucumbers and red onions that I'd tossed in Italian dressing.

"And?" I coaxed.

"Um." He pointed to his mouth. After he had swallowed, he said, "You're not going to like this. When we got there, the cupboard was bare."

"I hate riddles. What does that mean?"

"I find it hard to believe that you hate riddles. I mean he was gone again, Jenny, and so was she. Nobody home. There wasn't even a message on the door, telling us to have three pints and a loaf. What the hell's with Derek?"

I laid down my fork. "Damn. Geof, maybe *she* killed her husband? Look—she moves into a condo that's worth at least a hundred thousand more than the house she's leaving. How does she manage that? Did he leave her a lot of money, or property, do you suppose?"

Geof began sawing at his T-bone steak as if it had posed the tough question. I knew it was tender, so I figured he was taking out on it his general frustration.

"If Gardner left her anything but pregnant, we haven't found it," he said. "Besides, there was so much violence to the murder. It would have taken a fair amount of strength, so I have a hard time picturing the wife as the perpetrator. I have to admit, though, this latest disappearance raises some questions we didn't have before." He glanced at me, and his voice turned dry. "I'm sure you're real glad to hear that."

I shrugged, feeling helpless.

"Geof, I heard today that Sammie Gardner had an affair with Perry Yates. And that he is the ex-husband of Marianne Miller. Did you know that?"

"Yes," he said. "The detectives have been picking up a lot of neighborhood gossip."

"One of these days, I'm going to tell you something you don't already know. Oh, well, here's something—George Butts tried to make a pass at me today."

Geof looked up. "Are you all right?"

"Oh, sure, nothing happened."

"But it's lousy for you."

"Yes. I'm glad you understand." I smiled. "Maybe Butts did it."

Geof smiled slightly, too. "I'll have him picked up and we'll beat a confession out of him."

"That would be fine," I said. I sighed and picked up my fork again. "But you still think Mob probably did it?"

"Well, bloody fingerprints and a written confession do tend to incriminate," he observed dryly. "What I think, Jenny, is that I'd like to find him and ask him."

"Is MaryDell in trouble for, as they say, harboring him?"

"Yes," he said, as he popped a piece of steak decisively into his mouth.

"I wish you'd ask her why she wanted that old church for the recreation hall. I know she'll give you the routine about how it's such a good site, et cetera, but ask her why *she* thought to look there in the first place. I'm curious. There's no 'For Sale' sign on it, so how'd she even know to ask about it?"

"Why do you think she did?"

"I don't know; that's why I'm curious."

"Why did the Marlboro Man think to look there?"

I laughed. "Michael? He doesn't smoke, dear."

"Not even after sex?"

"Please," I said. "That is an old and terrible joke that only goes to prove how insecure you really are, and to which I will not deign to respond."

"Uppity broad."

He smiled at me. I smiled back at him.

"I don't really know why he looked there," I said, as I sliced my own T-bone. "But I think he was looking in the neighborhood anyway, and that building probably struck him as being a likely place to start his development. I suppose that could be more or less why it caught MaryDell's attention, too. . . ."

"I'll ask her," he offered.

"Did you bring dessert?" I asked him.

He spread his arms wide and grinned.

"I'm here, aren't I?" he said.

But dessert didn't turn out to be either cherry pie or sex. It turned out to be a visitor, who rang our doorbell at a most inopportune moment.

"Go away," Geof muttered when the bell first rang.

But our cars were in the driveway, and there were too many lights on—at least in other rooms—in the house. The bell chimed insistently. We looked at each other—something of an acrobatic feat at the time—and sighed. Luckily, we were still downstairs. It did take us a while, however, to put the cushions back on the couch and to get reassembled.

37

Geof went to answer the door and then came back into the living room with our late-night visitor.

"Derek!" I exclaimed.

He was alone, and stammering all over himself in apology to Geof. When I spoke, he looked up and saw me.

"Jenny, I'm sorry."

He said it so dramatically that it seemed to be an all-purpose apology—he was sorry for barging in on us, sorry for disappearing, sorry for everything. He was, I thought as I stared at him, a shocking, sorry mess. His sweater and trousers were rumpled, his blond hair looked greasy and unbrushed, his face had sagged into jowls like a much older man's. He was as jerky as a monkey. When we asked him to sit down, it seemed to take a force of will for him to remain seated.

"Derek, are you on something?" I asked him.

"No, no." He shook his head violently. "Listen. Please. I've got to get back, Sammie thinks I'm at the store, she'll be worried, I mean, after what happened to Rod . . ."

I opened my mouth, but Derek shouted, "Listen!"

Silently, Geof sank down beside me on the couch.

"I'm sorry," Derek said, miserably. "I didn't mean to yell at you. I've got to tell you this, that's all. I was leaving Marianne's house. It was about nine-thirty or ten o'clock, I guess, and I'm walking to my car, I see what looks like this man huddling in the doorway of the old church basement. Well, it was cold, you know, and it had been snowing for hours, and I figured it might be a bum. I didn't walk up to him right then, I mean I wasn't that crazy, for all I knew he might have mugged me, but I guess somewhere in the back of my mind, I kind of doubted that any mugger would be out on a night like that. So, anyway, I called out from where I was standing on the sidewalk.

" 'Hello,' I guess I said, 'are you okay?' "

" 'We're not bothering anything,' he says back to me, or something like that—"

"*We're* not?" Geof stared at him.

"Yeah, there was a woman with him—"

Geof's astonished stare swung toward me: a woman?

"She was dumpy; she seemed real shy. He did all the talking—what little we did—she never said anything and hardly even looked at me. I think she was scared of me, or at least I thought so then." Derek laughed a little, but bitterly. "I guess I should have been scared of her. Anyway, she was just this kind of cold-looking lump of a thing that clung to him the whole time I was there.

"He, the man, sounded scared to me, too—which goes to show how smart I am—and real cold. Well, hell, he was all huddled down into his coat, kind of hunkered down on his haunches. He looked like a kangaroo crouching in the dark. So, I thought, well this isn't right, something's weird here. And I immediately think they're bums or drunks who don't have anyplace to go, and I'm thinking, they'll freeze to death. I can't go on home and pretend I've never seen them.''

Them. I was still trying to digest that word.

"It was one of those things, you know, that would, like, haunt me. So I walked up a little closer to them and I asked him if he had anyplace to go. He shook his head, or said no, or something. And I'll tell you the truth, I really didn't want to offer to take them over to the mission in my car. I was a little afraid of him, I guess. Not that I had any sort of intuition or premonition, I didn't. It was just, here was this raggedy guy who I didn't know from Adam, crouching out there in the snow, with this woman with him, and there just wasn't any way for me to know what exactly I might be letting in my car if I gave them a ride.

"So, what happened was, I had the key to the basement that the landlord had given me. And, I knew I shouldn't do it—let them in there—but what the hell else was I going to do? Take him in my car? No way. Call the cops? I couldn't see doing that, I mean, they really weren't doing anything wrong, except maybe trespassing. So I thought, well what the hell, why can't they just spend the night in the church? They wouldn't be bothering anybody. I didn't see that they could do much harm in there." Here, Derek barked out another bitter, scalding laugh at himself. "What I thought was, well, it would be cold, but at least they wouldn't freeze. And I thought, I'll do one good thing. Here's one thing I'll do that's decent, that I won't fuck up.

"So I said to him, I asked him, 'You want to sleep in there tonight?' and he said he did. So I asked him to step over away from the door a few yards—I mean, it's not as if I really trusted him, I guess—while I unlocked the door. So I did that, and then I stepped back, and they went on in, and I asked him to leave before morning, so nobody'd see them, and he said okay, and that was it. I went on home and called you, Jenny.''

He rubbed his hands together and took a deep breath. "So I called you. At that point, everything was still okay." Derek shook his head, and half-smiled. "Right, I'd been fired, and I'd let these tramps into the basement, which I didn't have any legal right to do. But there wasn't anybody . . . dead yet.

"I had a hard time sleeping that night, partly because of worrying about finding a new job, but mostly because of worrying that I'd be in deep shit for letting that bum in. So I finally gave up sleeping, and about, I don't know, maybe five, five-thirty in the morning, I decided to drive back to the church, make sure everything was okay, and move the guy out of there with his woman.

"So. So I didn't want to be seen, particularly, so I drive up and park in the alley behind the church. And I see the back door's open, so I'm pissed, because he didn't close it, but I'm happy and relieved because at least he's gone. So I go inside, just to check things out—make sure he didn't set a fire in the wastebasket or anything, I mean, you wouldn't have believed the things I thought up while I lay awake, only murder wasn't one of them—and before I even get into the central meeting room, there's all this blood.''

Derek began to cry, so that his following words were choked out. "I've never been so scared, I didn't know what it was like to feel so scared. I thought I'd die right there, looking at all that blood. I mean, I just hauled ass out the back door, and I got in my car, and I drove away.''

"Derek," I said, on an intuitive impulse, "did you call me several times and hang up?"

He nodded.

So he was my anonymous caller.

"I wanted so bad to talk to somebody, but every time I

called, I couldn't do it, I couldn't . . . talk about it." He was making a heroic effort to control his emotions. Personally, I wished he'd let them fly; then maybe he could land on solid ground again. "Jenny, after I called the cops, I figured I was . . . finished. I still feel that way." Derek stretched out his arms and stared at the backs of his hands. "As if something's dying in me." He clenched his hands into fists and drew them up into his abdomen. "You'd already fired me. I didn't have shit in my life. And now I'd let this bum into that basement, and something really terrible had happened as a result, and I knew it was all over. I was scared, and I felt guilty, and I drove over to the office, and I just cleared everything out. And then I drove around in the snow for a long time, hell, I drove nearly to Boston that morning before I turned around and started back home. I figured I had to face up to this stupid thing I'd done. But then—"

He breathed in two shuddering, ragged gasps.

"Then on the way back, I heard on the radio that somebody had been killed at the church, and they gave his name, and it was Rodney Gardner, and I remembered that was the creep we'd interviewed, and I thought, oh my God, he's got a pregnant wife, and it's all my fault! Jesus, it's my fault!"

"Oh, Derek," I cried, and moved over instantly to sit beside him and to put my arms around him. He let himself be held, but when I murmured, "Poor Derek," he looked at me with horror in his eyes.

"Poor *Derek! No!*" he protested. "No, Jesus, Jenny, it was my fault! Poor Sammie, poor baby . . ." He laughed and sobbed at the same time, wildly. "Poor creep. Poor dead creep. Poor dead creep who'd still be alive if I hadn't let a couple of maniacs in to spend the night." Derek pulled away from me to place his face in his hands. Then he leaned his head back on the couch and spoke dully to the ceiling. "So I knew I was responsible. And how was that girl going to manage, no husband, a baby on the way? I had to help her. I had to do something. So that night, the next night, I called her from this motel room out of town, and I told her who I was, and what I'd done, and I said, 'Let me help you, please, I'll do anything.' And she told me to come over to her house and she'd talk to me. So I did, and she said she needed help, that I had to stay with her and help her now that Rodney was gone." Derek closed his eyes. "So I did."

"And now you can't get out of it," I said.

He sat up, looking angry for the first time and defensive. "I don't want to! It's my responsibility. It's the least I can do. I owe her."

"Your life?" I asked, incredulously.

"You don't understand," he said, leaning his head back and closing his eyes again.

Geof and I glanced at each other. We understood, all right. Derek was caught in a trap of sex, death, and guilt, spun by a seductive little blond spider who'd eat him alive if his soul didn't reject the poison of guilt that infected it. We didn't try to talk him out of that trap, not then. While I perked coffee for the three of us, Geof asked him concrete questions in a straightforward, matter-of-fact voice that acted more like a tonic on Derek than my coffee did.

"Derek, would you try to describe for me the man and the woman you admitted into the church?"

The man he described sounded like Mob; the woman sounded like Rosalinda.

"We needed this information, Derek," Geof said. "We knew about the man, but we didn't know about the woman."

"I'm sorry," Derek admitted. "I'm sorry about everything."

"Well, tell me what you noticed when you entered the back door the next morning. I'd like to hear about everything you saw, felt, touched, heard, or even smelled, Derek.''

Blood, what he noticed was the blood, the sight of which knocked out almost all other memory.

"Do you have the key to the basement with you?"

"Yes,'' Derek said, sounding almost calm now.

"May I have it, please? And Derek,'' said Geof casually, as he reached for the fateful key, "I'm curious about something—does Sammie own that condo?"

"Yeah."

"Pretty nice. How'd she manage that?'' Derek shrugged, as if he couldn't care less. "Money from an aunt of hers. Sammie and Rodney lived with the aunt. The aunt died and left Sammie some money, and they used it to buy that house they were living in, and then the condo."

"What was the aunt's name, do you know?"

Derek shrugged again, looking weary now and beaten down.

"I wish you'd go see my friend Marsha Sandy,'' I told him.

"I don't need a psychiatrist."

"The hell you don't."

"Jenny's right,'' Geof said.

Derek's answer was to push himself up from the couch and to insist on leaving. We let him go, but we stood at the window together, our arms around each other's waists, watching Derek get into his Toyota and drive off.

"Geof, I feel as if we're letting him walk back into a burning building."

"I know. But if we tried to stop him, he'd break away from us again. I suspect he'll have to find his own way out of this, Jenny."

"It's because I fired him . . ."

"Oh, come on, Jenny . . ."

"Let me finish. I mean, it's because of the emptiness he felt when I fired him. There was a void in Derek, Geof, and before anything good had a chance to fill it, little Sammie rushed in. Now he's got a commitment, all right, now he's got a cause. But it's awful, it's evil."

He shook his head. "It's his battle."

"But he needs help, and I played a part in this, and I care about him."

"There's nothing you can do."

"Oh, I don't know."

He sighed. "I was afraid you'd say that."

38

The next day Geof left early, saying he was headed for Marsha Sandy's house—to see if she'd talk to him about her client before he put out a pickup order on Rosalinda.

He was going to try bribing Marsha to get her cooperation: if she'd help him, he'd let her pick up Rosalinda herself and personally take her to the station to be interrogated as a probable witness to, and perhaps even participant in, the crime. Or crimes.

I went to the office, where I called Marianne Miller and asked her to telephone me immediately if she saw Sammie Gardner—alone—at her old house. She wanted to know why. I told her it was "foundation business." Well, Derek was still an employee of the foundation, so . . .

Marianne called me back at ten-thirty.

The merry widow had returned.

She didn't even look particularly surprised when she responded to the doorbell and found me standing there. If anything, she seemed almost pleased.

"May I come in?" I asked her.

236

Sammie Gardner smiled in her slow, sly way. "Why not."

"Where's Derek?"

"Pickin' up stuff from his condo."

Damn, I thought, he's really moving in with her.

Inside, the old saltbox was everything her expensive new home was not: slovenly, dirty, and scattered about with grubby, mismatched furniture that she wasn't even bothering to move out. The rooms I saw were "decorated" with graffiti, most of it either obscene or profane, that was scrawled across the walls in many different pens by many different hands, as if Sammie and Rodney—that fun couple—had invited their friends to have a go at expressing themselves. From what I read, their friends were barely literate, being unable to spell words longer than four letters.

"It's charming," I said as I stood with my hands in my coat pockets in the middle of the living room. "I don't know how you can stand to leave it."

She laughed out loud, briefly, holding her hands over her pregnant belly. Then she just stood, staring at me, and waiting for me to say my piece. Even as pregnant as she was, Sammie Gardner was God's way of defining sexy. The pregnancy that rounded her face and her breasts may have even added to her allure, sending out a message of ripe and ready fecundity. But it was the sly smile and the tumbling blond hair that really did it, that said, "Ready, honey, whenever you are." She was even looking at me that way, which had me shifting uncomfortably from foot to foot. Maybe Marianne Miller was right, maybe Rodney had watched, maybe the three of them—Rodney, Sammie, and Perry Yates—really had wanted to put together a quartet. Maybe she thought that I had come to apply for a spot in a trio.

Clearly, this was a doomed and idiotic mission to rescue a self-made hostage. I had been unprepared for the sheer unfeeling selfishness of the girl. Now I felt absolutely ridiculous saying what I'd come to say to her, which was, "Please let him go."

"Derek?" She smiled her sly smile. "You talkin' about him? Last time I seen him, he wasn't, like, locked up. He ain't wearin' no chains, you know."

"He feels guilty—"

"Yeah," she said petulantly, "he should."

"But he needs help; he needs counseling."

"Don't we all, lady. Me, I'm a grieving widow. Maybe he's my counselor. Maybe I'm his counselor." The smile disappeared into a yawn. She scratched her left breast and then lowered her bulk onto a sofa. Already, I was boring her. I decided not to wonder how Derek was managing to keep her attention. No wonder he looked so tired.

"I don't get it," I told her. "He doesn't have any money—"

"Yeah, well, I do."

"He doesn't have a job—"

"Thanks to you, right?"

"He can't be very good company—"

She laughed. "I don't require much in the way of what you call conversation, you know? Like, Derek's plenty good company for me right now. I need him, like. I got this move to make, I got things to do, and somebody's gonna have to take me to the hospital, and then look after the baby. I'm gonna get me a neat job, and Derek's gonna take care of things for me—"

"That's despicable, Sammie."

She looked as if she might get angry at that, but then she only smiled and said, "How do you spell that?"

So, I thought, you're ignorant, but you're not stupid.

"Where'd you get the money?"

I thought she'd tell me it was none of my business, but evidently she wanted to boast. "I had this rich aunt, see, and she left it all to me. Roddie and me, we was always real nice to her. We lived with her and took care of her, so now she's takin' good care of me." She patted her stomach possessively. "Me and her little niece. Bless my old auntie."

"What do you need Derek for, when you've got Yates?"

That didn't goad her either, but only twisted her smile up another notch. "I'll bet you been talkin' to that crazy wife of his, right? Did you know she's crazy? Like, when she threw him out, you know what that crazy bitch did? Threw all his clothes and stuff in his car and set fire to it! No shit! She really did! God, and it was a nice Chrysler, too. I couldn't believe it. I mean, like, she's Looney Tunes."

"When was this, Sammie?"

"Six months ago, seven, I don't know."

So that was Perry's leverage over Marianne, I thought.

"Did you ever see the man they're looking for—Mob?"

"Oh, sure." She said it casually, but then she didn't seem able to repress a shudder. "God, what a geek. He's crazy, you know? He used to hang around all the time, beggin' and stuff like that? My aunt used to give him doughnuts and coffee and stuff, God, she even let him sleep on our porch a couple of times. Gave me the goddamn creeps! I hated having that Looney Tune hangin' around me. God! She was crazy to let him hang around there, you know? I mean, God, look what he did to Roddie, I mean, like God, it coulda been me, you know? God!"

Her dismay over the fact and manner of her husband's death was, it seemed, relative to her own well-being.

"This was your aunt's house, then?"

"This?" She looked as if she were about to say something scornful, but then that sly, lazy smile reappeared on her face. "Nah, not this place."

"How long did you and Rodney live here?"

She shrugged. "Couple years, I don't know. Look,"

she said, suddenly impatient, "I got things to do." She flicked the fingernails of her right hand with her thumb, smiling her infuriating little smile at me. "Like Derek's waitin' for me, you know?"

"Oh, right." I gazed around me again, making my appraisal as insulting as possible. "This time, like use some of that money on like wallpaper, you know?"

"Fuck you," she said, and stuck her tongue out at me.

Amazing, I thought, as I walked out and closed her front door behind me: the only way to get a rise out of that girl was to criticize her interior decorating. But then she surprised me again.

"Hey, wait!"

I turned on her front walk to find that she had flung open the door to yell at me.

"Listen," she called out, "wait a minute, will you? I'll walk out with you, all right? Hold on."

It couldn't be because she liked my company, I thought; more likely, she wanted to taunt me some more about Derek. Still, curious, I waited until she appeared at the front door again, this time with her purse and a couple of paper bags. I walked back up onto the porch to take them from her and carry them to her car.

"That's the last of it." She nodded at the bags in my arms; they were full of small items of junk. "I ain't comin' back to this creepy place no more."

I anchored the bags down on the floor in front of the passenger seat of her MG and slammed the door shut. She got in and pulled away, with no thanks, only a wave that had more than a touch of bravado to it. I didn't wave back.

39

Two hours later, I had just invited Faye to step into my office for a little chat when Geof called from the station to tell me they had picked up Rosalinda and to tell me what she told them. It was, essentially, "I was there, but I don't know anything."

"She was fairly clear about it," Geof told me. "She told us that she and Mob went to sleep on the floor of one of those smaller rooms off the central meeting space. She says she didn't wake up until Mob woke her up, saying they had to leave immediately. It was still dark, she says, and he scared her because he had blood all over him—"

"Well," I said, as if that piece of evidence settled things.

Geof continued: "Rosalinda claims that at first she thought—vaguely, I gather—that he had somehow cut himself. Then she got really frightened because she thought he might have tried to kill himself. But he told her he was okay, and it doesn't seem to have occurred to her to wonder any more about it. He said he was okay, and she believed it. He said leave, and they left. He said, don't tell anybody we were there, and she didn't. He said, don't tell anybody where I go, and she won't. He told her not to worry about him, and I guess she hasn't. He seems to have guided her out of that basement so that she didn't see, hear, or touch anything incriminating.''

''Either he was being smart,'' I said, ''or protective.''

''Yes, and either she's smarter and a better actress than she seems capable of being, or else that woman really doesn't have the slightest idea what's going on.''

''Then why did she get so upset at your detectives when they came to question her here at the foundation?''

''Because they asked her about Mob. I take it that even she's afraid of his demons. He had told her not to talk about him, and so it upset and confused her to be asked about him.''

''Then how'd you get her to talk?''

''Marsha did most of that.''

''So did Rosalinda tell you where he is?''

''I don't think she knows.''

''I'm sorry. I thought this might be it.''

''Jenny?''

I waited, then said, ''Yes?''

''Uh.''

What's the problem? I wondered. ''Yes, Geof?''

''I'm not sure how to say this.''

''You want to know if I think there's any possibility that Marsha might be hiding him or that she might know where he is.''

''How did you know that?'' He sounded relieved, but then he sounded worried again. ''Yes. You mad?''

''No, it's a fair question. And the reason I knew that is because I've asked myself the same thing. Honey— Lieutenant Honey—I really don't think so. I can't imagine her doing anything as dramatic as harboring a fugitive, and I don't believe she'd take a chance of endangering the lives of other people by hiding his whereabouts. But why don't you ask her again?''

He said he would, after which he requested that I never again call him Lieutenant Honey, and then he hung up.

It was then, a little late, that I thought of an exceedingly slim possibility that nobody had yet considered.

I called Geof back to tell him, and then I called Marsha Sandy's house.

"Dr. Sandy's residence."

"Joe, is that you?"

"Yes. Who's this?"

I told him and then asked if I might drop by to see him immediately. "I have some questions about the recreation hall, and I want to take advantage of your vacation, to pick your brain." Sounding interested, he invited me to come on over.

I looked up, to find Faye standing in my doorway.

"Do you still want to talk to me, Jenny?"

She had waited patiently all that time.

"No, let's try again tomorrow." I was feeling jittery, and I wanted to get out of there before the phone could ring and detain me. "I'm sorry, Faye, but I have to do something for Geof right now."

"I understand," she said.

It's about time, I thought.

40

"Come on in, Jenny."

This time Joe was wearing Hush Puppies, blue jeans, and a pullover sweater, but no apron. He escorted me into Marsha's den, where he had a fire going, and offered me coffee, which I gratefully accepted. After a few sips, to warm my insides as well as my hands that held the cup, I put the coffee down, and leaned back against the pillows on the sofa.

"Do you mind if I just relax for a minute, Joe?"

"Course not." He was hunched over in his chair, elbows on his knees, coffee cup to his mouth. He looked tightly wrapped. Marsha had always liked them intense, I thought as I closed my eyes; she said their energy kept her awake when they otherwise bored her. I thought she held an altogether too detached view of men, but she claimed that was merely a side effect of her profession. "Shrinkage" she called it, saying that her knowledge of human behavior had an unfortunate tendency to shrink people into neatly wrapped and labeled packages that . . .

"Jenny?"

I opened my eyes. He was looking at me quizzically.

"You have some questions for me?"

"Uh-huh." Slowly, I worked myself back up to a sitting position. "I think my problem is, I'm starving. You wouldn't happen to have a sandwich or something hidden away in the refrigerator, would you?"

"Sure." He hid his exasperation pretty well and even pushed himself up out of the chair as if he were almost glad to have something to do to keep busy. "Tuna fish okay?"

"That would be great," I said. "I really appreciate this."

"Come on out to the kitchen with me," he suggested. "We can talk about your project while I put your sandwich together."

"Oh, no," I demurred. "If you don't mind, I think I'll just stay here and rest a while longer. It's been a hell of a week, you know? Being here feels kind of like being at home, it just makes me want to lie back and relax. You go on ahead, Joe. Take your time. Don't hurry on my account."

"Thanks," he said, with detectable irony.

Fixing the sandwich took him about ten minutes.

I consumed another twenty minutes in eating it, along with the chips and the pickles, which I ate slowly, one by one, as if they were delectable, individual beads of caviar. We chatted in a desultory fashion throughout, with Joe growing ever more fidgety. I, strangely, seemed to have been taken over by a torpor that slowed my speech and my movements. I knew I was driving him crazy, and I had to admire him for being so basically damn nice about it.

Finally, after I'd made a show of brushing off my hands, exclaiming over the crumbs I'd gotten on the carpet, and then insisting on finding Marsha's Dustbuster, and using it, he said in a clear, loud voice:

"What do you want to know about the recreation hall, Jenny?"

I looked at my watch: five-ten, which was almost a full hour since I'd arrived. Marsha tried to end her last appointment of the day by five, so I knew she'd probably walk in the door soon.

"Joe," I said, smiling brightly into his annoyance, "I'd like the benefit of your experience. What do you think we ought to accomplish for the clients at our recreation hall?"

He nodded, obviously relieved to have reached some sort of point, and said with a quick intensity, "Defend them, Jenny. Protect and defend them, because nobody else has and nobody else will. Jenny, you can't imagine how alone they are and how defenseless, especially when they're in an episode of their illness. They need some place they can go, at any hour, where they'll find somebody to whom they can say, 'Help me. For God's sake, help me.' "

I was listening, almost as intently as he was talking.

"This recreation hall of yours, Jenny, it'll be their safe house. Listen, if you want to make somebody—anybody— feel crazy, you take away all his security. Make him sick, make him unemployed, have society shun him, make him vulnerable, make him good and goddamned scared. That'll make you crazy. And what'll help you get sane again? Safety. Some safe place to start trying to be human again. You see what I mean?"

I heard a key turn in the front door. Marsha.

"Joe, you're kind of describing someone I know," I said, thinking of Derek. "But the funny thing is, you remind me of him, too. I think it's your good intentions . . ."

He was frowning, still caught in his intensity, when Marsha appeared in the doorway.

"Jenny!" she said warmly.

I looked at my watch—five thirty-five. If the phone

didn't ring soon, I was going to have to finagle an invitation to have dinner with them.

We broke off our conversation to greet Marsha and to hear about her day at the office. Then we talked about my question and Joe's answer. Joe fixed drinks. Marsha and I each had white wine; he drank a beer. We talked some more. I hung around, ignoring hints that they were hungry, until Marsha said, "I'd really like to ask you to have dinner with us, Jenny, but this is Joe's last night here." She winked broadly and nudged me. "Get it?" Joe laughed. I tried to think of something, anything to delay my departure. I was getting ready to offer to cook and serve for them when the phone finally rang.

"I'll get it," Marsha said.

In a moment she was back, smiling. "That was Geof, Jenny, he's going to drop by in a few minutes." She turned to Joe. "Can your stomach bear it a while longer?"

He smiled sweetly at her and said it could.

When the doorbell rang ten minutes later, signaling Geof's arrival, I grabbed Marsha's arm before she left the room.

"Marsha?"

She looked at me quizzically.

"Please. Remember that we've been friends a long time, and that I would never purposely do anything to hurt you."

She looked still more puzzled, then grinned over at Joe. "This girl always gets so damned sentimental when she drinks."

When she came back into the room, my husband was walking behind her.

Joe stood up, ready to shake Geof's hand.

Geof stood for a moment in the doorway, unsmiling.

"We've got Kitt Blackstone," he announced.

And then he looked directly at Joe Fabian.

Joe sank back in the chair, saying, "I'll explain."

41

The police in Joe's home city had, at the urgent request of the Port Frederick Police Department, arrested without a struggle the murder suspect, Christopher Blackstone, aka Kitt, aka Mob, at the home of Joseph Fabian.

"Did they hurt him?" Joe asked, with some belligerence.

"Don't be a bigger ass," Geof snapped. But then, seeing Marsha's expression, he relented. "No, he's okay. He's in custody up there now, but we'll have him down here as soon as the paperwork goes through."

"What kind of custody, Geof?" Marsha asked.

"Jail or hospital, you mean?"

"Yes. Which?"

"For right now, jail."

She made a distressed sound and turned away.

"Are you going to arrest me?" Joe asked.

"You're goddamned right, I am," Geof said. Making something of a show of it, he "read" Joe Fabian his rights. Then he said, "Look, you've got a right to call your attorney before you talk, but I don't have to call an attorney to tell you I think you're a son of a bitch. Who the hell do you think you are to harbor a fugitive from a murder warrant? You got it all figured out that he's innocent, is that it? Or maybe you figure he's so sick, he doesn't require due process. You have any idea how many hundreds of man-hours we've put in searching for that man? You got any idea how many scared people have been looking over their shoulders in this town? Are you related to him, or something, is that your excuse? Who the hell do you think you are?''

"Joe," Marsha said, "how was he when you saw him?"

He hesitated, looked at Geof, and then said, "He was in pretty bad shape, actually."

Geof quickly took out a pad and pen and began writing.

"He was scared," Joe said, "but not just of being caught. He told me that he saw a dead body in the old church basement, and lots of blood, and that he ran to his sister's, and she made him stay there. But he got scared again, stole her car, and left. That's when the police almost caught him, and then he was really frightened. He didn't know why they were after him, although he thought it probably had something to do with the body he saw. That's the night he showed up here." His glance at Marsha was a guilty one. "You were working late."

She only shook her head.

"What else did he see?" Geof asked.

"He told me there was somebody else in the church that night, somebody who hated him . . . ."

"That might be his paranoia," Marsha murmured.

"Did he name this person or describe him?"

Joe shook his head. "I . . . hid him in your basement the first night, Marsha. I'm sorry. But if I had told you, you'd be an accessory to what I was doing—"

"No," she said firmly, "I would not have been."

"Maybe if you'd seen him . . . he was so frightened. Anyway, after you went to work the next day, I drove him up to my place in Alban, and told him to stay there. There was plenty of food, you know. I called him regularly. But.''

"But," Geof said angrily. "But an old lady died."

"I know." Joe's shoulders slumped. "He told me he . . . well, I believed he didn't do it, that's all, I just believed him. But he was getting incoherent by that time, and—''

"And you allowed him to get sicker?" Marsha's voice rose.

He looked pleadingly at her. "They'd have killed him."

"Who?" Geof asked. "We would? Are you talking about us? The police? We wouldn't have killed him, Fabian. We'd have arrested him, that's all."

"Joe," Marsha said, "*you* could have killed him."

"I meant well," he said defensively.

"You meant well," Geof repeated, in a disbelieving tone.

"How'd you know?" Joe asked him.

"We thought he might try to reach Marsha," Geof said. "But Jenny told me that if he did, you were the one who'd be at home to greet him."

He and Marsha both looked at me, their expressions quite different from one another.

Marsha chose not to accompany Joe when Geof took him out of the house to the waiting police car, but she squeezed his hand and then reached out to hug him strongly as he walked by her. While they embraced, he whispered something to her that I couldn't hear. She nodded and smiled slightly. When they were gone, and she had returned to the den, she looked at me.

"He asked me to sneak a file into jail in a cake," she said.

"I think he ought to take this more seriously than that," I told her.

She nodded wearily. "I think so, too."

"Are you pissed at me, Marsha?"

"Don't be an idiot," she said simply.

"Well, but . . ."

"What will happen to Joe?"

"Probably nothing, considering the justice system."

"Oh. I don't know how I feel about that. I'm so tired." She waved a hand at me. "Go home. I need to think. We'll talk later, all right?"

Very late that night, she called me at home.

"Hi," I said, a little nervously.

"Hi," she said. "I've got permission to get in to see Kitt at that jail up in Alban. I thought I'd drive up there first thing in the morning. Is there any chance you could get away and go up there with me?"

"What time?"

"I'd like to pick you up at six o'clock, but, Jenny, if you think this might be too painful . . ."

"Because of my mom? I don't know; I can't predict things like that. But I'll be ready. After what I did to your love life this afternoon, it's the least I can do."

"You didn't do it," she said calmly. "And, no, it isn't."

It was the shorthand of friendship, and I understood it.

42

"Compassionate to a fault," Marsha said, during our drive up to Alban the next morning. "That's Joe. If he's not careful, he'll give bleeding-heart liberals a bad name."

"I hear you joking," I said.

"But not laughing," she concluded. It was another of our old lines, used for those circumstances when, as Adlai Stevenson once remarked, "It hurts too much to laugh, but I'm too old to cry." One of the reasons she was attracted to Joe, she told me, was that he cared so much about the same people who concerned her. "I knew he was a shade impulsive," she admitted, "not to mention being fanatical on the subject of fair treatment for the mentally ill, and both of those traits did give me pause, yes, they did. But . . ."

"I know."

"Well." She sighed, and downshifted around an icy curve on the two-lane highway. "His attorney will have to help him now. I can't. Frankly, the psychiatrist in me is sorely tempted to let him learn the hard way—to show him that one of the consequences of his actions is that I'm not so sure I want anything more to do with a man stupid enough to pull such a stunt. Anyway, right now I'm more concerned about Kitt. He's my patient and a good deal more my responsibility than Joe is. How do you suppose we'll locate the jail when we get there, Jenny?''

"Break a law," I suggested.

Kitt Blackstone had a court-appointed attorney who allowed me to watch through a two-way mirror with him while Marsha went into a small room alone with her patient. The attorney and several police officers tried to talk her out of it, saying the suspect was "crazy" and "out of control," but she calmly and firmly insisted that she could handle it.

"I'm his doctor," she reminded them.

"Well, fine," one of the officers finally said, throwing up his hands in evident disgust. "You do it. I'm glad if somebody can handle the crazy son of a bitch."

The attorney, whose name was Marty Burack, and I watched Marsha edge into the room, close the door behind her, and then lean up against it.

"Kitt," she said in a gentle, clear voice. "Hello."

In the room, there were two wooden chairs and a wooden table. Kitt Blackstone was crouched on top of the table. His head was tucked between his knees, so that I couldn't see his face. His arms stuck straight out from his sides like tree limbs, and his fingers were spread stiffly, as though someone were counting to ten on them. From the time Marty Burack and I had sat down in our room to the time Marsha spoke to him, Kitt Blackstone hadn't moved. The police officers had informed us that he had adopted that posture as soon as they had put him in the room and that he hadn't moved for them, either.

"Is it the demons, Kitt?" Marsha inquired, calmly.

No response. No movement. Nothing.

"Mob," she said in a louder voice.

The huddled figure on the table moved slightly. The top of his head was bald. I judged him to be about five feet eight inches tall. He was overweight, like his sister. His clothes looked as if they had been expensive, but now they were filthy and they hung in folds from his stiffened body like thin blankets.

Marsha moved close to him, so that she would be facing him directly if he looked up.

"Do you call yourself Mob?"

The figure moaned.

Beside me, the attorney breathed, "Fascinating."

"Why do you have your arms stuck out like that, Kitt?" Marsha asked. "Are you trying to hold the demons off?" She paused. "Listen to me, Kitt. I am going to help you. I have brought medicine for you. I am going to get someone to help me give you the medicine. The medicine and I will make the demons go away. Can you hear me, Kitt?"

The figure tucked his head down farther toward his crotch.

"My poor Kitt." Marsha walked over to the door and opened it. She called out into the hall for assistance, saying she needed at least three police officers. Together, with her instructions, the burly men managed to uncurl Mob just enough to allow her to give him two shots. While they did that, Marty Burack told me that he'd been appointed because the suspect was indigent. When I pointed out that his family wasn't, Burack shrugged and said, "You don't see them here, do you?"

We turned back to the tableau.

"I want him in the hospital," Marsha said. She looked commandingly up at the mirror.

The attorney beside me rose instantly and left the room.

"In the meantime," Marsha said, "could he at least have a cot in here?"

When the officers brought the cot in, they pushed it against a wall and then lowered Kitt Blackstone, still in his contorted position, onto it. Then Marsha shooed them out. She sat down in one of the chairs, to wait. The figure on the cot seemed to relax, too, though only slightly.

It was three o'clock in the afternoon before Kitt Blackstone woke up. The attorney had never come back, so I was the only one watching from the anteroom when the man on the table stretched slowly out of the crouch—in which he'd slept all that time. He lowered his arms as if they were jointed, metal attachments he could not feel. He brought his head up, and then he fell to his side on the cot so that he was lying sideways, his face toward me.

What I saw was an older-looking version of the face in the picture the maid had given me. His pale head was a moon—round, bare, and frozen. His expression was as stiff as a mask.

Marsha got up quickly and walked around so that she could see him, and he could see her. I thought I saw him flicker recognition at her.

"Hello, Kitt," she said.

Nothing. Frozen.

"Are the demons quiet enough for you to hear me? They will soon pipe down, Kitt. I promise you that. We'll keep giving you medicine until they do. Can you talk to me?"

I didn't see his mouth move, but I heard the sound, "Daaaa."

"That's right. Dr. Sandy."

She waited. Nothing.

Marsha looked up toward the mirror and shrugged at me. I thought she looked terribly sad and discouraged, a feeling I shared, since I had frequently seen my mother behaving like that. Kitt Blackstone, I recognized, was mired in a quicksand of insanity that had sucked him so far down that he was now virtually paralyzed; he still had his nose above the murk, he was still breathing, but that was all; the rest of him was pinioned by the great, compressing, terrifying mass of the quicksand. My perception was confirmed when Marsha left Kitt alone a few minutes later and joined me on the other side of the mirror.

"He's having a very bad psychotic episode, Jenny," she said, eyeing me at the same time, evidently to see how I was taking it. She must have been reassured by the view because she continued: "I haven't seen him this sick since the last time I put him in the hospital." She sighed and thrust her hands in the coat pockets of her suit. "This is really painful for me to see. He was making pretty good progress—*very* good progress, considering how ill he'd been. He'll be going back into the hospital now, and there's no real telling when he'll get out again. I hate this."

"Will we ever know what he saw or did?"

She shrugged. "I doubt it."

"Marsha, what's the importance of that biblical story to him? Is there anything more to it than the fact that he thinks he's inhabited by demons?"

She leaned the upper part of her body against the wall behind her and sighed again. Speaking slowly, as if trying to do him the honor of being accurate, she said, "He has always had an extraordinarily objective understanding of mental illness from the inside as well as the outside. He's quite intelligent and perceptive. He understands how other people view him. It is clear to him that when he's crazy the rest of the world views him with the same fear and loathing with which the townspeople in that biblical story viewed the man named Mob."

"In his story," I said, "are you 'Jesus'?"

She smiled a little. "When he started getting well, he was so grateful that at first he did try to turn me into Jesus, and when I wouldn't accept that, he wanted to think of me as his exorcist, but I couldn't allow that either. I believe it is more helpful to him to think of his illness as just that—as an illness and one that can be treated with the proper balance of medications and therapy, as migraines can be treated, or cancer. I believe in miracles, but I would rather that my patients think of their recoveries in a more mundane way, as something *they* can control on a day-to-day basis. I want them to take the responsibility rather than to be supine, waiting for miracles. To my way of thinking, taking that responsibility is usually miracle enough. If the hand of God shows in their cure, I believe it is at that intersection at which effective help is available and they are willing to take it.''

We were quiet for a few moments with our own thoughts.

I bestirred myself. ''Mother never felt capable of taking total responsibility for anything.'' I thought about that for another moment. ''Except when things went wrong. She always assumed responsibility for anything that went wrong—in all our lives. She was always apologizing for things she hadn't done and couldn't help.'' I looked up to find Marsha gazing at me. ''So who are the pigs?''

''In the story?'' She shifted against the wall, placing her hands flat against it as if she were pinned there. ''He didn't actually focus on that particular story until a few years ago, around the time he met that poor old woman who collected pigs. I think that through a process of simple association, he began to think of his demons as being the demons in the pig story. Anyway, in Kitt's view the pigs are all the people in the world who think he's crazy and they're not. He thinks, and I agree with him, that when normal people are around a crazy person, it turns them a little crazy with fear and loathing. We are so afraid of crazy people that our fear makes us crazy, he says.'' She looked back at the frozen man on the bed.

''You ready to go?'' I asked her.

''No,'' she said, still looking at him. ''But let's go.''

She had to leave him then, and hope for the best from that young, inexperienced-looking attorney, because she had other patients waiting. I was glad to be along to do the driving on the way back, so that she could rest. The sun was out, the temperature had risen, the snow was melting, and the drive was easier on the way home.

While she napped, I used the silence to think about those drowning pigs in Grace Montgomery's bathtub. I'd probably never know for sure, but I had a feeling that Mob had been in that house, that Mob had put them there, and that his message, as clear as he knew how to make it was: "Help me. Somebody else is crazy. I did not do this thing." Because my natural sympathies lay with him, this was one time when I didn't know whether to trust my own intuition.

43

I let Marsha off at her office and went to work myself. About an hour later, I heard a tentative:

"Jenny?"

It was Faye, who stood in my doorway smoothing her skirt with her hands, like a soldier trying to make a good impression on her commanding officer.

"May I talk to you, Jenny?"

"Sure," I said, halfway glad of a distraction.

Faye waited for me to gesture her into a chair before she took the liberty of sitting down. I sensed apology and mortification in the air.

"Derek finally answered the messages I've been leaving on his phone machine," she told me. "And he told me where he was staying, and I insisted that he let me visit him because I just wanted to be sure he was all right. And so this morning"—she glanced timidly at me, as if to say, do you mind?—"I went to see him at that girl's house." She said "girl" as others might say "slime." "I was absolutely appalled, Jenny, at what happened to him, at his reasons for being there, at *her* . . ."

"I feel the same, Faye."

"And I just want to tell you that now I understand that you aren't to blame. He's done this to himself. I don't know why; I don't understand any of it; it just seems so awful and sordid to me, but it's clearly Derek who's doing it, not you. So I thought I owed you more of an apology than I'd given you before. I was an idiot, and I hope you'll forgive me."

"It was understandable," I said, trying not to sound smug and magnanimous. "Perfectly understandable."

She screwed her face up in an expression of puzzlement and frustration. "Why? That's what I want to know. I understand why Derek's there—it's guilt and sex, if you ask me. But why does she want *him?*" She blushed a little and looked ashamed. "That sounds awful, and I don't mean anything against Derek; he's as cute as my boys, and I love him to death, but what could she see in him? He's too nice for her! She's just a greedy little . . . little *bitch* . . . and he doesn't even have a job now. So what does she want with *him?*"

I felt myself staring at her. "That is a very good question, Faye. That is probably the most intelligent question I've heard in the last month." She was staring back at me as if she expected me, like Sister Ignatius, to explain it all to her. "I wish I had an equally intelligent answer."

But that wasn't why she was looking at me expectantly. It was Faye who had the answer. She was merely waiting, politely and diplomatically, for me to voice it first. When I didn't, she cleared her throat tactfully.

"It's because she's scared," Faye said.

"Scared?" I was startled. "She? Who?"

"The girl, what's-her-name—"

"Sammie."

"She reminds me of my children when they were afraid of the boogeyman, and they'd resort to practically any trick to keep me in their bedrooms, so they wouldn't be alone in the dark. Didn't she make you think of that, Jenny?''

"No," I admitted.

"Well," she said kindly, "you're not a parent."

She was exactly right: The day I had talked to Sammie Gardner in her former home, she had been jittery, had even seemed reluctant to lose my loathsome company. Much like Marianne Miller had seemed after the murders, and as Grace Montgomery had seemed when, in her crazy way, she had tried to persuade me to stay and sleep on her roof. None of them had wanted to be alone with the boogeyman.

"Who's the boogeyman?" I asked Faye.

"Oh, it's just her imagination," she said dismissively.

But on that point, I thought she was wrong.

"If we want to help Derek," I said, thinking out loud, "maybe we'd better learn a little more about Miss Sammie."

"What can I do?" Faye said quickly.

Another good question, I thought, gazing at her. "All right. First, let's find out about that aunt who left her all the money. Can you telephone and ask Derek?"

"I don't think he'd be alone."

"Well, I don't know who else to ask, except maybe her old neighbors. I'll call the artist, see what she knows." I snapped my fingers, suddenly inspired. "Faye, I know what you can do, and you'll love it." I smiled at her. "Call Michael Laurence at his new real estate office and see what he can find out for you about the sale of Sammie's old house and the purchase of her new one. It's probably a wild-goose chase, but we might learn something interesting about why she moved and how she financed it. It's certainly better if you ask Michael than if I do—he likes you."

She wisely refrained from editorializing on that comment and simply got up from the chair and strode purposefully back to her desk.

"Faye, there's something else you can do."

She looked back at me.

"I want you to advertise for a new secretary for the foundation." Before her shock had a chance to turn to dismay, I continued: "We'll need one immediately, what with you being promoted to assistant director."

She was staring openmouthed at me. I smiled at her. She closed her mouth and then, with an impressive show of dignity and restraint, smiled back.

"Thank you very much," she said. "I'll try to deserve it."

44

Marianne Miller was home, working, when I called, but she sounded uncharacteristically abrupt, almost rude. This time, she seemed very much to mind the interruption.

"I'll be brief," I promised, feeling guilty at disturbing an artist in mid-inspiration. The idea of Artist At Work created a sort of awe in me; the whole process seemed so far removed from my left-brained person, so important and mystical, as compared to my own calculating way of being. My rationale for interrupting Marianne was that it might benefit her eventually—if only Faye and I could retrieve Derek from Sammie Gardner. "Can you tell me anything about Sammie Gardner's aunt, the one she and Rodney lived with?"

"Dorothy Rhodes," Marianne said, in a snappish tone that carried oddly over her next words. "Nice lady, I liked her a lot, as different from that little tramp as you can imagine. But she never could see anything wrong with Sammie, or with creepy Rod either, for that matter. Mrs. Rhodes was so kind to them. She gave them the run of her house for, I don't know, I guess at least three years."

"When did she die?"

"Oh, I guess it's been two or three years now."

"And she left Sammie a lot of money?"

"Yeah, I guess so." Her voice shook with what sounded like anger. "That's what I heard anyway; that's what Perry said, and he ought to know." She laughed briefly, bitterly. "After she died, they took the money and bought their house."

"Why didn't they just live in her house?"

"What?"

"I said, why didn't Sammie and Rod continue to live in Mrs. Rhodes's house after she died? Wouldn't that have been logical?"

"Well, it would if there was still a house, I guess. But her house burned down, you know—"

"No. I didn't."

"Yeah, that's how she died, in the fire, it was awful. *You* know, it was the house on the empty lot next to the church basement. Oh, Christ." She astonished me by starting to cry. "Oh, Christ, so many awful things have happened; I just want out of here so bad . . ."

"Marianne, what's wrong?"

Through her tears, she said in a hopeless voice, "Have you seen Derek? Does he say anything about me?"

I'd made a mistake, I realized, in not telling her the truth earlier; she was suffering, and this unrealistic pining for Derek only exacerbated it. "Marianne, I should have told you this earlier, but I didn't want to hurt your feelings. Derek is living with Sammie Gardner, in her new condo—"

"*What?*" She shrieked it, and then, unaccountably, began to laugh and cry at the same time. "Oh, thank God, thank God, thank God . . ."

She hung up, leaving me staring at the receiver in my hand.

When I had finished shaking my head in amazement,

and when my mouth finally closed, I pressed another phone line into service and called the police department.

"Geof," I said, accusingly, "did you know that Sammie Gardner and Rodney used to live with Sammie's aunt, a Mrs. Dorothy Rhodes, on Tenth Street, and that the house burned down, and she died in the fire?"

"Yes," he said, sounding puzzled that I'd even brought it up. "Of course I know that. But Jenny, there wasn't anything to that fire—it wasn't arson, if that's what you're thinking. I wasn't on that case, but I talked to the detectives who were, and they said it was a case of faulty wiring in an electric stove. We double-checked with the fire department, and they told us it was tragic, but it was definitely an accident. She died of smoke inhalation. I believed them, and I think you ought to believe me. I'm sure about this."

"All right," I said, reluctantly, "I believe."

"It never hurts to ask me, though," Geof said, in the nice way he has of making me feel less foolish. "Oh, and I did ask MaryDell Paine why she chose that site."

"What'd she say?"

"She admitted that even if it hadn't been the best site in town, she would have rammed it through her committee, because it was a place where her brother had been happy. She thought he'd be more likely to go there again, since he knew it from the time it was a church. And it was for sale, had been for some time."

"And that was it?"

"Well, it was comparatively cheap, too, which was important if she had to ask her husband for some of the money."

"Since he hates her brother."

"Yes," Geof said, drawing it out, "he does."

I hung up just as Faye walked back into my office.

"Michael asked around," she announced, with a familiarity that made me smile inwardly, "and then he called me back. Michael says that Rodney and Sammie Gardner originally bought their house on Tenth Street and then resold it to the same person.''

She handed me the telephone-message sheet on which she'd written a name. I felt the third point of a triangle snap into position. One. Two. Three. As easy as . . .

''I think this ought to mean something,'' I said, looking up at Faye.

''If it does, I'm sure you'll think of it,'' she assured me, sounding very much like my old grade-school teacher and some of my trustees. It seemed like misplaced faith to me, but maybe Geof could make something of it. I decided to pay him a visit instead of simply calling him with this new and possibly worthless piece of information.

He didn't think it was worthless.

In fact, we spent the rest of that afternoon hashing it over with the other detectives.

What did it mean? How did it fit?

Answering those questions required other phone calls, as well as a couple of additional interrogations by the police of certain persons who had already been thoroughly interviewed. All that effort, carried late into the evening, eventually resulted in a single theory.

It sounded good to me. More to the point, it sounded plausible to Geof and to the other detectives. But proving it, aye, that was the rub.

45

Life goes on. Even in the middle of a murder investigation—one that was winding to a resolution—there were still meals to eat, people to see, bills to pay, and foundation business to conduct. The appraisal on the old church basement had come in, and it was satisfactory. A title search had shown the property to be free of liens. We were set for closing, and I was now anxious, after all that had preceded this moment, to get it over with, once and for all.

I called the landlord's house, and again got Mrs. Butts on the line.

"Triple A Realty," she said, sweetly.

"This is Jenny Cain, and—"

"I'll get him!"

I nearly laughed. Such is the power of the threat of a lawsuit these days. When her husband came on the line, I said, "How would you like to be tens of thousands of dollars richer today, George?"

He opined as to how that would be lovely, and he promised to meet me at the church basement.

As I approached the double front doors, I was nervous: so many things had conspired against this moment, that I couldn't trust it. Though not ordinarily a pessimist, as I walked in I found myself expecting things to go awry. At the last minute, he might find something unacceptable about the deal; or, all things considered, I might even chicken out. I doubted that I would—too much preparation had gone into this moment, and the cause was too dear to my heart—but you never know what might happen next in any real estate transaction. Hell, old George might keel over from a heart attack; stranger things have happened. . . .

"Howdeedo," he said at once, as I walked into the kitchen, where he sat at the same big old table. He twinkled at me; I twinkled back, to the best of my ability, and waved the check at him.

"Let's get this over with," I suggested.

His face fell in comical mock dismay. "What's the hurry? Like I said, I kinda like doin' business with you."

He reached out for the check, but I held it high, and tut-tutted him. "You're the one who seems to be in a hurry for cash. Not so fast, George. Contracts first. Money later."

We settled across from each other at the table to iron out the last details of the purchase. When we reached the subject of title insurance, I said, "Did you have enough insurance to cover your loss on that property next door?"

He made a sound something like "huh." Then, quickly, he said, "Ain't never enough to cover a loss like that. A woman died in that fire, you know. Can't cover a loss like that."

"You're a sensitive man, George," I remarked.

He eyed me, grinning slightly. "That I am."

"You owned that property; I'm surprised you didn't notice that old wiring and replace the stove before something happened."

"Hell, I tried." He leaned back and stuck his thumbs in his belt loops. "Gardner tried; that cute little Sammie tried. But the old lady liked that damned old stove, and she wouldn't hear of me taking it out. Hell, even if I am a landlord, I'm not heartless, you know? I didn't want her carrying on, so I left the damn thing in the house. Shouldn't never have done it, I know that, and I feel damn bad about it, but Rod Gardner'll tell you, like he told the fire investigators, she wouldn't hear of it. Hell, if I'd been at fault, he'da sued me, you can bet on it."

"I guess he can't tell me, being dead and all."

"Yeah." Butts rubbed a hand against the stubble on his face. "Pretty sad. Lotta tragedy in that family."

"That's pretty valuable information," I commented, and he looked puzzled. "That information Rod had about what a thoughtful landlord you were; why, information like that could be worth quite a lot to a fellow. Might even buy him a house. Course, if he's a greedy sort, it might not be a good enough house, he might decide he wants an even better one, maybe even an expensive new condo for him and his wife and the baby. . . ."

I brightened, as if struck by an idea.

"I guess Sammie could tell me, though." When he cocked his eyebrows again, I said, "About what happened in her aunt's house, I mean; about how the old lady wouldn't let you replace the stove, like you wanted to do. It might have looked pretty bad for you if the truth was, say, that she had asked you to fix the wiring, but you had refused to do it. As the landlord, you might have been charged with manslaughter, or worse, I suppose."

"Yeah, 'spect so." He sat up straight in the chair, slapped his big hands down on the tabletop, and said jocularly, "If that were the case, which it ain't." He chuckled. "That Sammie, she's a cute one, all right, just a cute, scared little rabbit, but she's got herself a nice little nest now, so I 'spect she's happy. Well, you got my signature on the contract, how's about giving me yours on that check now?''

''And Mob would know,'' I said.

He blinked. ''Mob? What? What would he know?''

''About how much Dorothy Rhodes supposedly loved that old stove, and how much you supposedly wanted to replace it. She used to give him doughnuts and coffee; she even let him sleep on her porch in rough weather. I expect they talked a lot; I expect she would have mentioned to him how dearly she loved that old stove. Don't you expect so?''

He was squinting slightly at me and clicking his front teeth together in a thoughtful kind of way. Finally, he said, ''That boy's crazy, ain't nobody gonna believe a word outta him, 'specially since he killed young Rodney. You don't want to be believin' anything that boy says.''

I nodded. ''You're probably right.''

He shoved the contracts across the table toward me with a brusque movement. I put my hands on them and pretended to look them over in order to gather my thoughts. I lifted my pen and started to sign my name, but then I put the pen back down again and looked at him.

''Grace Montgomery might have known, too.''

His fingers, which lay flat on the tabletop, drew back like crab's legs.

''She and Mob were friends,'' I said. ''It was an odd friendship, but a pretty close one, I suspect. He might have told her, oh, all sorts of things.''

George Butts pushed himself back from the table, overturning his chair with a crash as he did it. I stood up, too, glad of the table between us.

''And actually,'' I said, ''Sammie might be more scared of going to jail than she is of you. She might be scared enough to tell the police how Rod had an appointment with you that night, and how he was going to tell you the new condo wasn't enough, and that they wanted cash on top of it, claiming it was for the baby—"

"Greedy," he said, in a strained version of his old jovial tone. "You're greedy, just like them two. Think you're going to hand me a check, and I'm going to hand you some cash, is that it? Well, I don't think I like doin' business with you so much, after all—"

But instead of moving toward me, he moved backward.

"Mob's out of custody, you know," I lied, as evenly as I could. "That's what sometimes happens when people cooperate with the police. They tell everything they know, and they get—"

"Mob's out?" The twinkle had long since disappeared; now it was openly replaced with an expression that was hard and frightening. "Funny they'd let a madman like that out on the streets again. He might go crazy again. Might kill somebody else, maybe even do it right in here, just like last time. . . ."

He reached for the butcher knife on the wall at the same moment I started backing out of the kitchen. I was screaming and running, and he had it in his hand, holding it out in front of him as he rushed after me into the hallway. The police who were waiting there let me run on by them. It was only George Butts they stopped—for good.

If he hadn't turned instinctively and lunged toward one of the detectives when he saw them, they never would have shot him. But he did, and they didn't miss. In the big meeting room down the hall, I was still screaming. I couldn't stop.

Epilogue

Sunday afternoons I usually reserve for a drive to the Hampshire Psychiatric Hospital to visit my mother. This Sunday Geof wanted to accompany me, after brunch with Marsha Sandy and Rosalinda McInerny, at the C'est La Vie restaurant down by the harbor.

We had thought about inviting Derek and Marianne Miller, but it was all too awkward. I'd heard from Marianne that she and Derek had dated a few times. Derek had gotten away from Sammie Gardner—but only because she kicked him out as soon as she knew she had nothing more to fear from George Butts. The girl claimed—and there was no one now alive to refute her—that she had only guessed at the real reason for the payoff, and for the later blackmail, between her husband and Butts. It was on the basis of that "guess"—to which she admitted at the police station—that I had leveled my accusations at Butts. It was he who was the link to the odd series of real estate transactions on Tenth Street—he had owned the house that burned, the church where Rod Gardner was killed, and he had not only sold a house to the young Gardners but had

273

later bought it back from them as well. There was no one alive, either, to tell us why he killed poor old Grace Montgomery, although we felt the answer lay in the probability that she knew something about the fire or the murder that he couldn't afford for her to know.

Sammie Gardner had only wanted Derek around because she was frightened—and for kicks. Once Butts was dead, she quickly decided she wasn't interested in supporting a bodyguard, even if he was good in bed. Derek was now collecting unemployment, but at least he was using some of it to pay for counseling from Marsha.

As for Marianne Miller, she was still a little shaky, too, recovering from her terrified assumption that her former husband, Perry Yates, might have been the one who killed Rod Gardner in order to get Sammie for himself. That was why she'd been so relieved when I told her that Derek was living with Sammie—if Derek had her, then Perry didn't. And if Perry didn't, then his children probably didn't have a killer for a father. A jerk, maybe, but at least not a killer. Poor Marianne still suspected the unborn child might be Perry's. It probably wasn't, I had told her, or Sammie would have been after him for support payments by now.

This particular Sunday was about a month after George Butts's death, a month of watching Faye adjust to her new authority. I'd cheated her, in a way, because I had not hired a new secretary; I had merely enlarged her duties and her salary. The foundation had, for some time, needed to cut back on personnel expenses, so she and I and Marvin, our accountant, were all taking up the slack. Sad to say, we hadn't even noticed it very much, since we'd been doing most of Derek's real work all along.

It had also been a month of watching Marsha rebound from ending her relationship with Joe Fabian. During the meal, my old friend was vivacious in her anticipation of the imminent opening of the recreation center—which Mrs. Butts had unaccountably decided to sell us, after all.

My new "Friend," Rosalinda, was peaceful in her understanding that Kitt was doing as well as he could be expected to do at another hospital. Because of all the recent trauma he'd endured, it was doubtful that he'd be out again soon, if ever, but Rosalinda didn't know that.

Geof laughed a lot during breakfast and seemed a bit hyped up himself. He had spent much of the month watching me as I tried to bounce back from the unexpected depression into which so much death and fear had plunged me. I was glad to see him enjoying himself for once instead of worrying about me. On this Sunday, I tried to rise to the mood, but Sundays wear me down, even before I get to the hospital.

"Love to your mom," Marsha said, with a hug and kiss, as we left the restaurant. "I'll visit her the next time I'm up there."

"Bye, Jenny Friend," Rosalinda said, shyly.

I was glad to let Geof navigate the long drive, to put a Paul Simon cassette in the tape player, to travel in companionable silence, and to close my eyes most of the way. But when the car started bumping in an unfamiliar way, I opened them. I looked out to find evergreens and bare maple trees close by on either side of us.

"Are we lost?" I inquired, not really caring.

This road was not the two-lane blacktop highway to the hospital; this was more like a private road, dirt and rocks, curving through the trees toward the ocean.

"I decided to take another route," Geof told me. "Pretty drive, isn't it?"

"Yes, it's nice, but what is it, a county road?"

"Not exactly," he said.

We were coming to a clearing, and soon there was the ocean in front of us, along with a glorious, clear-blue view of sky. There was a house set off to the left of us, just in front of a lovely stand of Norwegian pines. It was a small-ish but charming old place of stones and timber, well kept, set among pleasingly wild bushes and flowers. It seemed so pretty and so *homey* that it brought tears to my eyes. How very fortunate the people were who owned this place, I thought, with self-pity. They had lights on in the house, and there was smoke coming from one of the two chimneys. If Geof knew these people, it was news to me, but good news. I knew I'd like them, whoever they were.

"Friends of yours?" I asked him.

He smiled over at me. "I called ahead. I thought you'd like the surprise. Do you mind that we'll be a little late to see your mom?"

"No. We're the only ones who'll know the difference."

He parked in the graveled circle drive in front of the house, which was really more like a large, two-story cottage, and then, in an unusual gesture, walked around the car to open the door for me.

"Why, thank you, kind sir." I managed to smile at him.

He held out his hand to me, to help me "alight," and then kept hold of it as we traversed the flagstone path to the front door.

"Who are these people?" I whispered.

But he only smiled and knocked.

When no one responded, he pressed gently against the door. It came open to his touch, revealing a charming but empty living room. I would have felt like Goldilocks, except that not only was there no one at home, there was no furniture either. There were only logs, burning in the fireplace.

"Geof?" I said, turning to frown at him. "What *is* this?"

He pulled me into the living room, then closed the front door behind us. He put his hands on my shoulders and turned me around so that my back was against him, and I was facing the beautiful living room.

"Do you like it?" he asked.

I twisted back around, to look at him. "Geof?"

276

"Do you *like* it?"

I nodded. "Geof, who got the fire going?"

"Would you believe the three bears?"

"No."

"Spontaneous combustion?"

"No!"

"Okay, then. The real estate agent."

I surprised myself, by laughing.

"Is she hiding upstairs?"

"Well, yes," he admitted, looking sheepish. "And I asked her to hide her car out back. Shall I call her down now?"

"In a minute." I moved in close to embrace him with all the strength I had. With my face buried in his chest, I murmured, "You'll have to give me a minute."

"We have lots of time," he said.